For Edi

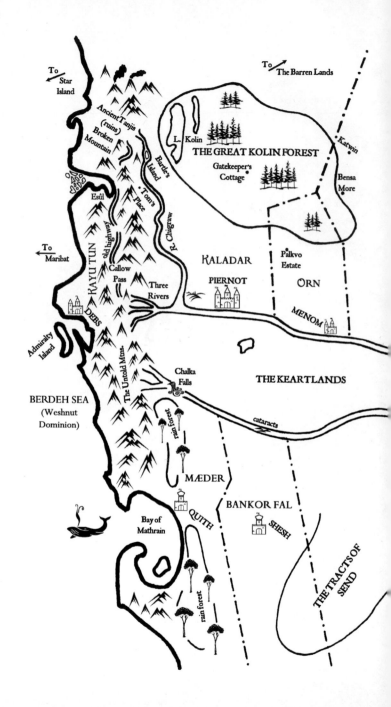

THE SPANISH GATEKEEPER

BOOK I

Empire of the Ulfair

a science fiction fantasy

by

Bernard Dukas

Kaladar Books ◆ San Francisco

www.thespanishgatekeeper.com

The Spanish Gatekeeper Book I—Empire of the Ulfair

Library of Congress Control Number: 2010942303

ISBN 978-0-9831929-0-9

e-book format ISBN 978-0-9831929-1-6

1. Science Fiction 2. Fantasy

Published by KALADAR BOOKS – San Francisco
www.kaladarbooks.com

First paperback edition printed in the United States of America by arrangement with Dakota Press

♻

Contents

Book I

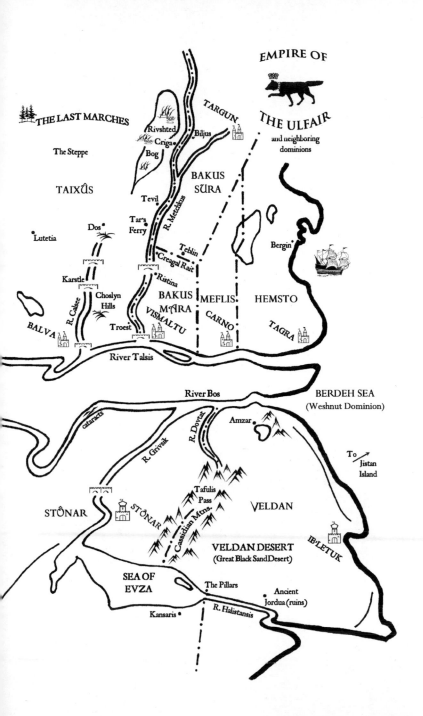

Chapter 1

The Ruin in the Meadow

Peter de Soto was just beginning to doze off, chin upon his chest, when Herbert (a first cousin on his mother's side) thwacked him aside the noggin with a well worn copy of *Tit-Bits*. Surprised and more than a little disoriented, Peter pulled himself bolt upright. His assailant sat directly across the swaying compartment, a satisfied grin plastered across his enviably handsome face. Not for the first time, it occurred to Peter that his appointed "guardian" for the trip to northern Spain was, for all intents and purposes, twenty-two going on eight.

"Gawd I'm bored," groused Herbert, forcing a yawn and stretching his arms from side to side.

"Then why don't you read a proper book?" suggested Peter, peevishly rubbing the injured side of his head.

"And why don't you stuff it, you little twerp."

In this pleasant manner, more or less, the cousins traveled together from London to the family's *pazo* or manor house in Galicia, first by boat to Coruña, then south by train to Ourense and finally the long coach and carriage ride east, all the way to the village of Caxide on the Ribas do Sil. It was relatively speaking an arduous journey, but entirely worth the hardship, for a summer in Galicia, especially in the *cañón,* was something Peter would never willingly miss. The Sil River Gorge, with its ruined monasteries, sweeping vistas, and haunting forests was without question one of the most beautiful and enchanting places on the planet. What's more, it was where Peter's younger cousin, *Bonifacia* (his dearest and closest friend in the world), called home.

Stepping at long last from the carriage and gazing up the walk to his aunt's door there was no escaping the fact that the summer of 1900 would be a bittersweet sojourn, for it was to be Peter's last long holiday in Spain. Since early childhood it had been his father's practice to send him to his Aunt Generosa—a second home a world away from the sooty skies and hurried streets of London. But he'd come of age in a manner of thinking and in the approaching year was to begin a part-time apprenticeship with his father's firm, the first small step toward assuming the corporate mantle that would one day be his to bear. Peter's idyllic summer routine was coming to an end. *But not yet,* he reminded himself. This summer had barely begun, and he had much to look forward to.

He ambled up the steps to the *pazo* and was nearly bowled over by Bonifacia, a precious girl only a few months shy of his own age. "Cousin Peter!" she cried, her face flush with glee. Casting aside all decorum, she clasped him to her breast and kissed him affectionately on both cheeks. "Welcome! My goodness, how you've shot up!" she remarked in mildly accented English. "I have missed you so. Hello Herbert. *Come,* you must be tired. Both of you. I'll help you settle in. Ah, but first you must pay your respects to Mama. I expect she'll be having chocolate on the patio."

Bonifacia's nervous chatter brought a smile to Peter's face. He couldn't help but notice how very little she had changed over the intervening months. The same lustrous russet-colored hair, deep-set dimples and delicate features so typical of López women. Still a young girl in outward appearance, Peter knew first hand never to under estimate his younger cousin. Bonifacia possessed a keen intellect and indomitable spirit well in advance of her tender years. To his embarrassment, he'd gained in comparison several inches in height, developed an angular chin, and altogether lost his boyhood complexion. He felt rather like a newborn giraffe, awkward and gangly, as if discovering the ground beneath his feet for the very first time. If Bonifacia noticed his discomfort, she never let on.

Despite an English upbringing, Peter regarded Caxide as his principal home. He was happy for yet another chance to escape incessant reminders of the war and the peculiar rules and expectations of public school life. In his aunt's house he'd always been free to play and roam about, unmindful of the world at large. Occasionally, Peter and Bonifacia did get themselves into trouble, in their exuberance trampling a prized begonia or one of Generosa's favorite chrysanthemums. They were, despite these minor incidents, generally well-behaved if untidy children.

"Come, Peter. You can help me catch a Gatekeeper," announced Bonifacia after breakfast one morning. It's the only *Satyridae* missing from my collection." Without waiting for a response, she took Peter by the hand and led him from the room. They passed Herbert in the corridor looking especially dapper in knee-high riding boots and silken top hat.

"Where are you children off to?" he demanded to know.

"To catch butterflies in the west mead," replied Bonifacia.

Herbert rolled his eyes. "How exciting."

Peter had to wonder at his father's judgment. *Whatever possessed him to entrust my care to this loathsome ninny?*

"I'm bored half silly," pronounced Herbert, dusting some invisible object from his jacket sleeve. "Tell your aunt, I'm off for a ride."

"Tell her yourself," railed Peter.

Herbert's reaction was swift, seizing his cousin by the shirt collar and lifting him up to his face. "Look, you little piece of scat. You'll do as I tell you, understand?"

"Stop it! Leave him alone!" shouted Bonifacia, putting up her hands to push Herbert away. But he brushed her aside, as one might fend off a troublesome midge. Although developing rapidly, Peter had only just turned fifteen. Herbert was still a good head taller and blessed with an athletic build. A blind man could see Peter lacked the requisite muscle and physical coordination to stand up to his elder cousin. A confrontation would only end in grief.

"Fine. I'll do it," bellowed Peter, swallowing his pride. "Just let me go."

Herbert tossed him back with a smirk, poking the end of Peter's nose with his index finger for added measure. "Don't do anything I wouldn't do," he quipped, and walked off with a swagger.

"What's that supposed to mean?" shouted Peter after him.

Herbert chortled a reply without bothering to look back. "You know what they say about kissing cousins!"

"Moron!" retorted Peter, his face going red with embarrassment. He had no intention of informing his aunt about

Herbert going out for a ride and in short order Peter and Boni-facia were happily scouting the distant fields and lanes for unsuspecting butterflies, putting Herbert, and every other un-pleasant distraction, out of their heads.

"Remind me, Bonnie. What exactly are we looking for?"

"I told you," she replied, with evident exasperation. "The Spanish Gatekeeper—*El Lobito Listado.*"

"Brown did you say?" He struggled to remember the rest …Something about *eyes.*

She frowned, disappointment writ clear across her lovely face. "*Orange,* Peter, with a broad brown border, and *eyespots* up near the tips of the forewings. Really, you must learn to pay more attention. Keep searching, will you. Try over there by the bushes."

Dear delightful Bonifacia, in general rather used to having things her way. Obediently, Peter searched the berry bushes, in the process pricking a finger and adding a number of unpleasant scratches to the back of his hand. "Bonnie!" he cried, catching sight of her elusive Gatekeeper. "Come quick!"

She scampered over, net in hand, carefully avoiding the bramble. "Look there," he said, pointing in triumph at a crea-ture with impressive orange-brown wings.

Bonifacia was crestfallen. "Oh Peter, that's *Pyronia tithonus.* I need *Pyronia bathseba.*"

It was his turn to frown. "Well, how was I to know?"

"*Bathseba* has a very distinctive white stripe on the underside of its hind wing," she instructed. Did I not tell you? It's quite impossible to miss. Go on. Keep looking."

Underside of the hind wing? Peter bit his lip and continued searching through the wild flowers. Before long, another pair of orange wings caught his notice, flitting about a dense thicket set in a slight depression and enclosing on all four sides the crumbling walls of an old ruin. This time he hesitated. "*Tithonus* or *bathseba?*"

The moment he settled on *bathseba* the butterfly lifted its deli-cate frame and fluttered over the tumbling ramparts. "Bollocks!" cried Peter, trudging after it. He scrambled down the hollow, heels first.

"Heavens, Peter. Whatever are you doing?" shouted Bonifa-cia from above.

"I've found your bléssed Gatekeeper. It's gone over the wall."

"Are you certain?"

"White stripe underside the hind wing?" he asked.

Quickly assessing the situation, Bonifacia clambered down the slope to join him.

"What is this place? Do you know?"

"I'm not sure," replied Bonifacia. "Maybe part of the old monastery of Santa Cristina. There's bits of it hidden all about. Mama would know for certain."

After a few minutes spent reconnoitering the surrounding thicket, Peter and Bonifacia surmounted the broken wall in tandem. It was not especially high at the one point and thick-stemmed ivy provided ample foothold. Still, the climb, or rather the descent, presented some unforeseen challenges. The ground was lower on the inside of the ruin than they had accounted for and the interior decidedly murky as much of the good light was blocked by the height of the intervening wall. Peter landed first amid the brake and offered Bonifacia a helping hand, which she politely but flatly declined.

"Where, exactly, did you see that Gatekeeper?" she asked.

Peter was about to point toward the very spot when something entirely unexpected caught his eye. "*Wolf!*" Taken by surprise he fell back with a cry.

"*Dios mío!*" shrieked Bonifacia, tumbling after him.

In a corner of the ruin, half hidden in shadow, stood a large black wolf. Peter, now flat on his back, held Bonifacia tightly by the wrist. Slowly he recovered his wits. "Just a moment…" There was something very odd about that wolf. Something, in fact, quite beyond the realm of possibility. "Bonnie, do you see? That wolf…it's wearing a crown!"

"Yes," she whispered in bewilderment, "and a gold chain about its neck."

As they watched, the creature began to take on a strange transparent quality and then to waver, like candle smoke upon a breeze. A second later, it was gone.

Stunned beyond words, the companions slowly regained their feet. Peter made to step forward, but Bonifacia pulled him back. "Peter, don't!"

"It can't have been real," he replied.

"Just the same…" she started to say, but he let go her arm and stubbornly crossed the distance to where the phantom wolf had stood just moments before.

Peter inspected the ground, but there was no hint of the creature's presence, not a bent blade of grass, nothing at all to indicate the animal had ever existed.

"I don't understand," said Bonifacia. "Was it real?"

Peter turned toward the wall and brushed aside the dense ivy. "Something else here," he announced. Together, they cleared away the foliage. Peter chuckled despite his recent fright. "Not what I'd expected."

Indeed, parked against the crumbling wall was the diminutive form of a *gnome* fashioned entirely of gray stone, his right hand thrust forward, palm up, as if awaiting payment. Typical of his race, the gnome's distinguishing features included an over-blown face, long beard and tall pointed cap. But this was no lovable character from the pages of some children's fairy tale. The little man's expression was unmistakably malevolent.

Bonifacia gaped anxiously at the carving, so out of place amid the ruins of an ancient monastery.

"Hey, you've cut your cheek!" exclaimed Peter, truly noticing Bonifacia for the first time since their confrontation with the wolf.

She put her hand to her face. "I must have clipped it when we fell." Bonifacia removed a kerchief from her pinafore, hold-ing it to her cheek and then examining it for blood. "It's nothing, Peter. Just a scratch. What about the wolf?" she asked, changing the subject. "How did it disappear like that?"

"You sure?" asked Peter, uncertainly, but Bonifacia waved off his concern. Reluctantly, he continued. "A trick, I think." He pointed to a spot directly behind the gnome where a rectangu-lar plate was fixed to the wall. It had the appearance of smoked glass. Taking his pocket knife Peter edged all round the object, prying it lose. The cover popped to the ground trailing an as-sortment of wires. "Just as I thought," said Peter. "Some form of projection. I've seen the like in London—a chap named Lumière. Father took me to see him. He loves that sort of thing. Anyhow, this Lumière fellow, he put on a moving picture of a train pulling into a station, all performed with lights and mirrors. I can't remember the name of the device, but it must have been very similar to this." Peter ran one hand down the nape of his neck. "That wolf, crown or no, could have fooled me."

"Well it *did* fool me," replied Bonifacia, dabbing her injured cheek. She paused to consider Peter's explanation. "But Peter...no one in Caxide has electricity. *Not a single soul.* Mama says it will be years before they build a hydro-electric dam above the Sil."

He was momentarily at a loss for words. "Well someone must. Just look at those wires. That projection wasn't powered by gas." There was silence between them. "Who here could afford to bring electricity, and moreover, has the influence to make it happen?" They both knew the answer to that—their neighbor, Don Modesto. "How far are we from the Rodriguez estate?" asked Peter.

Bonifacia pointed more or less at the gnome. "That way, beyond the edge of the field, where the tree line begins."

"So this ruin falls on our lands?"

Bonifacia nodded.

"Well, there you have it, Bonnie. Don Modesto installed all this to scare the likes of us away. And it almost worked," he added.

"But why here, Peter?"

He cast about for an answer. "Because Don Modesto has discovered something valuable and wants it for himself."

"Such as?"

"Treasure," he replied. "The abbots of Santa Cristina must have buried their gold here and then lost track of it. Don Modesto found it and doesn't want anyone, especially your parents, to know. Look there..." He indicated another unusual feature at the base of the crumbling wall—the top of a large rectangular stone, like polished obsidian, just visible above the foundation. "It's a door. I'm sure of it. Behind that is a vault. That's where the treasure lies."

"You've lost your marbles," croaked Bonifacia. "I've never heard anything so ridiculous."

"Do you have a better explanation?"

She frowned. "No. Not yet, but I'll think of one. Now please, let's get out of here. Dinner will be waiting and we've got ourselves a good march home."

Walking back to the *pazo*, Peter and Bonifacia continued to debate their encounter with the wolf. Bonifacia was steadfast in her belief that Don Modesto could not possibly have had anything to do with the goings on at the ruin. "But it's odd, I'll admit. Mama has never mentioned any work taking place out there, let alone involving electricity. Even if she had authorized it, I don't see how work of that sort could take place without all of the *cañón* knowing about it. Now that I think on it, Mama couldn't possibly have anything to do with this."

"Well then, what about your father?" asked Peter, determined to nose out every possibility. "Maybe he arranged for whatever's going on down there and forgot to mention it to your mother."

Bonifacia furled her brow. "I shouldn't think so, Peter. Papa hardly takes any interest in the *pazo*. He never has," she added glumly. "That just doesn't fit."

He had to agree. Peter's Uncle Ramón lived in Madrid for most of the year, together with his cursèd mistress. He was almost as much a stranger to Bonifacia as he was to Peter. He couldn't think what else to suggest. "Did you have a clear look at that wolf?" he persisted. "I know this sounds odd, but there was something about it that seemed awfully familiar."

"Same here, but I can't quite place it." She glanced up at the midday sun. "Dinner will be ready. Just look at us. We had better get cleaned up or Mama will have a fit."

She was right, of course. Her smock was a complete shambles. His own breeches and jacket were caked in dirt at the knees and elbows. They tidied up as well as they could and went to join Bonifacia's mother for lunch on the patio. Peering at them over the edge of her newspaper, Generosa dropped it quite suddenly to the flagstone.

"*Aye! Dios mío!*" she cried. "What has happened to your face child?" She seized Bonifacia by the chin, turning her head from side to side, examining her intently. "Scratches! All over scratches! And you too Peter! What have you children been up to?"

Bonifacia was uncertain how much she should tell her mother.

"Come now. What has gone on?" she demanded.

"*Pódollo explicar*. I can explain, Aunt Generosa" stammered Peter. "We were after a butterfly for Bonnie's collection and fell amongst the thorn-brake."

"Dear Lord! Where did this happen?" she demanded.

"In the West Meadow," he replied.

"You weren't playing anywhere near that old ruin, were you?" His silence told her everything she needed to know. "The ruin! What were you thinking?" she berated. "Those walls could have toppled on you. Then what? At your age. Honestly, you behave like little heathens, the two of you. Keep away from there. Do you hear? Both of you!"

Peter opened his mouth to protest, but nothing came out.

"But Mama, we saw a wolf!" blurted Bonifacia. "And there was a little man carved from stone, *and electricity!*"

"A wolf in broad daylight? And electricity?! Such an imagination!" exclaimed Generosa, dismissing her daughter entirely. "Look at your precious face. Promise me, you won't play there any more."

"Mother, you don't understand. We weren't playing…"

"Promise me."

Bonifacia's shoulders slumped under the sheer weight of her mother's persistence. "Yes Mama."

"You too Peter."

Peter knew from long experience that it was quite hopeless arguing with his aunt. He hung his head in defeat. "Yes, Aunt Generosa. I promise."

"*Vale*. Finish your meal and go play like normal children."

They ate their lunch in glum silence and then excused themselves from the table. Together, they walked side-by-side back up the high steps to the verandah.

"So what happens now?" asked Peter.

"Nothing. We forget all about it" murmured Bonifacia. It's none of our business. I should never have said anything."

"But Bonnie, you can't mean that? Someone—probably Don Modesto—has been poking about that old ruin without your mother's knowledge. It wasn't our imagination. You were right to say something. I just didn't have the courage."

She made no reply and they settled quietly in the rocking settee overlooking the garden and stables. From where they sat, they could see Generosa's grizzled groundskeeper, Carlos, pruning faded blossoms from a salmon-colored camellia. Peter put his foot out to stop their swaying. "Look there," he said, pointing a finger in the direction of the stable manager leading two magnificent palfreys by the bridle. "Visitors."

Their guests turned out to be *la señorita* Doña Lucia, Don Modesto's youngest daughter, and her chaperone, Maria-Jésus. The Rodriguez family owned the very old and very grand *estado de país* neighboring their own lands. Lucia was an exquisitely charming, sophisticated, and affable girl, every inch the Spanish aristocrat. She'd met Herbert the previous summer, and was evidently taken by his good looks and splendid manners. It didn't take a genius to realize he'd engineered his morning ride on the outside chance he might once again encounter her.

Peter and Bonifacia followed their unexpected guests into the parlor and sat cross-legged on the floor listening to Lucia, Maria-Jésus, Herbert and Generosa make idle conversation. "We were out for a ride and had the pleasure of renewing our acquaintance with young Mister Holcolmb" said Lucia, by way of explanation. "I hope his offer of tea was not too presumptuous, Señora Espasande?"

"Certainly not, Doña Lucia. You are always a most welcome guest in this house. Besides, Herbert is a member of this family and quite within his rights to invite whomever he wishes for afternoon tea, or hot cocoa if you prefer."

Herbert, as usual, made a complete ass of himself while they waited on the tea. Peter was soon bored to tears and about to make his apologies when Bonifacia elbowed him in the ribs, gesturing with wide eyes toward a little enameled wolf resting on top the sideboard where it lay suspended from a stand beneath a protective glass cloche. Now there was something interesting!

Peter got up from where he sat and strolled casually around the room, pretending to admire all of his aunt's collected knickknacks, pausing at last in front of the wolf. Now he understood why the wolf in the meadow looked so familiar. The resemblance was uncanny, right down to the crown resting atop the creature's head and the gold chain or collar fashioned around its neck. Thinking no one was paying much attention, he gave the protective dome an exploratory tap.

"Peter. Do be careful with that," admonished Generosa before he was able to lay another finger on it. "It has been in our family for a very long time."

He decided to exploit the sudden turn in conversation. "Aunt Generosa, why does the wolf wear a crown?" Queen Victoria's lion, he remembered, wore a crown much like it. He had seen it once, painted on the side of the queen's carriage as it trundled up The Mall.

No one immediately spoke up, but Lucia and Bonifacia came over to where Peter stood. "*Con permiso?*" asked Lucia. Generosa nodded her approval. Carefully removing the wolf from its protective glass, Lucia examined it gingerly. "It is the *Reíña Loba,*" she replied in answer to Peter's question. "The Wolf Queen."

"Wolf Queen?" snorted Herbert from the far side of the room.

"A local myth," explained Lucia.

"The Wolf Queen is progenitor of the house of López," interjected Generosa, with evident pride.

"Ah, yes, a quaint story," smiled Lucia. Peter's aunt, however, found nothing amusing apropos the López family history. She frowned her displeasure. "Oh dear. I am sorry." Lucia dipped her head in apology. "I meant no disrespect Señora Espasande." Lucia gazed at the pendant lying in her palm. "It's certainly a rare and beautiful object. An exquisite example of early modern Galician folk art. Pity the chain has gone missing."

"Señorita, *por favor,*" pleaded Maria-Jésus. "It is not well to touch the figure." She made the sign of the cross.

Peter stared at Lucia in puzzlement.

"She is afraid of it," laughed Lucia, sensing Peter's confusion. "The Wolf Queen is not an object of Holy Mother Church. Maria, you see, still believes in *lobishomes.*"

"*Lobishomes?*" he prompted.

"It is the Galician word for werewolves," replied Generosa.

He looked again at Maria-Jésus. This time in astonishment. *Blimy,* he thought. *Werewolves! This is 1900. Can people still believe in such things?*

Generosa raised herself up from the settee to join the others gathered at the credenza.

"What about the scales?" asked Bonifacia, gently fingering the pendant still resting in Lucia's open palm. Unlike the black wolf in the meadow, the jeweler who had designed this little figure had placed, in addition to the crown and collar, a set of scales within the animal's out thrust paw. "Why would anyone portray the Wolf Queen with a set of measures?"

"I'm not certain," said Generosa. "The scales of justice perhaps."

"Oh! What's this?" exclaimed Lucia. She opened her hand to reveal a kind of silver disk or token. It had fallen from the belly of the jeweled wolf.

"Ah, you have discovered the Reíña Loba's little treasure," said Generosa. "Look here…there is a small cavity in the stomach of the wolf. If you press just at this point the coin is released."

Peter took the object from Lucia and held it up between his thumb and forefinger, then passed it to Bonifacia to examine. It was embossed on one side with the likeness of a gate or doorway. On the other, with a comet or shooting star. There was no inscription, at least none that could be easily identified. "It doesn't look much like any coin I've ever seen," remarked Bonifacia.

Generosa shook her head. "Grandfather called it a 'key.' But if that's what it is, it's a very odd sort of key, don't you think?"

Peter and Bonifacia turned to one another in a flash of realization. *A key!*

Generosa took the coin, or "key," from Bonifacia and pressed it back into the vacant slot beneath the wolf's belly. With obvious reverence, she then placed the wolf back on top the sideboard beneath the glass cloche. "The key remains," she said, "hidden within the *Reíña Loba,* but I'm afraid the object to which it belongs is lost forever."

Bonifacia pinched Peter to gain his attention. Her thoughts echoed his own. *Forever is a very long time.*

Peter ventured one last question. "Aunt Generosa, do you know anything about the old ruin in the West Meadow?"

She crooked her head to one side, clearly unhappy about the question after their morning's folly. "It was once part of the *Mosteiro de Santa Cristina,*" she answered, "like so much of the lands around Caxide. The walls are very ancient, some of them as old as the *Reconquista,* I think."

"Much older below ground," added Lucia. "When he was quite young, my father conducted a few limited excavations of the site, with Señor de Soto's permission, of course. The foundations go back as far as the Suevi, and before that, the Romans and possibly the Celts."

Ah-ha! So Don Modesto is interested in archaeology! thought Peter triumphantly. That *had* to be at the root of all of this. He made up his mind then and there. Señor Rodriguez had found something important, perhaps of great value, out there in the meadow and was trying to keep it secret. He had rigged some elaborate protection, perhaps using electric batteries, to invoke a facet of local lore in the hope of scaring away any would be interlopers. It all made perfect sense.

After their guests' departure, Peter and Bonifacia spent the remainder of the afternoon arguing back and forth the significance of what they'd both seen and learned and how they should best proceed. How much did Lucia really know? How far would she go to protect her father's activities, now she knew Generosa had a key to the hidden vault? Peter did his level best to persuade Bonifacia to his own way of thinking. Bonifacia remained unconvinced.

"But it's as plain as the nose on my face," he moaned. "The abbots of Santa Cristina buried their gold down there, deep in the dungeons of the old monastery—loot from the Spanish Main I'll wager. Don Modesto intends on digging it up in the dark of night and doesn't want your mother, or anyone else, to know."

"Piffle," admonished Bonifacia. "You've been reading *The Boy's Own* again. I do believe there is something very serious going on here Peter, but I fear we may be quite out of our depths."

And so Peter and Bonifacia went to bed that evening divided on what to do. Bonifacia slept soundly until awakened sharply from her slumber.

"Bonnie, wake up!"

Her cousin was standing over her, a taper draping his frame in pale yellow light.

"Peter! You scared me half to death. What's happening?" she asked. "Why are you dressed?"

"I can't stand it. I have to know. I'm going out there."

She rubbed the sleep from her eyes, eventually gaining his gist. "You can't mean it? Let's go wake Mother. We'll tell her everything this time." She stood up and donned her dressing gown, but Peter held her back.

"But don't you see? This is our chance to find out if the coin is truly connected to whatever lies behind that door in the hollow."

"Peter, we mustn't," pleaded Bonifacia.

He was intent upon the mystery. "Then you stay here. I'll go see for myself."

Bonifacia chewed her lip in frustration. "All right. I'll go with you as far as the outer thicket if you insist upon being so stupid. But any sign of trouble and I'll cry out. I warn you."

To Peter, that seemed like a wise precaution in any case. "Put on some proper clothes. I'll meet you outside the front door in two minutes."

He crept quietly down the steps and into his aunt's sitting room. The tiny enameled wolf sat on top the credenza, just as they had left it. He lifted off the glass dome and slipped the pendant into his pocket.

Bonifacia was waiting for him outside. "Do you have the coin?" she whispered. He lifted the little wolf from his pocket to show her. "You took the whole pendant? We only need the key!" She looked terribly cross. He shrugged a tepid apology.

It was a beautiful star filled evening under a waxing moon, warm enough to meander out of doors without overcoats. Armed only with a small lantern and shovel, they traveled down the garden path past his aunt's carefully tended beds, sculpted cypress trees and the moss-flecked statue of San Xoán, a finger raised in perpetual admonition. The smell of summer flowers hung thick in the air. A nightjar called softly through the darkness.

A simple gate set amid a shiven slate wall marked the boundary between the formal garden and the western mead. They stepped through, following a well-beaten trail through tall grass, bramble, and wild flowers. A weathered outcropping provided the only clear landmark in the open meadow. From it, they took the less traveled path to the left, heading down the incline to the ruin.

Reaching the thicket, Bonifacia gave Peter's hand a worried squeeze, or perhaps it was the other way around. "Remember," said Bonifacia, "any sign or sound of trouble and I shall cry out for help."

He nodded. "We've only the one lantern between us. Best you keep it."

"No. I'll be fine. You'll need it to see your way over the wall."

"I can't carry it *and* the shovel. Anyhow, the moon's bright enough tonight."

"Very well. Have it your way." She kissed Peter on the forehead and he set off to scale the crumbling perimeter, leaving poor Bonifacia alone in the dark with only a small taper lantern for comfort.

Hampered by the shovel and the darkness, his progress was much slower than it had been that very morning, but he mustered his resolve to push forward and was soon up and over the old wall. On nearing the spot where he'd seen the wolf he slowed his pace to a dead crawl, listening and watching intently for any sign of movement, making absolutely sure no one else was about. The wolf, he knew, was not likely to reappear. He'd pulled apart the mechanism that had given it life.

But there before him stood the gnome looking all the more menacing in the pale moonlight, and Peter's courage suddenly waned. For the longest time, he stood stock-still, urging his legs to carry him forward. He managed two or three steps when he heard a rustle in the shrubbery behind him. His heart near skipped a beat at the sight of Bonifacia's terrified face poking abruptly over the wall, the lantern casting her profile in eerie shadow.

"What's wrong?" he hissed.

"Nothing. I couldn't let you go alone." Her love for him had apparently outweighed her fear.

Together they advanced, halting in front of the preposterous little sentinel. "I don't much care for the looks of him," whispered Bonifacia. "This is a really bad idea."

"It's just an oversized garden gnome. Hold the lantern up for me, will you Bonnie. I'll try to dig some of that earth away from the door."

She did as he asked, doing her best to avoid getting the way. After ten long minutes, sweat tumbling from his brow, Peter had had enough. "I've barely made a dint!" he exclaimed. The door was still more than half buried in the ground. He put his hand to it, feeling its polished surface, cold as a winter's day.

"I've had just about enough of this place and it's getting very late," said Bonifacia, with growing impatience. "Please Peter, let's get away from here before someone comes along."

He glanced once more at the unfriendly face of the gnome, feeling less and less certain, but his sense of curiosity was enough to keep him from losing his head entirely. He drew the little enameled wolf from his pocket and pressed down on it as he'd seen his aunt do. The small silvered disk dropped easily into his hand and he held it aloft for Bonifacia to see.

"We've come this far, Bonnie. Let's at least give it a try." He pressed the coin to her palm.

She hesitated.

"What are you waiting for?"

Bonifacia held her breath and dropped the token into the gnome's upturned hand. It stuck suddenly as if grabbed by a strong magnetic force. In the blink of an eye the door vanished, removing the one thing holding back the earth below their feet. They'd no time to react. Bonifacia and Peter tumbled right along with the ground beneath them, straight down and across the threshold.

Lying on her back in a great heap with the broken lantern at her side, Bonifacia shouted, "The door!" Before Peter had time to twist round and see for himself, it winked back into existence. Instantly, the light of the moon was quenched and they were thrust into a black expanse as dark as the deepest ocean.

"Fool!" he shouted, cursing his own stupidity for not having had the sense or foresight to anticipate the subsiding ground. "Plonker! Idiot!"

"Stop your cussing, Peter, and find us a light," shouted Bonifacia, her voice echoing fearfully in the void.

"Are you okay Bonnie?"

"I'm fine Peter." There was the slightest hint of panic in her voice. "Just find us a light!"

"Did you bring along a packet of lucifers for that lantern?" he asked.

"Oh. Right! Give me a moment." She pulled a small box from her pinafore and struck up a match with a trembling hand. Holding it up toward the door, an electric lamp mounted just to the left flickered on, blinking weakly.

"Ah. Thank God for that," sighed Bonifacia. She shook her fingers to put out the match. "See if you can find any way to get that door back open," she commanded. Together they scaled the earthen rubble inside the entrance, searching in vain for a way to trigger the mechanism.

"But there has to be some way out," she cried. "There just has to be. We're not looking in the right place." They searched again, but there was nothing. The door was smooth and seamless, like polished glass. No handle. No key hole. Nothing at all on which to gain a grip. "What sort of door is this?" bawled Bonifacia in exasperation. "Did you see how it just blinked in and out of existence?"

A trap door, thought Peter, but dared not utter it. Taking a deep breath, he turned and stared down the dark passageway beyond. "This isn't a vault, Bonnie. It's a tunnel. There's nothing else for it. We must go forward."

"I suppose," she replied gloomily.

Peter put on a brave face. "I shouldn't worry. There's sure to be another door at the far end. I expect it will lead us out somewhere on the Rodriguez estate."

"I hope so," she replied. "It would be lovely to emerge from this dreadful place into Lucia's welcoming arms." It went through Peter's head that they might just as easily find themselves walking straight into Don Modesto's decidedly *unwelcoming* embrace.

"Peter, if Don Modesto has something to do with opening up this old tunnel, why didn't Lucia mention it this morning?"

"Covering up for her papa, I expect. We can ask her to her face when we're home free." Peter took the box of lucifers from Bonifacia and struck up another match to light their way. "Be careful where you plant your feet Bonnie. I wouldn't want you falling down any holes." He'd made one terrible mistake already and desperately wanted to avoid making another. They'd hardly taken a single step in the other direction when a light came on overhead.

"Is someone there?" shouted Bonifacia. Her own voice reverberated back down the empty corridor.

Peter shook his head. "Keep going," he urged.

As it turned out, there was no need for matches to light their path. Every few paces another electric lamp mounted to one of the innumerable bowed pilasters running the length of the tunnel turned on above their heads as the one behind switched off.

"How do the lamps know to do that?" asked Bonifacia in astonishment.

"I'm sure I don't know," he replied. "I've never seen anything like it, even in London." Another question for Don Modesto.

Hand-in-hand, they walked the cold dank corridor in silence, breath rising from their lips in tiny short-lived clouds. Peter draped his coat over Bonifacia's shoulders doing his best to fend off the chill, but it was little comfort overall. Water dripped, *blop, blop,* from the vaulted ceiling creating small pools on the floor and echoing softly first in front and then behind them. The tunnel just seemed to wind on endlessly as if excavated by some colossal worm.

"How much farther can it be?" groused Bonifacia. "I'm beginning to feel a bit woozy."

"I am too and it's not just from being tired. There's a vibration under the floor and in the walls that wasn't there before. Like trains rumbling through the Underground. Do you feel it?" Bonifacia nodded unhappily.

The vibration twisted into an audible hum that rang uncomfortably in their ears, growing louder and louder with each step. "Peter, if it doesn't stop soon I think I shall faint!"

Cupping their hands over their ears, they hustled forward at a trot. The disturbance eventually subsided, allowing them to resume a more sustainable stride. On and on they walked. How much time and how much distance they covered was difficult to say. After a very long while a light literally appeared at the end of the tunnel. Picking up the pace they soon reached the other doorway, this one also lit by an electric lamp mounted to one side.

"Merciful God!" cried Peter.

"I just pray there isn't a tunnel like this one on the other side," remarked Bonifacia.

Peter stopped dead in his tracks. The idea had never occurred to him. He suddenly envisaged an endless series of doors and tunnels leading nowhere—a cruel joke devised especially to torment overly inquisitive adolescents. "There's no handle here either," he carped. "Cold to the touch and just as smooth as the other one."

"I won't stand for it!" cried Bonifacia angrily. "Not again! I want out!" She lunged forward, probing the edges of the door with her tiny fingers. Peter began to give into his own worsening fears and scrambled to do the same on the side nearest the lamp. Averting his eyes from the flickering light, he reached over top of it thinking there might be some mechanism concealed there. His hand inadvertently brushed against the fixture and the door blinked out of existence, just as its counterpart had done when Bonifacia inserted the key.

There stood suddenly revealed a wide wood under a starry sky. That surprised Peter, quite frankly. They'd walked for so many hours he half expected to be greeted by the dawn. A rough trodden path led from the foot of the door to a small cottage some distance off, the glint of firelight shining through an unshuttered window and a wisp of pallid smoke issuing from the chimney top.

"What did you do?" demanded Bonifacia.

"Nothing."

"But why did this door open from the inside and not the other?" she persisted.

"I've no idea. I just brushed against the lamp."

She regarded him with unmistakable disappointment.

"How was I to know? It never occurred to me to mess with an electric lamp. I was looking for a button or a knob."

"Perhaps we should go back and give the other door another try," she suggested, her voice quavering in the darkness.

He gaped at her in disbelief. "And what if it makes no difference? We've been at this for hours, Bonnie. I'd sooner ask Don Modesto for a little charity. I'll tell him he can have his blasted tunnel. There's nothing to it but misery."

Deep down, Bonifacia must have felt as tired, hungry, and discouraged as Peter because she readily conceded the point. They'd been up since well before midnight and the prospect of trudging back through that dreary passage only to find the door on the other side still barred was too much to contemplate.

Peter looked out toward the cottage. "If this door is anything like the other, it will close right after us. Should we care?"

"I don't see how it matters now," replied Bonifacia. "Let's just get out of here."

They stood hand-in-hand and jumped together across the threshold. As expected, the door rematerialized behind them, but accompanied this time by the blast of a shrill horn in the distance. It reverberated through the forest, scattering animals in the darkness.

"What was that?" asked Bonifacia, taken aback.

"Dunno. Coachman's horn, maybe?" Peter turned to survey their surroundings. The tunnel emerged from the side of a small hummock framed in fine dressed stone. Like the entrance on the far side, it too was flanked by a diminutive sentinel carved of granite, the little fellow's palm raised upward to accept payment.

"We should recover that key from the other door when we get back," said Bonifacia. "Mama will be furious with us if she finds her precious wolf without it. You do still have the wolf, don't you Peter?"

He rummaged through his pocket to make certain it was still there. "Yup."

"I don't recognize this place," said Bonifacia, casting about. "I thought I'd seen most of the Rodriguez *estado de país* at one time or another. I can't think where we might be."

All at once Peter's legs began to buckle and he pointed with a trembling finger toward the night sky. "Oh dear God in heaven!"

She followed his glance. "How can it be?!" stammered Bonifacia, suddenly perceiving the object of his fear. They both sank to their knees.

"Two moons Bonnie! There are two moons in the sky!"

"What is this place?" she cried, taking firm hold of Peter.

They settled on the ground, balled up together with their backs to the tunnel door for safety, too frightened and too terrified to even move or speak. In an instant, a mere breath of time, the quiet wood, the sound of peeping frogs and crickets, the cottage, the starry sky, all of it took on a new and sinister bent. Even the air they breathed seemed suddenly a chancy thing. Their minds raced, chock-full with the worst sort of imaginings.

"Peter," said Bonifacia, "I want to go home."

Chapter 2

A Humble Paladin

Peter had no notion of how they might accomplish that. Two very solid doors blocked the tunnel behind them and the key, he presumed, remained stuck to the gnome's hand in the far meadow. His coat still draped across Bonifacia's shoulders, Peter raised his shirt collar and huddled against the chill night in sullen silence, brooding over the distant cottage and the tantalizing trace of smoke rising from the chimney top. They sat together like that for a very long while. Then finally, girding up his courage, Peter struggled to his feet.

"Don't even think it," piped Bonifacia, reading his mind.

"But it's doing us no good just sitting here," retorted Peter. "We should find out more about this place."

She regarded him with a pained expression. "I'm quite happy right here, thank you. If you had any sense at all you'd stay put too. Someone will be along in due course. Someone who can tell us what is really going on here and put things right." She wrapped her arms about her knees and hugged them to her chest.

Gazing at her, Peter was reminded of her mother and his aunt's cautionary words about staying away from the ruin in the meadow. There was precious little he could do about that now, save beating himself up for breaking his promise. To make matters worse, he'd made off with Generosa's precious little wolf (albeit with every good intention). How could he have foreseen the outcome? *How could anyone?* Still, Peter was filled with remorse, not the least for his precious cousin, whom he'd led, quite literally, down the garden path.

"You can stay here if you like, Bonnie, but I'm going to have a look about." He pointed across the clearing. Pale fingers of milk-white mist coiled round the boles of the distant trees, timidly probing the open sward and the lonely cottage, then backing suddenly away as if they'd trod on something unpleasant.

"Don't you even dream of leaving me here alone!" she exclaimed.

He offered her his hand. "Come along then."

She accepted, despite a powerful inclination to keep very near the tunnel entrance. Cautiously, they made their way across the field under the azure-tinged light of the twin moons.

"It all seems normal enough," remarked Bonifacia in an effort to reassure herself.

Peter glanced uneasily at the cottage and the wood beyond. "I suppose," he replied.

The dwelling was a modest affair, built of rough fieldstone capped with a wood shake roof, well-worn from many years of exposure to the elements. Nothing about the place struck Peter as particularly extraordinary or "other-worldly."

A glint of firelight shone through diamond-shaped panes set between narrow muntins. Together, they crept toward the window and clinging to the outer sill, quietly pulled themselves up on tiptoe to peer inside.

No one seemed to be about. The cottage, although cozy by any standard, was furnished with several fine pieces, including two commodious rockers, carved from dark wood in broad ivy patterns. Strings of onion and bundled herbs hung from low rafters next to a brace of coneys awaiting the cooking pot. A fire blazed to one side of the room, iron kettles on the boil. In front of the hearth lay a long table fashioned from two planks flanked by benches, hinting at the possibility of regular visitors. A bed, sideboard, and pantry box rounded out the dwelling's major furnishings. Aside from an odd sort of post or pedestal near the fire, the cottage would not have seemed much out of place in Britain or the Continent.

They were taking all this in when a single clear note, like the "*toot*" of a child's flute, sounded from somewhere close behind. Peter was in the course of turning about when something seized him firmly by the ankles and pulled him sharply to the ground. He landed with a pronounced thud that so startled Bonifacia she lost her breath and nearly toppled. Dragged off by his feet, Peter twisted around to see who, *or what,* had nabbed him. A shadowy figure stood calmly to one side clad in a coarse gray habit edged in faded blue piping. A deep tippet hood completely concealed the man's face (Peter at least *presumed* it was a man). But most alarming to Peter and Bonifacia was the creature sitting just to the fellow's right, a thing that could only be described as a "toad." And not just any ordinary toad. The size of a Saint Bernard with enormous saucer eyes and vibrant yellow skin bathed in rust-colored patches, the beast (to Peter's great horror) had him by its massive tongue and was in the process of reeling him in, rather like a fish on a line.

Bonifacia screamed for Peter to hold on, doing her utmost to rescue him by grasping his shoulders and pulling back with all the strength and determination she could muster. But she was just a sprig of a girl, after all, probably no more than six or seven stone in stocking feet. Her strenuous efforts on his behalf were woefully inadequate. Peter was, by this point, lamenting his untimely end when the habit-clad figure raised his tiny flute and gave it another short "*toot.*" The creature immediately released its grip on Peter's ankles, swiftly spooling back its gargantuan tongue and clamping shut its mouth with a resounding "*glop.*" All things relative, Peter breathed a heavy sigh of relief.

Winded from her exertions, Bonifacia stood at Peter's side, cheeks stained with tears, her tiny frame shaking with equal amounts of fear and vexation. As their assailant stepped forward, Peter couldn't help noticing the man's hands, human-like for the most part, but entirely sheathed in a coat of tawny fur! This was no Galician friar.

The figure gathered his staff from where it lay propped against a tree and motioned with one end in the direction of the cottage door. Peter got to his feet and dusted himself off. Meekly they went along, the way a cockerel goes quiet when carried off to the chopping block, no thought of bolting in either of their tired empty heads.

Bonifacia pulled the latch and together they stepped inside the cottage, the giant toad-like creature close upon their heels. A sennit mat lay to one side of the door and the monster nestled atop it, much the way a cat might knead its bedding before settling down for the night. There the beast remained ensconced, utterly rigid except for the act of breathing. Every so often it would blink, its two gigantic eyes never veering from them, even for an instant. They found its continued presence within the room, to say the least, unnerving.

Their captor herded Peter and Bonifacia toward the far end of the table, then gestured toward their pockets with his stick, evidently desiring them to empty out the contents. They obliged under the circumstances. Bonifacia had in her possession only a fine lace handkerchief, still marked with blood from her tumble in the ruin. The first item Peter laid out was a small folding knife.

"You might have used that to free yourself from the beast," remarked Bonifacia under her breath. Peter cast her a sidelong glance and continued to empty his pockets: a well-used hankie, a half-consumed box of matches, some string, and then with no little hesitation, his auntie's enameled wolf.

This last object elicited an altogether surprising reaction. The hirsute friar stood stock-still, then brought himself to his full height and solemnly bowed. When he raised his head again they caught a fleeting glimpse within the hood of deep-set eyes the color of liquid amber.

Bonifacia gazed at the fellow in bewilderment. After such rude and threatening treatment, this was hardly to be expected. Not knowing what else to do Peter reciprocated with a hesitant bow of his own and Bonifacia followed suit with a grudging but practiced curtsy. Wondering what could possibly happen next, they watched with growing curiosity as the owner of the cottage walked over to the sideboard, opened a drawer and removed a heavy brass key suspended from a chain, which he promptly slipped about his neck.

"Peter! The *Reíña Loba!*" gasped Bonifacia.

Indeed! Fixed to the top of the great key, right above the clover-shaped bow, was yet another variation on the running wolf—the *Reíña Loba*. The similarity to their own little wolf (the one Peter had nicked from his auntie's credenza) was beyond refute.

"What's it supposed to mean?" asked Bonifacia.

"It means, my dear Bonnie, that this chap, whoever he is, is somehow tied to the tunnel we came through and, quite probably, the door on the other side."

Their status suddenly (and inexplicably) elevated in the eyes of their jailer-cum-host, Bonifacia and Peter were permitted to reclaim their belongings and invited with a sweeping gesture of his furry hand to sit at the table. There being no obvious harm in it, they went along, enduring all the while the fixed gaze of the amphibian monster seated beside the door. The table was then set. Laying two large bowls in front of them, the voiceless specter spooned out a quantity of steaming broth that looked and smelled to Peter and Bonifacia remarkably familiar. Without bothering to serve himself, their host took up a seat at the far end of the table nearest the door.

Although they could not precisely see his face, they could tell he was watching them intently. For their part, they sat on their hands examining the fare upon their plates with a great deal of skepticism. But it smelled *so* good and *so* familiar. The companions had not slept nor eaten in many an hour. Their stomachs grumbled involuntarily and for the first time the thing in the corner croaked, probably out of empathy.

The cowled figure nodded encouragingly and Peter at last relented. Bonifacia watched wide-eyed as her cousin lifted his spoon and timidly sampled the broth. "It's *caldo,*" he pronounced and promptly availed himself of more.

"Pardon me?" replied Bonifacia.

"Not much different from your mama's." Peter spooned through the contents of his bowl, talking with his mouth half full. "Faba beans, a toadstool of some sort, pork, blood sausage, onion, garlic. Even a few leaves of *grelos*. It's *Caldo Gallego* all right, and blesséd good!"

"But how can that be?" Bonifacia picked up her own spoon and gave the soup a tentative sip. "Hey! You're right," she exclaimed. "*Moi bo!* But our host doesn't seem to be up on his etiquette, does he? *Caldo* is properly served as a winter dish."

"Fine by me," muttered Peter. "Maybe it's winter here …wherever *here* is." Hungry as little wolves, they lapped their meal down, forgetting for just a moment their far reaching troubles.

"That sort of makes up for things," quipped Peter, once they were finished.

Bonifacia set her soupspoon down on the table, gazed at their curious host, then back at Peter between puckered brows.

"Peter, where in heaven's name are we? What sort of place is this?"

He wiped his mouth with the cuff of his jacket. "I'm just as confounded as you, Bonnie. But I'll say this, if anyone can tell us how to get back home, it's this chap. Look at that key around his neck. He's involved with that tunnel, no mistaking it."

"I doubt he understands a word of what we're saying. If only he could speak," sighed Bonifacia.

"You haven't tried conversing with him in Spanish," prompted Peter, "…or Galician. He certainly knows how to cook like a Gallego."

Bonifacia cleared her throat. "*Perdoe,*" she said. "*Chámome Bonifacia. Perdinme. Necesito axuda.*"

If the fellow understood, he gave no sign of it. Instead, he got up and frittered about the sideboard. Removing the lid from a plain ceramic canister, he reached in and pulled out a quantity of glistening black beetles, placing them in a sticky heap atop the pedestal near the hearth. The big toad croaked in anticipation. "I wonder…" said Peter, watching all this with growing fascination.

The peculiar friar gave his little flute another "*toot.*" In the instant it takes to crack a coachman's whip the big toad's tongue lashed clear across the entire room, snatching the lot from atop the pedestal. It was over in the blink of an eye. Neither Peter nor Bonifacia had any time to react. The monster licked its lips and promptly reverted to its former condition, motionless except for those great blinking eyes.

"Ah Yuch!" cried Bonifacia, regarding the beast with new-found disgust. This newly revealed talent did nothing to enhance Peter's own regard for it. He reached down and self-consciously rubbed his ankles.

Following this little demonstration, their companion went about his housekeeping, afterward pulling up two rockers before the fire and motioning for the pair to reseat themselves. They obliged yet again and were rewarded with warm quilts to cover up. Peter could not say what hour of the day it was. Certainly many hours past midnight. It had been a very long journey to wherever it was they were—a remarkably good repast, a comfy chair beside the fire and the two young travelers were beyond all resistance. Peter was asleep the moment the blanket fell across his lap. Only once was he disturbed by voices in the night. *Voices?* thought Peter, but he was too exhausted to even raise his head. *In the morning,* he told myself and drifted back into a deep, deep sleep.

Peter was awakened by a gentle nudge upon the shoulder. A hint of morning sunshine greeted his eyes obscured by passage through leaded window glass. Shaking the cobwebs from his head he looked up to find himself staring straight into the face of a most unusual man. He called him a "man" because he had no other measure to go by, and he was for the most part very like one, possessing square cut features, penetrating corvine eyes, but most astounding of all, the largest, bushiest eyebrows one could ever imagine. To say this was no exaggeration. The fellow's brows nearly filled his forehead and were so long at the points nearest the ears that the individual was able to twist and wax the tips in such a way that they dipped far down and away from his face, like a magnificent set of drooping ram's horns.

Peter was naturally startled to be awakened by such an outlandish fellow, but the man smiled reassuringly, stepped back, removed his hat and bowed with a courteous flourish. Replacing his hat, he spoke with a lispy almost Castilian accent. "Lord Arbiter, we are honored to receive you. I am Dashwan, your servant."

Lord Arbiter? Peter pulled the quilt that still covered him up closer to his chin.

"I must first of all apologize for your treatment last night, but there was no way for Biixwaw to have recognized you. You look…" he hesitated as he searched for the right words, "…*different* than we expected." He cleared his throat before continuing. "I do understand you must be tired from your long journey, but nevertheless, we must make haste."

Peter took the opportunity to study in larger detail the man who had addressed him in so peculiar and so formal a fashion. All in all, he cut an impressive figure. Not yet middle aged he guessed, tall and slender, fair of skin, dressed in a splendid blue and silver embroidered coat open at the front and so long that the hem swept upon the ground. He carried a sword at his hip, but it looked more like ornamentation than anything to worry about. On his head sat a high circular hat of matching pale blue felt, a shiny black peak trimmed in argent and a badge above. There again, the running wolf!

He was not alone. Near the door stood another chap with the same sort of long spreading eyebrows, but groomed without pretension. This one obviously a military man, but of a sort centuries out of fashion on the Continent, replete with feathered casque, levelar armor and chain mail. In sharp contrast to the courteous ease of his companion, there was no smile upon the soldier's face. He stood all somber and business-like with one hand resting firmly on the hilt of a sword that looked anything but ornamental.

Their shadowy host, the enigmatic friar, stood off to one side in silence, no more revealed than the night before, the awful padde-like beast conspicuous in its absence. Peter glanced over to the chair in which Bonifacia had been sleeping. She was sitting bolt upright, watching these curious newcomers with wary fascination.

"I beg your pardon," said Peter. "I believe you may have me confused with someone else."

The grand-looking fellow, *Dashwan,* canted his head to one side as if to consider the possibility. "Are you not Manuel López?"

"Manuel López? No sir. My name is *Peter* López de Soto, and this," he added, gesturing toward Bonifacia, "is my cousin Bonifacia Espasande." A fantastic story Bonifacia's mother once shared about the supposed origins of the López family fortune suddenly occurred to him. "An ancestor, our great-great-great grandfather, was named Manuel López, but you couldn't possibly mean him. He died over two centuries ago."

Dashwan's face was a mask of utter indifference. "You are from the realm that is called *Gallaecia,* are you not?"

"Well, yes. That's true," replied Peter, a little surprised. "It's called *Galicia* now. Has been for a very long time."

"And you have the chain? The wolf I mean."

Peter removed the pendant from his pocket. "Do you mean this?"

"Precisely," answered Dashwan. He rested his chin on the tip of his index finger. "I am only a humble paladin of the court and do not claim to understand these matters. Whatever your true name may be, you have in your possession the token of office, came in response to the summons, and were permitted passage. Others more qualified will have to be the judge of you. We must proceed, my lord. We dare not tarry. The empress awaits."

"The empress?" interrupted Bonifacia, rising to her feet. "We will *not* proceed anywhere without more explanation. Do you understand? Peter is not your *arbiter,* whatever that is supposed to mean. He's just a boy, hardly fifteen. We only want to go home."

Peter threw off the quilt and walked over to stand beside his cousin in a demonstration of unity. Dashwan's expression went from vacant to something like pity. "Sweet girl," he said, "that will not be possible."

Those were *definitely* not the words she wanted to hear.

"Not possible?" repeated Bonifacia.

"I'm afraid not. The portal was set for travel only in one direction."

"The portal? You mean the tunnel?" corrected Bonifacia.

"Yes, I suppose you could call it that."

"Well then, you can bloody well set it back in the other direction, can't you?" she commanded, losing her patience altogether.

"Only a wizard can do that, and he would need the key."

"Isn't he a wizard?" asked Peter, pointing at the impenetrable figure who kept the dog-sized toad on a mat beside his door at night.

"Him? No. Biixwaw is a *gatekeeper,*" replied Dashwan, with a respectful dip of his head in the latter's direction. "Perhaps the last." The gatekeeper inclined his cowled head in acknowledgement.

"Then where do we find a wizard who can open the portal for us?" persisted Peter.

"Alas, wizards are very few these days."

"God in Heaven!" cried Bonifacia. "Is that all you can spout? Obfuscation? I can't take any more of this nonsense!" she shouted, stamping her foot in anger. "Wizards and portals and gatekeepers!" She stormed suddenly across the room, past the astonished soldier and out the door. Peter hurried after her.

There was a troop of horsemen waiting outside, all of them with brows like Dashwan and the captain, but plaited in a tight braid drawn back over their ears. They stared after Peter and Bonifacia in confusion as they trotted from the cottage toward the tunnel entrance. Peter could hear the lot of them trailing behind. It would have been simple enough for so many grown men to bar the way to two adolescent children, but none prevented them.

Bonifacia stopped at the tunnel door with Peter standing next to her. Dashwan, the captain, the horsemen and the gatekeeper formed a ragged line in front. "Open this door!" she bellowed.

No one made a move. No one said anything in reply.

She pointed at the gatekeeper, Biixwaw. "You! Come over here and open this door. Do you hear me? I want it opened this instant!"

Biixwaw only spread his arms in apology.

"My lady," said Dashwan. "It simply cannot be done. Not without a key. And even then it would require a wizard to make the necessary adjustments."

"Then find us the key and bring a wizard!" She began to cry.

Dashwan just shook his head.

She sat down on the ground and buried her face in her hands, sobbing. Peter knelt down beside her and wrapped an arm around her, feeling horribly guilty and utterly responsible for their predicament.

"My lord and lady," said Dashwan. "You must understand. It is dangerous for us to linger here. We must go."

"Dangerous is it now?" Peter gaped at the man with growing disbelief.

"The alarm was sounded last night when you came through the portal. We did not think to silence it and Menom has spies everywhere. Come," he pleaded, "the hour is late and the rebellion fast becoming unmanageable. The empress will be much relieved to hear of your arrival and, no doubt, desires your counsel. My lord, please. No more questions. We must make haste."

Peter turned to Bonifacia. "He must be soft in the head," he said with growing exasperation. "I'm not Manuel López."

She rose to her feet, wiping the tears from her eyes. "Of course you're not, Peter. But it seems we're not being offered any choice."

Peter, for his part, could think of no alternative. They obediently followed the others back to the cottage. His head felt as though it were filled with pieces of broken glass. Some mistake had been made. That much was obvious. Other than that, he could make no sense of what was going on. Spies from Menom? What was that supposed to mean? All he really understood was that there was no going back, not without help. And rescue seemed unlikely. Who would find the portal door within the ruin and come looking for them? Certainly not Cousin Herbert.

The gatekeeper prepared two small horses. "You heard Dashwan," said Peter as they saddled up. "The empress or this so-called wizard can get us home." It was an encouraging thought.

"Maybe," replied Bonifacia. "I just don't fancy the idea of losing sight of that tunnel. It's the only way back, as far as we know. We don't even know for certain where these people are taking us, do we?"

"To the empress," answered Peter. "That's what Dashwan said."

"This is insane," countered Bonifacia, looking both frustrated and angry. "How's it going to be when she finds out you're *not* Manuel López?"

Peter blinked. "I don't like it either Bonnie, but clearly we need some answers and I don't think we're going to find any lounging about here."

"You keep saying that. It's just the sort of thing that got us into this in the first place."

She was right, of course. If it weren't for Peter's stubborn curiosity they'd never have ventured beyond the west mead.

Under the watchful gaze of the soldiers, they tightened their girths, adjusted their stirrups, and mounted with a helpful leg up from one of the troopers. Dashwan, the only member of their party with a smile on his face, got astride his own beautiful dappled gray while showering the two wayward companions with blithe words of encouragement.

At a signal from the captain they rode off under escort, four troopers riding point, the others in tandem behind, their burgee-tipped lances fluttering in the morning breeze. Peter turned to watch the hooded gatekeeper standing like an old elm beside the doorway to his cottage, and for some inexplicable reason, waved goodbye.

Chapter 3

Separate Ways

The road was evidently little traveled. And although their pace was undemanding, they halted only for a cold repast or to briefly rest and water the horses. If they looked to either side at any time, they might have thought they were still at home in Galicia, the landscape flush with twisted oaks and chestnuts amid gray outcroppings of lichen-covered granite. But looking forward, all they could see were the backs of a medieval captain of horse and a flamboyant paladin. It was a stark and visible reminder of where they were, or rather, where they were not. If that were not enough, they needed only to glance up at the night sky.

Weary after countless hours in the saddle, the party encamped on a brae above a picturesque brook, the soothing purl of its dark waters dampening the voices of the soldiers as they arranged a picket for the evening and set a campfire. Their meal consisted of seed cake and mild cheese accompanied by sea-blue eggs fried up open face in a pan set over the fire. Bonifacia could only bring herself to nibble at the cake.

"Queer as they are, these eggs are actually pretty damn good," said Peter, happy to have a bit of hot food in his belly after a long ride. "You really ought to give them a try."

"I haven't seen a hen the entire way, or even a farmhouse," retorted Bonifacia. "And I especially don't care for the look of those eggs." She grimaced. "You don't know how safe any of that food is to eat, do you Peter? You're not one of *them.*"

Peter shrugged. "Suit yourself. I don't know about that gatekeeper back there, but these blokes look human enough for me. I'll take my chances." He greedily downed the rest of his supper.

That night as the twin moons rose above the treetops, Dashwan and the other soldiers, save one, gathered together in a tight circle. At first, Peter and Bonifacia thought they were preparing to discuss their plans or the route for the next day. To their surprise Dashwan and the others stood shoulder to shoulder with arms entwined, like schoolboys arranged in a scrum, and commenced to pray. The odd man out, meanwhile, settled himself beneath a tree some distance away and began to play a sorrowful tune on a small bulb-shaped ocarina that hung from a rope about his neck.

Bonifacia and Peter were accustomed to saying their prayers before bed. Not wishing to embarrass themselves by appearing any less devout in the eyes of their escort they indicated their desire to join the circle and were rewarded with an invitation to stand alongside. Peter and Bonifacia couldn't say from the words spoken that they were praying to the same god, but a prayer is a prayer after all.

"Dashwan?" asked Bonifacia, as they sat together about the dying embers of the fire.

"Yes, my lady?"

"What did you mean when you said that we responded to a summons?"

"Not *we,* my lady. The summons was specifically for the lord arbiter. If you'll forgive me, these are perilous times." His eyes fell on Peter. "You should never have permitted Her Ladyship to accompany you through the portal. That was very ill-advised, my lord."

"I don't understand much of what you're saying," replied Peter. "Summoned by whom, and why? I'm not even sure how. And just what perils are we facing exactly?"

"You're trying to trap me?" he asked suspiciously. "These are trick questions?"

"I'm telling you, we don't understand anything of what's going on here. We wouldn't be asking otherwise."

Dashwan frowned uncertainly. "Very well, I'll go along, but I caution you, I was very young when all this was arranged, just a lad not even arrived at court. Captain Gothrain may know more about it than I…"

Gothrain, his heavy gray brows dancing in the embers' light, only shrugged. "There was a lot of fighting going on back then, so close on the heels of the Og'yre War. What I know now, I learned much later from others."

Dashwan took that to mean no. "The answer to your question," he continued, "surrounds a dispute over the territory called the Keartlands."

"A dispute between whom?" interjected Bonifacia. So many questions were racing through her head. Now that she'd had a little food and rest, she could hardly get them out fast enough.

Dashwan's left brow rose so high that it threatened to topple his beautiful blue hat. "*Between whom?* my lady. Why, the Empire of the Ulfair, of course, and the four dominions."

"I see," she replied. "And this place, I mean where we're sitting right now..." she pointed toward the ground, "...lies within the Empire of the Ulfair?"

"Certainly."

"Just go on," prompted Peter, casting Bonifacia a beseeching glance.

"Well, as I was saying, it began as a dispute over control of the Keartlands, the lands between the rivers Talsis and Bos. The territory has been the root of many wars over many ages. The last war was particularly trying."

"Pah!" spat Gothrain. "An understatement if I've ever heard one."

This time, Dashwan ignored the captain. "Matters were escalating beyond all reason with neither side gaining the upper hand. Desperation and hopelessness led to criminal acts of a most appalling kind. It was then, a little over fifty years ago as fate would have it, that a most remarkable man, Manuel López, came into our midst."

Peter perked up. "Wait a second. There, you said it again— *Manuel López.*"

"Yes."

"But don't you see? That's not possible. He died over *two hundred* years ago, assuming we're talking about the same chap. How can he have been tripping about this place *fifty* years ago?"

"That is curious, isn't it?" replied Dashwan.

"Curious? It's preposterous!" blurted Peter. "The name is common enough. It can't have been *our* ancestor. It was obviously someone else."

"May I see your chain again, the wolf I mean?" asked Dashwan. Peter humored him, drawing the little enameled wolf from his pocket and holding it out for all to see. "Well," said Dashwan. "It's missing its chain, but there's no mistaking that, my lord. One of a kind. The arbiter's token of office. A gift from the young empress. As I said, not fifty years ago."

Peter rubbed anxiously at his own brow. "But that can't be."

"Peter," said Bonifacia, resting her hand on his arm. "I'm beginning to wonder. Do you really think it preposterous? We're in a land with two moons, giant yellow toads and God knows what else?"

He turned to face Dashwan with his enormous drooping eyebrows. "But Bonnie…"

"Let Dashwan tell his story, Peter. I'm sorry I interrupted him earlier. Maybe there's a clue within it that will help us find our way home."

There was no sense arguing that.

"Where was I?" said Dashwan, clearing his throat.

"You were telling us about Manuel López."

"Ah, yes. The war was going very badly, for both sides, and there seemed no way out. Hopelessness and despair were the order of the day. Then, as it happens, a wizard came through the portal, the very same one you both emerged from. Only, the wizard did not realize he had been followed, by several off-worlders much like yourselves—no eyebrows to speak of."

Bonifacia could not resist interrupting one more time. "*Off-worlders*. That's what you call us?"

"Your planet circles a different star, does it not?"

She sighed. "I'm beginning to think so. This is all so bewildering. Do go on."

"Cunning these off-worlders must have been to accomplish such a feat. The portals are designed to prevent such trespass. The intruders overcame the gatekeeper and set upon the countryside hereabouts with an eye to harry and plunder. With the army serving far off, there was little could be done to prevent them at first. But one by one the brigands were hunted down and slain, with one exception—Manuel López.

"López was captured and taken to Piernot for interrogation. I don't know how it came to pass, but after a period of imprisonment he was released and placed in the service of the emperor, Kansôr IX. It would seem López was blessed with a silver tongue and convinced the aging sovereign that he could do something to bring about an end to the war. Kansôr, for reasons I cannot know, believed and trusted this foreigner. He was granted a commission and sent under the protection of a white flag to parley with Kor Sook Far XVI, ruler of Bankor Fal.

"Against all odds López obtained a truce with Sook Far who recommended him to others. López returned to Piernot with a miraculous wide-ranging offer of peace. *Lord Arbiter* López spent the next ten years of his life enjoying the fruits of his splendid achievement."

"But what then?" prodded Bonifacia, taking a keener interest. "What became of Manuel?"

"You really don't know? The old emperor died and his daughter, Xhôn, assumed the throne. The lord arbiter appealed to the new empress explaining his earnest desire to return home. Alas, he had never been pardoned for his earlier crimes and by law could not be released from his obligation. The empress, bless her heart, took pity on him, granting López leave until summoned back. It was understood this would occur just about the time our treaty with the four dominions was due to expire."

"So he went back through the tunnel?" prompted Peter.

"Yes. Nigh on forty years ago."

Gothrain cut in, "The empress, forgive her, waited too long to issue the summons. The treaty will expire in a matter of weeks and the rebellion has got out of hand. I fear it is too late, even for the lord arbiter." He lifted his head to gaze directly at Peter. It seemed to Peter that the captain's brows bore the great weight of many years and a great many battles.

Dashwan nodded in agreement. "What's more, the portals are aging and little maintained these days. I should think they will be entirely unworkable once the wizards have altogether vanished from this world. I was surprised to learn a wizard could even be found when the order came down to issue the summons. You are lucky to have got through."

"Lucky?!" exclaimed Peter. That was a perspective he didn't quite appreciate.

Dashwan's eyes shifted between Peter and Bonifacia. "We've been waiting nearby ever since. Nearly a month now. Not too close, mind. Didn't want to alert Menom. Not if we could help it. Stupid of me not to have remembered the alarm."

"I'm curious. What form did this summons take?" inquired Bonifacia. "How would it have seemed to us?"

"You must have recognized it. The badge of the Ulfair Court. A black wolf, of course, ensigned with the imperial crown." He pointed to the emblem on his hat.

Bonifacia rolled her eyes. "The wolf in the ruin!" Peter blanched with embarrassment, recalling his theory about treasure and their good neighbor, Don Modesto.

"This is an interesting game," said Dashwan, by way of apology. "Have I answered all your questions? It is getting rather late and we have a long ride ahead of us tomorrow."

Peter and Bonifacia crawled under their blankets next to the fire. "I should like to meet this Empress Xhôn after all," announced Bonifacia. "I think you're right Peter. If anyone is likely to have some proper answers for us, it will be her."

"Dashwan isn't very forthcoming, is he? He and Gothrain keep talking as if *I'm* this lord arbiter fellow. Nothing I say seems to make any difference to them."

"Peter?"

"Yes?"

"I'm sorry I acted so badly earlier. Like a spoiled child. I should be more courageous."

"Don't be ridiculous," he replied. "I think you've been very brave indeed. I'm frightened too, you know. This is an awful mess I've got us into."

The dimples on her cheeks accentuated whenever Bonifacia smiled. It made Peter feel better somehow to know that she was coping with her fears. He was grateful in a sense for her company. *Together,* they would work this all out. He was sure of it. But now he had a question for her. "Bonnie? Where do you suppose we are?"

"Somewhere amongst the stars I should think." She looked up into the clear night sky. "*Boa noite,* Peter."

He followed her gaze upward. "Good night, Bonnie."

They rose with the first sound of birdsong, shaking the dew from their blankets. Peter noticed as he went about feeding and grooming the horses that the one young soldier who had set himself apart during prayer the evening before had spent the night well away from his companions. He noticed too that his uniform was nowhere near the make or quality of the others, well worn at the knees and elbows. He found this contrast peculiar enough to ask Gothrain about it.

"That one?" The captain's face displayed equal amounts of disdain and pity. "He's an akritar, a frontier guard, not one of us."

"What's he doing here then?"

"The rebellion has taken its toll on the Household Guard and regular army. Standards call for a minimum of twelve to a half troop so they're filling the ranks with simpletons from the country. Orders say we've got to take him along, but that doesn't mean I can force my men to associate with the likes of him, nor would I want to."

Peter watched the akritar as he cared for his horse and fixed his own morning meal, never once asking for or receiving support from his comrades. They breakfasted and once again took to the road, four horsemen up front, followed by the captain, Dashwan and themselves, eight riders including the akritar pulling up the rear. The road through the forest was now much more defined, leading their column past the occasional woodsman's cottage, each with no more than a small garth, pen and smokehouse. Every so often the road transformed into a series of switchbacks lowering them down the side of a sheer dell, where they clattered across a rough hewn bridge or splashed through a shallow ford and up again on the other side. In this way the hours passed, the forest never much altering from the twisted roburs and chestnuts so like Galicia and the *Ribeira Sacra*.

Bored, Peter nudged his horse alongside Dashwan, thinking to pick up their conversation where it left off. "Aside from the fact that I keep telling you my name is Peter López de Soto, not Manuel López, does it not strike you that I'm a tad young to have negotiated a peace treaty some fifty years ago? From what you've told me, your lord arbiter should be well into his seventies by now."

"That, as I have said, is for others to decide," replied Dashwan. "My task is to see the lord arbiter delivered safely to Her Imperial Majesty." He smiled at Peter, content in his duty as he saw it.

Peter decided he was wasting his breath on the man and fell back to ride alongside Bonifacia. He griped, "I can't seem to get anything of substance out of Dashwan."

"Keep trying," she replied. "He's polite enough, but finds my questions tiresome and seems altogether displeased that you brought me along." She pointed at a stone wall in passing. "I've been trying to fix certain landmarks in my head. I thought we could retrace our steps if necessary, but now I'm not so certain. We've made so many twists and turns I can't retain them any more. If we can't get hold of an actual map, I think we should draw one up for ourselves."

Peter thought that was a capital idea and was about to suggest a way in which they might accomplish it when a cry rang out from the horsemen to their rear. They immediately turned in their saddles to see what had happened. Four of their column lay on the ground, pierced through the chest with fletched arrows! As Peter and Bonifacia watched, the remaining horsemen reined in their rearing animals lowered their lances, and charged off in pursuit of their attackers hidden amid the trees.

Captain Gothrain and Dashwan immediately drew their swords. Gothrain turned to look for his scouts, but they'd imprudently allowed themselves to round a bend in the road and were now nowhere in sight. Gothrain's face was flush with anger. He brandished his sword, dug in his spurs and rode swiftly to Peter and Bonifacia's side, Dashwan riding hard at his heels. A heartbeat later, a bolt passed directly through the poor captain's neck, toppling him from his horse. He managed to crawl a few feet, then moved no more.

All this happened so fast. Peter had never seen a man die. He felt more shock than fear or terror, having no other instinct than to stay close to Bonifacia. Of the horsemen that thundered off into the woods, only one returned—the young akritar, his lance and helmet discarded and hell-bent on escape. He reined in his excited horse beside Dashwan.

"Take the girl!" yelled Dashwan, still brandishing his own weapon. "Ride!"

The akritar reacted like a shot, never hesitating. He had no difficulty plucking Bonifacia from her saddle in one fell move. With a swift kick to his horse he bolted off and away into the trees, Bonifacia tucked firmly under one arm.

"No!" screamed Peter, turning his horse to ride after them, but Dashwan had anticipated his move and seized his animal by the reins.

"You will get yourself killed that way. These people will not harm the lord arbiter."

"Bonnie!" he cried until he was hoarse in the throat and tears flowed down his cheeks in torrents.

Their opponents meanwhile revealed themselves, moving slowly out of the forest to surround them. Plainly, this had been a well orchestrated ambush. They were bowmen for the most part, draped in russet-colored cloaks and arrayed in fine corium armor. Gothrain and his men never stood a ghost of a chance against so many, so well prepared.

From around the blind corner that had spirited away their scouts there rode a small party of dark-clad horsemen. The first of their number raised his hand to halt the others. He was an imposing figure, as much or more a warrior from his appearance than the late Captain Gothrain. The man said nothing in the way of greeting. Instead he drew his sword and approached the comely paladin. Dashwan, in turn, gestured for Peter to stay back and rode forward to meet him. "Dashwan!" shrieked Peter, realizing what was about to take place.

The courtier turned to Peter at that very moment and winked a telling smile. Then, spurring his horse forward, clashed with the enemy. As it happens, Dashwan was no stranger to the blade. He fought bravely and with a degree of ferocity Peter had not thought him capable. But the end was a foregone conclusion. Dashwan fell defending his "lord arbiter" and all that Peter could do about it was sit his horse and weep helplessly.

When it was over, Dashwan's murderer rode leisurely toward him. Peter thumped the flanks of his horse, urging her to gallop off in pursuit of Bonifacia. But it was a small matter for the foe to cut off his escape and rein him in.

The warrior removed his helmet revealing a hard-edged and cruel face, his unkempt and sweated brows plastered down the two sides of his jaw. "*This* is the lord arbiter?!" the man laughed disdainfully. "A bobtail boy!" Taking off a heavy gauntlet he mussed the hair atop Peter's head with mock affection. Peter recoiled and spat on him. Instinctively, the destroyer's arm went up to bash him, but he held back at the last moment and laughed again. "Gag him and tie the boy's hands."

The bodies of Peter's hapless escort were kicked to the side of the road and left to rot on the cold ground. The vanquishers marched off in a narrow column through the woods, leaving the road behind. Bonifacia did not return. She had succeeded in making her escape together with the young akritar. That, at least, is what Peter chose to believe.

They traveled slowly, the majority of their party on foot, a bowman leading Peter's horse by the reins. Peter occupied his time twisting at the ropes that bound his wrists, and watching for landmarks he could employ to guide himself back after he'd made his escape. It was foolish thinking of course, but his pride blinded him to all other possibilities. Dashwan, he remembered, had mentioned something about 'spies from Menom.' He couldn't tell from that if Menom were a person or a place. He thought, perhaps, the sadistic brute that led this band of cutthroats was the man himself. There was no telling, his demands for information ignored at every turn.

On they wound in silence through the indecipherable forest, rarely breaking for rest or refreshment. In the dark of night they stopped to eat and sleep without making camp. Each evening Peter was routinely tied to a wide bole and given a single scrap of stale bannock to gnaw on. With his aching back pressed against the tree he would drift to sleep only to be awakened a short time later with a rude kick to the shin. The bowman assigned to him would then untie his legs and gesture for him to mount up, a clumsy procedure with both hands bound, but accomplished nevertheless. Off they'd go again, the sun not yet risen above the horizon.

It was hard for Peter to stay awake. Each time he nodded off, he nearly tumbled from the saddle and had to wrench himself upright. His body ached from the continual strain and effort.

The company regained the road at last and the endless gray forest slowly gave way to fields of freshly tilled soil and verdant pasture just new to leaf. Farmers and townsfolk suspended their labors to watch them pass.

Mentally and physically exhausted from the journey, Peter was actually relieved when the column finally turned up a wide drive at the end of which stood a great stone manor behind a sturdy foss and rampart. The soldiers formed ranks and a small squad that included himself and the bowman under whose charge he'd been given advanced within the gates, led by their odious captain. They were met by the manor guard who kept a wary eye upon them.

A thin sallow faced man stepped forward, bowed deferentially, and was addressed by Peter's malefactor. "Where is your master?" his kidnapper demanded.

"Lord Palkvo welcomes you to his home, Captain Menhar, and awaits you in the Blue Room."

Menhar. Peter deliberately fixed the name in his mind.

"Bring him," commanded Menhar. The bowman hauled Peter down from his horse and prodded him to follow along. He'd been in the saddle for such a long time he felt weak in the knees and struggled to remain upright. The lord of the manor, Lord Palkvo, was in conference with two other men when they entered the room. He finished his conversation before looking up. *Whoever this man is,* thought Peter, *he's no friend of Menhar and important enough to risk slighting him.*

"Palkvo, gracious as ever," sneered the captain.

"Forgive me Captain Menhar, you were not expected. To what do I owe this pleasure?"

Menhar beckoned for Peter to step forward. He obliged, opting to avoid the indignity of being further prodded. "I have a task for you from the Duke of Menom. You are to keep the lord arbiter here until he arrives."

So Menom is a man, thought Peter. *Not a place.*

"The lord arbiter?" exclaimed Palkvo. "Why this is a boy! I met the lord arbiter once, many years ago. This boy is not he."

At last, someone talking sense.

"Whoever he is, he arrived through the portal in response to the witch's summons. Dashwan had him under escort."

"And what of Dashwan?" inquired Palkvo.

"He has gone to meet his maker," replied Menhar, icily.

"You murdered him in cold blood!" shouted Peter.

This time Menhar did not hesitate, knocking Peter to the floor with an iron fist. Palkvo did nothing at all to intercede. He spoke with a measure of self-control. "Killing Dashwan was unwise, Menhar. The empress will not take his death lightly."

He scoffed. "What of it? She and her kind are finished."

Palkvo looked uneasy. "As you wish. I will care for the boy until Lord Borganin arrives. Are the bindings really necessary?"

"His gob is more trouble than his hands. See that he is not harmed. The duke has plans for him."

Palkvo proffered Menhar a modest bow. More, Peter presumed, out of obeisance to the Duke of Menom (or "Lord Borganin"?) than the evil captain.

"The Bakan, Joshkar, will remain here with the boy," added Menhar, nodding in the direction of his myrmidon bowman, "as will a company of my soldiers. You will see to their accommodation and provision."

"A company!" protested Lord Palkvo. "I will not stand for it!"

"You will do as you are told, Palkvo. They will be withdrawn after Lord Borganin has seen the boy."

Palkvo was livid, but obviously powerless to prevent the de facto occupation of his estate.

"See that he is not harmed," repeated Menhar, taking his own leave. He spun about and departed the hall with a gratuitous sneer in Peter's direction.

Palkvo turned to Peter's freshly appointed guardian. "Remove his restraints," he ordered. The bowman, *Joshkar,* brandished a swift knife, slicing the ropes from Peter's hands. He rubbed at the raw skin on his wrists. His reluctant host looked squarely at Peter. "What is your name?" asked Palkvo, levelly.

Peter had no reason, as yet, to offer Lord Palkvo any offense. "López de Soto," he replied. "*Peter* López de Soto," he added for emphasis.

"López de Soto?" Palkvo seemed genuinely surprised. "You are the *son* of Manuel López?"

"I beg your pardon my lord, I believe he was my great-great-great grandfather."

Palkvo raised a questioning brow. "Indeed? Amran, be so kind as to escort our guest to his room and see to his wrists."

Still sore, Peter did his best at a bow, which Palkvo returned in kind, and then followed Palkvo's steward, Amran, out of the hall with his own personal guard and perpetual shadow, Joshkar, in tow.

It was evidently not the first time this sort of protective arrangement had been used in the old manor house. Peter's room was high up in one corner of the structure beneath the rafters. It was well enough appointed, but only a small window, hardly wider than his head, provided light and fresh air. To get to this room from the inner corridors of the manor it was necessary to pass through an intermediate room, which was, of course, assigned to his taciturn jailer, Joshkar. Peter's one consolation was that Joshkar's abode, owning to its remoteness, was hardly more accommodating than his own, possessing no window at all.

Peter was permitted a few hours each day to wander a secluded garden within the towering walls of the manor. Whenever Joshkar had some errand or other to attend to, he was locked unceremoniously in his room with nothing to do but lie on the bed and stare up at the ceiling. These were occasions for Peter to worry about Bonifacia and wonder at her fate—an effective antidote for wallowing in self-pity. He missed her terribly, no less her always prudent counsel. These solitary hours also afforded him plenty of time to go over the things he'd learned, or not learned, about the circumstances of his own captivity. He still had many more questions than he had answers, but one thing was abundantly clear, knowledge was the key to his well-being. He was determined to learn all that he could before the arrival of the enigmatic duke. The question was, *how?*

A key rattled in the lock. Joshkar stood in the doorway.

"Lord Palkvo desires to speak with you."

Peter sat up in his bed. "Ah, so you can speak," he teased. "I was beginning to think Menhar had cut out your tongue."

Joshkar did not dignify his taunt with a response, only motioned toward the door.

"Very well turnkey," said Peter, falling in step. Palkvo greeted him coolly. Peter, for his part, bowed respectfully. "My lord."

Palkvo cut directly to the chase. "You say you are the great-great grandson of Manuel López?"

"Great-great-*great* grandson," he corrected. "He's been dead for over two hundred years."

"You have proof of what you say?"

He had to think about that. "No, not especially. I can recount for you my lineage. It is something Galicians are generally good at."

Palkvo scratched thoughtfully at his salt and pepper brows. "That will not be necessary."

It was Amran's turn to ask a question. "How was it that you came through the portal, young de Soto?"

That was easy. "We had the key."

"We?" replied Amran.

They don't know about Bonifacia! Peter wondered if there was any good reason to hide her presence from them. He decided not. Borganin would tell them soon enough. "My cousin, Bonifacia, and myself. This all started because we were chasing butterflies and stumbled on the black wolf."

Amran cast Lord Palkvo a furtive glance.

"Where is this cousin now?" asked Palkvo.

"She escaped with one of our escort when our party was beset. I could not say where she is at present. Safe I hope."

"And you say you have a key to the portal?"

"*Had,* my lord. It was left behind." Peter reached into his pocket and removed the *Reíña Loba*. Menhar, for whatever reason, had thought to leave it in his possession. "The key belongs with this. It has been in our family for generations."

Palkvo rose from his chair at the sight of the little jeweled wolf. "Bring it here."

Peter hesitated.

"Don't worry. I shan't take it from you."

He held the little wolf out for him to see. Amran and Lord Palkvo examined it carefully, then handed it back.

"That is a pretty treasure you have there, Lord de Soto. Mind you take great care of it. The Wolf Queen does not bestow such tokens lightly."

"Wolf Queen?" he exclaimed. He'd heard that name before.

"The Empress Xhôn," replied Palkvo.

"The empress is the Wolf Queen?"

"It is a sobriquet for any female who sits upon the throne of Kaladar."

Peter thought he was beginning to understand a little of this place, but now he was thoroughly confused. "Are we in Kaladar?" he asked. "I thought this was the Empire of the Ulfair."

Palkvo looked slightly amused. "No and yes child. You have crossed into the province of Orn. Kaladar is where you were captured. Both Kaladar and Orn are part of the empire, at least for the present."

Confused and frustrated. "Can you arrange for me to be sent back to Kaladar? I should very much like to speak with the empress" said Peter.

Palkvo's face grew decidedly grim. "Did you not hear Captain Menhar's instructions? You are to wait here for the arrival of the Duke of Menom."

"I just thought…"

Palkvo cut him off. "You thought wrong. You will remain here as our guest until the duke's arrival."

Peter stood in silence for a moment, biting his lip. "If I may ask, my lord. Who *exactly* is Lord Borganin?"

"The Duke of Menom, Governor of Orn. Our prince."

"Does the empress not rule Orn?" he asked.

"Such an inquisitive mind," observed Palkvo. "Have you not put all the pieces together? We are in rebellion. The Queen of Kaladar—the empress—reigns in name only. Lord Borganin will soon unseat her and rule in her place. It is only a matter of time."

Peter could only imagine someone trying to overthrow Queen Victoria. *The very idea!* However little he knew Dashwan and Captain Gothrain, he perceived them to be decent men and understood they were loyal to the empress. Unable to mask his revulsion, he sputtered "I thought you were different, but you're just like Menhar. Aren't you? A worthless self-serving traitor!"

"You go too far!" roared Palkvo. "Someone take the boy away before I do something I may regret!"

Chapter 4

Henrik

"Stop! Stop! Let me down!" screeched Bonifacia as they zig-zagged through the wood at a mad gallop. Brown sweat and foam from the straining beast clung to Bonifacia's pretty blue pinafore. A buckle on the soldier's cross belt jabbed her shoulder while the pommel worked against her lower back imparting a mean black bruise. But the akritar forged on, holding her tight in the saddle before him.

Grasping limbs from the surrounding forest streaked perilously close to Bonifacia's face and she winced and wiggled to prevent fragments of brake and branch from striking her. "Oh stop!" she cried.

The horse grunted with each long stride, snorting loudly as the akritar reined first left and then right, narrowly avoiding trees and outcroppings, once or twice even jumping a fallen timber. They rode on at this interminably breakneck pace, Bonifacia bumping against the akritar like a raggedy doll.

"Oh *Dios!* Stop!" she pleaded in agony and fear, but on he pressed into the forest until the horse could give no more. At last they slowed to a trot, then a walk and then a halt somewhere deep within the wood. She could feel the akritar loose his grip, letting her slip slowly to the ground.

Brushing herself off and wiping away the tears, Bonifacia forced herself to her feet, almost toppling in the process. "I've lost my hairpin," she sniveled. The akritar remained slumped in the saddle. For a moment she wondered if he'd been injured and started to worry, but he stirred finally and slowly lowered himself from the horse.

With his eyes fixed upon her, he bent at the waist to catch his breath. Pulling himself back up to his full height, he returned to his horse where it rested amid the trees, its long neck stretched low to the ground. The animal's powerful chest and shoulders still heaved from the monumental exertion of its run. It raised its head at his approach and the akritar scratched the animal affectionately between the ears. Then moving around the horse as if in slow motion he reached under, undid the girth, and slipped off the saddle. For a long drawn out moment the akritar stared at Bonifacia, tears welling in his bloodshot eyes. He pulled a long knife from the top of his boot and studied it carefully.

Bonifacia stood stock-still, not fully comprehending. She watched him reach for the reins, tap the horse behind one knee and then gently coax it to the ground. The reason was now apparent—a thick quarrel protruded from the animal's flank. She gasped at the sight of it.

The akritar got down on one knee, cradling the horse's head in the crux of his arm. The animal gazed calmly up at him, regarding its master with unreserved love. With one quick motion of his knife the akritar slit the creature's throat, cosseting its head until the lifeblood drained away. Bonifacia shuddered and turned her head.

"Girl," said the akritar, regaining his feet.

She faced him, unable to look upon the lifeless creature.

"There is a house some ways from here where we may find safety for a time. With luck we can make it there in a few days. Can you walk?"

"Yes, I think so," said Bonifacia, though her body still ached from their harrowing ride.

He pulled a water bag and satchel from the saddle and tossed them to her. "I can't carry everything."

Bonifacia tugged the straps over her head.

"Ready?" he asked. She nodded, following after him in silence.

They walked deeper and deeper into the forest. There were no roads, no trails or footpaths that she could discern. Even the sound of birdsong evaporated. In a way, she found the undisturbed forest comforting. It seemed unlikely the enemy would pursue them into a place so far removed.

"What's your name?" she asked the akritar, shattering the dense stillness.

"Henrik," he replied, never breaking his stride.

"My name is Bonifacia," she said.

"I know."

"Where is it we're going?"

"Someplace," he said.

"That's not very helpful."

"Helpful?" He stopped short and turned on her. "Girl, do me a favor. Stop your garrulous prating and just keep up."

Bonifacia glared at him. "As you wish."

They carried on, slowly but steadily, picking their way through the forest until darkness fell and they could go no more. In the shelter of a tapering dingle, Henrik called a halt for the night. "We'll camp here," he said, searching about for a level place to make their beds. "You can use my cloak for cover."

"No thank you," said Bonifacia stubbornly.

"Just take it, will you."

"If you insist." She kicked some fallen leaves into a tolerable mattress and laid out Henrik's cloak, which was large enough to cover four or five Bonifacias.

"You haven't answered me," said Bonifacia before going to sleep. "Where are we?"

"Kaladar," replied Henrik.

"I suppose that's an answer," she said. "And who were those men that attacked us?"

"Ornish rebels. Borganin's men. Now go to sleep. We still have a long walk ahead of us."

Bonifacia pouted. "Do you not say your prayers before you go to bed?" she asked.

"That's none of your business. You're welcome to do as you please."

Stars twinkled between the overhanging branches, the moons hidden temporarily behind the forest canopy. Bonifacia said her prayers and crawled up under Henrik's immense cloak. She fell asleep to the sound of insect song, the peaceful rustling of leaves in the treetops and Henrik's ocarina carrying a cheerless tune into the night. *Where is Peter?,* she wondered.

"Get up," commanded the akritar, after what seemed only moments, but the sun was out. "We can eat as we walk."

Bonifacia rubbed the sleep from her eyes and crawled out from beneath her soldier's cloak. It was far too long and heavy for her to carry on her own. Henrik rolled it up and strung it across his shoulder together with his haversack. "Take this." He handed her a mound of sticky paste and a handful of dried currants on top a broad green leaf.

"What is it?" she asked, giving the paste a tentative sniff.

"Breakfast. Don't eat the leaf." He strolled off, Bonifacia tripping after him.

"Breakfast?" She was famished and her stomach grumbled at the mere mention of food. "It looks like soggy bread." She poked at the viscous glop with her little finger.

"Not bread, strictly speaking," said Henrik. "It's called *melat*. Made from the pulp of a fruit. Much better than shorka eggs. Now eat up. It will give you strength."

"I don't think I'm familiar with shorka eggs."

"Sure you are. The household guards were eating them."

"You mean those funny eggs? The blue ones?"

"Yeah, that's the ones."

"And what exactly is a *shorka?* Some kind of chicken?"

"I can't say I know *cheek-hen,*" replied Henrik. He stumbled on the pronunciation. "Have you not seen a shorka? Yellow padde-like creatures with big buggy eyes."

Bonifacia started to laugh. "What's so funny?" he asked.

"Nothing," replied Bonifacia. "Just that I know someone who really enjoys eggs. He's in for a big surprise when he finds out." She dipped her fingers into the melat and gave it a taste. "Hey! Not bad," she exclaimed, smiling widely. "A little like lemon custard. You must show me how to make this." She paused, becoming suddenly very serious. "I'm sorry about your horse."

"Me too," said Henrik.

They walked together through wooded glens and steep river valleys for more days and nights than Bonifacia cared to count. Her feet were sore and hurt with every step. "Does this forest have an end?" she bleated.

"We're almost out of it. Can't you hear the birds?"

"The birds?"

"Just listen."

She was so intent on putting one foot in front of the other that she hadn't noticed the birdsong. Except for the occasional woodpecker, heavy silence pervaded the deepest parts of the wood, every sound absorbed by the damp moss and lichen-covered trees. But here, at the eaves of the forest, where the trees were thinning, the sun reached through the canopy and the birds were once again all a twitter.

"The walking will be easier once we're clear of the trees and back on level ground. With luck, we should be able to make our destination before nightfall."

"You still haven't told me where our destination is," retorted Bonifacia, trying her hardest not to sound querulous.

"My uncle's cottage," said Henrik. "He lives alone and doesn't receive many visitors."

The conversation died there. Bonifacia needed all the strength she could muster to soldier on, but the sun on her face, the pleasant singing of the birds and patches of fresh wildflowers put her in a much better spirit. Near noon they shared a meal of melat and wild berries while seated atop the rocks beside a crystal rill.

"I'm so sleepy," sighed Bonifacia. "And my shoes are in absolute tatters."

"Not much farther now," replied Henrik. "Do you want me to carry you?"

She couldn't tell if he were serious or not. "No thank you," she replied. With the collection of things Henrik was already carrying, she would have been a dreadful burden. "I will manage, but I don't think I can go another day like this. It's three steps for me to every one of yours."

"Like I said, it's not much farther. We'll cross this brook," said Henrik, gesturing with one hand, "then pass through a stretch of lowland fen, but it soon turns to mire and will pull you under if you step badly. You must be extra careful then and mind you stick to the track."

Bonifacia did not at all like the sound of that. "Your uncle lives in the morass?"

"Uncle Bartle likes his privacy. He sells peat from the turbary...amongst other things."

After their meal, she removed her shoes and followed Henrik across the brook, picking up the narrow track again on top of the slippery brae. As Henrik foretold, the terrain altered rapidly, trees abandoning the land in favor of sedge, tussock and spindly willows interspersed amongst pools of still dark water thick with blooms of green-blue algae.

They wended their way carefully through the growing miasma, the smell of swamp gas turning their noses. As the sun began its descent the sound of peeping insects grew louder, pressing in about them. The air grew dense with beleaguering midges that flitted annoyingly about their eyes and lashes.

A deep throated croak rumbled somewhere off to their right, the creature hidden by the rushes and tall marsh grass, answered by another somewhere in the distance. "I know that sound," said Bonifacia, anxiously scanning the swamp. "What did you call it? A shorka? Are there many of those horrid beasts out here?"

"Some. They sound a lot closer than they really are. Come, keep moving."

They hurried along the winding trail as best they could, keeping a wary eye on the setting sun. "Over there," said Henrik.

The trail ended abruptly at the edge of a swift moving stream, edged all round in tall grass and reeds and shrouded in a dense mist. A bollard rose amid the tussocks. Fastened to the top of it were block and tackle, and three thick ropes projecting out across the stream, their end points lost in the heavy fog. From one of these ropes lay suspended a bosun's chair with a wood slat for a seat.

"Get on. I'll pull you across the water."

"*Caray!* Are you mad?" exclaimed Bonifacia.

"It's perfectly safe. I've ridden it a million times."

Bonifacia remained steadfastly unconvinced. "I don't care if you've ridden it ten million times."

"I can go first if you prefer."

"That suits me fine," she said.

"You'll have to wait here on your own till I'm across," warned Henrik.

"If I must, I must. Just get on with it," replied Bonifacia, irritably.

Henrik let drop his haversack. "Give me the satchel and water bag." Bonifacia unhooked the items from her shoulder and passed them to Henrik, watching as he hid them behind some reeds. "My uncle has a boat on the far side of the river. 'Safer that way. I can come back for these things later."

Henrik swung himself up between the folds of the ropes, settling himself on the narrow seat. The aerial device drooped along the catenary with his added weight. "See, nothing to it. If I pull on this second line it will take me across, then I'll send the chair back for you. When you're ready, just give the line a solid tug. Mind you hold on to the ropes with both hands and I'll pull you across from the other side. All right?"

"Fine," said Bonifacia.

He reached up and drew on the line. The bosun's chair lurched forward over the water, swinging from side to side as it went. Hand over hand he hauled on the overhead line and slowly Henrik and the odd contraption disappeared into the mist.

Bonifacia stood by the edge of the river listening to the roar of the water. Between the dusk, a cloudy sky, and the thick gray mist, she felt alone and vulnerable, as if standing in a dimly lit room. The wait was interminable, and she remembered the feeling she had when Peter slipped over the wall in the hollow leaving her on her own, frightened in the darkness with only a taper lamp. She trembled at the memory.

At last the empty aerial chair came bumping out of the mist, swinging wildly. It stopped abruptly when it reached her side of the brae, knocking up against the block and tackle.

Bonifacia took a deep breath, crossed herself, and slowly climbed out onto the wooden slat that barely sufficed for a seat. The chair hardly dipped at all from her added weight. Tugging hard on the line and hurriedly entwining her arms around the two ropes on either side, the aerial device lurched forward. She closed her eyes tightly, feeling the seat pull out over the water with each steady jerk of the rope. Part way across she gained the courage to open one eye and glimpsed the swift flowing stream only a few feet below her dangling legs. Ahead of her, she could see only fog and the churning water.

Bonifacia's imagination immediately got the best of her. She had no certain knowledge that Henrik had arrived safely on the opposite bank. It might not even be Henrik hauling now on the rope. Who might she find when she alighted on the other side? Panic welled up inside her. She called out, "Henrik! Henrik!" but there was no answer to be heard above the burble of the stream.

At length the chair emerged from the mist and she found herself hanging above dry land, Henrik standing at ease beside the reciprocating bollard.

"Not so difficult, eh?"

Bonifacia scrambled from the flying chair, happy to have two feet planted back on *terra firma* (or the nearest equivalent).

"The cottage is down this way. You can just make out the light from here."

It was very dark by this point, clouds having moved in to obscure the night sky. Henrik set off at a brisk pace for his uncle's cottage. They stopped just outside a low rail fence. "Best wait here a moment," cautioned Henrik. He hopped over the fence and headed toward a small wood frame house raised on stilts. There were voices in the dark, a little laughter, and a few moments later, Henrik was back at the rail.

"No worries," he said. Reaching over to grasp her under the arms, Henrik lifted Bonifacia up and over the fence. "This way."

The door was open and they went directly in. Henrik's uncle stood stooped over the fender tinkering with an iron kettle. For a moment, Bonifacia worried that his long white brows might catch the flame, but something about the old man gave the impression of long practice and quiet competence.

"Tea will be ready in just a tick," he said. "Take a seat at the table." That's when Bonifacia noticed the pedestal behind the old man. Instinctively, she whirled about to face the doorway. Despite what she knew she'd find there, she still gave a start at the sight of the enormous blinking eyes of a shorka watching her from a mat beside the door, just as they had at the gatekeeper's cottage.

"I should have warned you," apologized Henrik.

"Ah," said Henrik's uncle, seeing her recoil. "That's just Strella. Take no notice of her."

"I don't care much for shorka either," admitted Henrik. "Uncle Bartle captures and tames them for market."

Bartle joined them at the table. He walked with a perceptible limp.

"You mean to say the creatures aren't domesticated?" exclaimed Bonifacia.

"No. 'Course not," replied Bartle. He smiled, displaying a mouthful of crooked yellow teeth. "They only breeds in the wild and very particular about it."

"We heard them calling to each other in the quagmire beyond the river," remarked Bonifacia.

"Just so," said Bartle. "No place for young'ins like yourself to go wanderin'."

"Why's that?" asked Bonifacia, not sure she wanted to hear the answer. "The gatekeeper in the forest used his shorka to subdue Peter, but in general they seem pretty docile."

"Docile?" exclaimed Uncle Bartle. "Pah." He massaged his leg thoughtfully.

"They're not?"

"Natural cannibals, given the opportunity. A little thing like you. A pair would have you by the shanks and splayed in two in no time at all."

"Uncle!" protested Henrik. "I'm sorry Bonifacia, he's not used to decent company and likes to frighten people." It was the first time Henrik had called her by her proper name.

Bartle sniffed the air. "The truth ain't always pretty," he said. "Ah, the kettle's up."

Bonifacia watched the shorka in the corner watching her as Bartle poured the tea.

"Don't worry about Strella," said Henrik. "She's very old and set in her ways. Once tamed, shorka get very lazy and quite docile, despite what Uncle says."

Bartle chortled. "So, Henrik, what's the story here, eh? Too busy being soldier. You haven't come to see your old uncle in ages, and show up now with this little thing in tow. Not from here, is she? Someone's took her eyebrows, poor darlin'." He examined Bonifacia in the firelight. "She could stand a bath."

Bonifacia reddened.

"She's been through a lot, Uncle." Henrik recalled their story from the point where he'd encountered Bonifacia and Peter at the gatekeeper's cottage.

"So it's come to that," quipped Bartle, learning of the Ornish attack. He gazed down at Bonifacia. "You came through a portal?" he asked.

"Yes, sir."

"Please, call me Uncle Bartle. Why would you want to do a thing like that?"

Bonifacia sighed. "Enter the tunnel? I don't know really. It was a mistake. We didn't fully comprehend." Her eyes welled with tears.

"Damned fool wizards, always muckin' about," cursed Bartle.

Henrik interrupted the conversation. "We'd like to rest here with you for a while, if you don't mind, Uncle. Think on things for a bit. Decide on our next move."

"Of course, Henrik. You're always welcome." He turned to Bonifacia, his leathery features flushing warm and sincere. "And you too little darlin'. Stay as long as you like."

Chapter 5

The Assassin

Peter sat slumped on a lion-footed bench in the tranquil atrium of Lord Palkvo's fortified manor watching big smaragdine bees and variegated butterflies flit from flower to flower. *A pleasant enough prison, but a prison all the same,* he thought to himself. The bowman sat on the step opposite him attending to his weapon, nearly oblivious to his presence. In the endless days and weeks since his capture Peter had hardly heard more than two short sentences from the man's lips, or anyone else's, repeated over and over again: "Get up, you" or "Come along now, quickly!" The few hours he spent each day in Palkvo's garden did nothing to boost his spirit. With little to occupy himself his mind drifted.

"You all right?" came a voice, shaking him from his dark reverie.

"Hmm?"

"I asked if you are all right. You looked as if you were about to keel over," said the bowman, gazing quizzically at him from his stone perch.

Peter looked up in surprise. This was the first time the fellow had taken even the slightest interest in his welfare. "Joshkar—that's your name isn't it?—would you talk with me? If you don't, I swear, I shall go stark staring mad!" Peter was only half joking. Like any schoolboy, he'd grown accustomed to the playing fields. Guilt plus days of endless solitude and inactivity were taking their toll on him. It was doing him no good whatsoever rehashing old events. He needed something else to occupy his brain.

The bowman shrugged noncommittally, propping his weapon against the atrium wall. "Very well. What would you have me say?"

"Ah. There's a start at least. I'm like a fish out of water, Master Bowman. I could stand a little advice. It would seem you're the only one I have to turn to."

It was the bowman's turn to look surprised. "Turn to? Me? You're daft. How'd you come to settle on that idea?"

"I don't know. There's something about you, if you don't mind me saying. You're not like the others."

"It's the accent," he replied.

"No. I think it's something more than that."

Joshkar stroked the corner of his mouth with a thumb the same butternut hue of bowstring wax.

"What's wrong?" asked Peter. "Is someone preventing you from speaking with me?"

"Pfah!" scoffed Johskar. "I'm no one. Who gives a hang about what a Bakan might have to say to you, or anyone else?" He leaned a little ways back and squinted at Peter through one eye. "You want my honest advice?"

"I'd value it."

"Go home."

Peter shook his head in exasperation. "Can you please be serious?"

"I *am* being serious." His expression was surprisingly grave. One might even say compassionate. "You don't want to get yourself tangled up in any of this."

"So what am I to do? I can't go back. Can I? Not unless you've got a key to that ruddy portal in your pocket. And you don't have one, do you?" He felt the sudden urge to kick the fellow, but restrained himself. "If you've got no proper advice to offer, I suggest we talk about something else—this place, this blasted world you live in. That would be a useful start." He clutched a hand to his aching head. "I can't seem to get a handle on any part of what's going on here."

From his demeanor, the bowman found Peter's outburst amusing. "Well, I suppose that much I can oblige." He drew a long knife from his boot and kneeling forward, sketched the outline of a rough map in the rose-colored gravel of the garden path. "There are seven provinces that together make up the empire." He pointed out each one with the tip of his blade. "Kaladar, Orn, Taixûs, Bakus Mara, Bakus Sura, Meflis and Hemsto. All of them, except Bakus Sura, front the River Talsis."

"You're from Bakus?" asked Peter.

"Bakus Sura," he corrected with a nod.

Peter studied his map. "Which way is north?" he asked.

"*North?* I know nothing of *north.*"

"South then, or east and west."

He shrugged his shoulders, not comprehending.

"Well, up or down then. You must provide directions somehow."

"Ah," he said, at last taking hold of his meaning. "Toward."

"Huh?"

"*Toward* Menom, for example." He thrust the point of his blade into the ground, displacing a few bits of gravel to indicate the location of the capital city of Orn. Peter gathered from his words that Menom was both a person *and a place.* "You might also say above or below, or beyond or this side of Menom. It depends on the context, you see."

"I'm not sure I do. I'm to say *toward* Menom if pointing someone in that direction?"

"Precisely. You'll hear folk sometimes refer to the upper or lower latitudes, but that's an old term, not much used anymore. There's a stone marker at the center of the Keartlands from which the logicians took their measure in days gone by."

Peter took a moment to digest all this. He was inclined out of habit to call the top of his map north, even if true north proved to be on the bottom. Pursuing the matter seemed rather pointless when no one else could follow his meaning. "Have you no compass?"

The bowman's response was just another of his Frenchman-like shrugs.

"How terribly cumbersome. What's this area over here?" He pointed past the far right-hand edge of Joshkar's drawing.

"That's the ocean, dominion of the Weshnut. The Berdeh Sea and the River Talsis are all controlled by the Weshnut samkan, Lord Admiral Tosha."

He drew a long line nearly straight down the left side of his map. "And here," he said pointing with his knife, "tall mountains skirt the opposite coast. They go by many names, most often the Untold Mountains. We call the narrow land beyond Kayu Tun in the old tongue, literally 'beyond the peaks.' It is home to the Weshnut and their capital, Debs."

"These Weshnut, they control the entire ocean? On both coasts?" Peter was astounded. It then occurred to him that England and the Royal Navy had come very close to achieving much the same.

"There are reasons for everything," was Joshkar's cryptic reply.

"And down here, below the River Talsis, that's the Keartlands?" prompted Peter.

"Ah. You do know a little of our geography." He was impressed.

"Very little, but I'm beginning to catch on. Who lives there?"

"Nowadays, no one. 'Used to be home to several clans under the old Kaladwen Empire, but they're all gone now. By treaty it forms a sort of buffer between the four nations that occupy the lower latitudes and the empire."

With the point of his knife he extended the lower boundaries of his map. "The River Bos frames the far side of the Keartlands, almost parallel with the Talsis. It's fronted by Madær, Bankor Fal, Stônar and Veldan—our traditional enemies."

"So they control the Bos?"

"The Bos is mostly unnavigable. No one controls it."

Peter ran his finger along the outlines of the map, doing his best to absorb the geographic makeup of the alien world in which he'd inexplicably found himself. "And that's the size of it all?" he inquired. "No other landmass or continent?"

"The Berdeh covers most everything else, as far as I know. There are islands, of course, but none of much import. There's also more to the extreme latitudes than I've drawn here, but they are barren desolate places, largely unexplored."

"There isn't much to your world compared to my own," observed Peter. It was a stupid insensitive thing to say and he wanted to take back his words the moment they came out his mouth.

Joshkar straightened to his full height and glared down at him. "I think that's enough geography for one day." He sheathed his knife and commenced to erase the map with the toe of his boot.

As usual, they dined alone for supper, Joshkar sitting next to Peter about midway down the long table. Peter picked up the thread of their previous conversation while prodding unenthusiastically at his plate. Joshkar seemed to have forgiven his earlier transgression, although he hardly deserved it. "Does this planet have a name?" he asked.

Joshkar paused mid bite. "Now there's a question I've never been asked. We usually just speak of it as the *World*. Occasionally it's referred to by another name, though I scarcely know where it comes from or what it means."

"And that is?"

"TNX-37B."

"Come again?" Peter shook his head. "What sort of name is that?"

"I told you, I don't know. The Ulfair sometimes call it that."

"I thought *you* were Ulfair. That's the name of your empire, after all. They must be an interesting bunch, these *Ulfair*."

"Interesting is not the word I would choose to describe them," he rejoined. "They are off-worlders like yourself. They came through the portals generations ago."

"Really? Through the portals?" That certainly piqued Peter's interest. "Tell me more."

"Some discussions are better suited to the garden," he replied under his breath.

"All right," he sniffed. "So, if you're not an Ulfair, what are you?"

"What am I?"

Peter pointed to his own brow and then to his. "You lot. Those with the big bushy eyebrows. Do you have a name for yourselves, *your species?*"

"Ah," he said, self-consciously twisting the plait of his long brow between his thumb and forefinger. "*Gwellem*. And you? What do your people call themselves?"

Peter replied after a moment's thought, "Human beings, I suppose."

"*Hu–man.*" Joshkar tasted the word for the first time. "We don't seem much different from one another—humans and Gwellem, I mean."

"Hmm. I guess that remains to be seen," said Peter.

"The Ulfair," Joshkar added as an afterthought, "they *are* different."

Peter was about to ask him just what he meant by that, when Lord Palkvo's steward entered the room. As a general policy, Peter held his tongue in front of Palkvo's staff.

For some reason or other, Peter didn't see Joshkar all through the next day and consequently spent the whole time involuntarily locked in his room. "I've had about all I can stand of that," he blurted when next they met. "You must find me some books to read or something decent to occupy my time. Anne Boleyn had it better than I do."

He smiled at Peter with evident pity. "You are just a boy, aren't you?" He escorted Peter down to the garden. Miserable and depressed, Peter slumped on his customary bench.

"So what ails our lord arbiter this day?" asked Joshkar.

"I wish you wouldn't persist in calling me that. You know I am no such thing."

"I do not know that. You arrived here through the portal when summoned, carrying, no less, the Wolf Queen's token of office. What's more, you were being escorted by her liegemen when you were captured. Is that not so?"

"I've heard all that before. Well, except maybe that last bit. It was all an accident. A misunderstanding. Nothing more."

"It little matters. The people believe you are the lord arbiter and that's what counts. Word is already spreading of your return, with a little encouragement from the duke, I dare say. They expect you will resolve the current crisis, as you did once before. You may not realize it, but for many Gwellem you represent the last great hope for peace."

"You're joking?" His words shook Peter to the core. "Why isn't anyone telling them the other part? That I'm Peter López de Soto, not *Manuel López*? That I'm fifteen years old. Why doesn't someone tell them that?" He was incredulous.

"People don't generally take much stock in trifles."

"Trifles?" he roared.

"The portals are places of magic," explained Joshkar. "There are many stories and legends surrounding them. People go in and come back flying serpents, or so it is said. What is it to them that the lord arbiter went away a man and came back a boy?"

"Joshkar, you must put them straight!"

He laughed entirely at Peter's expense. "And how does the lord arbiter propose I inform the people of our world that you are not who they think you are? By what means? Shall I summon His Lordship's crier?"

Peter was flummoxed. "Surely Borganin will disabuse them of this absurd idea!"

"I think that is unlikely. Understand, young master, that if the people believe you are the lord arbiter and you choose to endorse Lord Borganin's bid for the imperial throne it would go far to legitimize his position."

"Endorse his bid for the imperial throne! You can't be serious?"

"You keep saying that. I am quite serious. A heavy responsibility rests with you."

"I won't do it! Never!"

Joshkar's face grew grim. "The duke will endeavor to persuade you...by whatever means."

Peter's mouth went suddenly dry. "Joshkar, you wouldn't permit him to do such a thing, would you?"

He spoke plainly. "I am a soldier in the service of Orn."

Peter looked at the bowman through fresh eyes. *You mustn't lose your head,* he told himself. *Joshkar is your only hope.* "You needn't take any special risks on my account," said Peter. "But you can help me understand what is going on here. I mean *really understand.* No more trifling geography lessons. I'm asking you as a personal favor. As a friend. My *only* friend. *Please.* You can do that much, can't you?"

Joshkar studied Peter's face for a very long while. It took all of his resolve not to melt under that penetrating gaze. "All right," he said at last. "I'll share what I can."

"Oh. Thank you!" cried Peter.

"As for the rest, I'll be straight with you...whether you live or die is largely dependent on how well you comport yourself over the next few days and weeks."

Peter suddenly felt that his legs might go out from under him. "I'll do my part," he replied. In truth, the mere prospect of failure chilled him to the bone.

"Time will tell. So, just what is it you think you still need to understand?"

"Borganin's rebellion, for example. What's that all about?"

"That's as good a place as any to start," he agreed.

Peter was, of course, curious to know why Joshkar would ever consent to abet him in this manner. He had no good reason to believe his (frankly pathetic) overtures had swayed the Bakan in the slightest. Whatever his reasons, Peter was grateful and under the circumstances, much too relieved to press him on the matter.

Joshkar had barely begun to explain to him the origins of Borganin's rebellion when he heard approaching footsteps. Lord Palkvo stepped from behind the encircling covered walk. "Make yourself presentable," he barked. "We have visitors."

Peter had long since decided there was no point in contesting each and every order demanded of him by his jailers. He would pick and choose his battles carefully. He did as he was instructed, then followed Joshkar down to the reception hall surrounded by trophies and keepsakes belonging to the ancient house of Palkvo.

Palkvo gave him a cursory inspection, nodding his grudging approval. Peter was directed to seat himself in a preposterously opulent chair set for the purpose beside Lord Palkvo. Their visitors were delayed for some reason or other, so they sat biding their time in awkward silence, the members of Lord Palkvo's retinue lining the walls with nothing better to do than cast disapproving glances in Peter's direction.

A herald finally appeared at the entrance and announced with all the pomp and solemnity he could muster, "His Grace, the Duke of Menom, Master of Orn and the Upper Talsis."

Peter was stunned. Borganin? Having just learned what he had from Joshkar, his mind was in turmoil. How was he to behave? He needed more time to think.

Palkvo stood and gestured impatiently for Peter to do likewise. Into the room walked the infamous Duke of Menom—Lord Borganin. He was dressed in burnished mail and wore a forest green surcoat magnificently embroidered with silver acanthus leaves. His brows were blond and his face smooth and rather on the youthful side, all to Peter's great surprise. He'd imagined Borganin to be a dark and brooding fellow, like his brutal lieutenant and never thought to ask about his actual appearance. He was wrong in almost every respect. The man was merely young and ambitious, rather dashing in reality.

Peter was relieved not to find the despicable Captain Menhar in the duke's company. He bowed deeply, taking his cue from Palkvo. "Your grace," said Palkvo. "Welcome." He hesitated just a moment, but couldn't resist asking, "Master of the Upper Talsis? This is a new title, my lord?"

"Your impertinence is noted, Palkvo, but you are quite right." Borganin smiled, amused by his own effrontery. "Come, let's not beat about. Introduce me to your guest."

Palkvo turned to Peter, "I have the honor of presenting the lord arbiter imperial." By this time Peter was becoming rather used to such nonsense. He bowed once again with an even greater flourish. Borganin returned the courtesy with an indifferent wave of his hand.

"I was forewarned of this. You are very young in appearance," stated the duke.

"I am but fifteen, my lord."

He raised one scrupulously groomed eyebrow, but made no comment. "Seat yourselves," he instructed. Peter looked to Palkvo for confirmation. He nodded and they obliged. "That's better. Now we may talk as friends."

Borganin gestured toward a member of his entourage and a chair appropriate to his stature was brought forward for his convenience.

"Would you care for some refreshment, my lord?" inquired Palkvo.

"Kind of you Palkvo, but I am well provided for. He motioned and a chalice was produced for the duke's pleasure. He sipped silently, his gaze never wavering from Peter. "Where is Manuel López?" he asked.

Peter replied that his great-great-great grandfather was many years in his grave. This began a rather lengthy interrogation, one which he'd been through several times already. Borganin seemed not the least surprised by all he had to say and Peter imagined, hope of hopes, that here at last was one man who understood and would pronounce all this a great mistake. He would, he thought, be denounced as a fraud and (very happily) sent on his way, no serious harm done.

But yet again, to Peter's enormous frustration, his story seemed to make no difference. Borganin continued to address him as "Lord Arbiter." Peter's mind was lost in thought and he missed Borganin's last words.

"López de Soto," he repeated, with gathering vexation. "This girl that came through the portal with you, *Bonifacia Espasande,* do you know where she has gone?"

Peter replied with all honesty, "I have no idea, my lord. I know nothing at all of the soldier that carried her off."

Borganin twisted his jaw to one side, considering perhaps if he should believe him. *What interest could Bonifacia possibly be to him?* wondered Peter.

"Enough," said Borganin, rising suddenly from his chair. "Prepare the boy. He will accompany me to Menom. We leave within the hour."

Peter rose from his seat filled with an irrational urge to flee. He was certain that nothing good would come from going off with this man. Palkvo had not been the most gracious host, but neither was he cruel. He could not say the same of Borganin with any confidence. The duke glared at Peter, as if daring him to protest. Peter said nothing and Borganin turned to leave the hall.

Just then Peter heard a peculiar, barely audible, "*swish*" and immediately felt as though someone had clapped him on the shoulder. He looked over to see a small feathered dart protruding from the region below his collarbone. He looked up in amazement.

Borganin gazed at him with equal surprise. Had the dart been meant for him? He turned to face the direction from which it had come. The assassin, one of Palkvo's retinue, appeared not the least bit concerned. He stood openly against the wall, boldly gripping the small tube that had concealed the barb. As

Peter slumped to the floor and his vision began to swim and then fade, the last thing he saw was one of Borganin's men sever the fellow's head with a remarkably dexterous swipe of his blade.

Chapter 6

Uncle Bartle

Bartle set out a hot bath for Bonifacia in a large copper tub behind the cottage together with a battered tin basin to launder clothes. Her ablutions complete, Bonifacia slipped on a borrowed shirt with sleeves that hung straight down past her fingertips. Then for modesty's sake she wrapped a length of striped toweling about her waist like a girl from the East Indies. "Goodness, what an ensemble," she muttered aloud. "What would Mother say?" She laughed heartily at herself.

Barefoot, she entered the cottage to find that Henrik and Bartle had fixed a comfortable bed for her on a straw filled paillasse in the loft. The bed was reached by way of a wooden ladder worn smooth from years of use.

"Strella can't climb, can she?" asked Bonifacia, casting the yellow monster an anxious glance.

"No, not no more," assured Bartle, "the old girl's grown too fat and lazy. If she worries you though, you can hook the ladder off to one side once you're up there."

"Where will you sleep, Uncle Bartle?"

"Here, just below you." He pointed toward an alcove at the back of the cottage directly opposite the door, barely large enough to contain a single cot and nightstand.

"And Henrik?"

Henrik entered the cottage just as she spoke. He'd been to the washup, his flaxen hair still dripping wet and his slick long brows pulled back over the top of his ears. "Someone's taken all the fresh toweling from the bath," he grumbled, then noticed Bonifacia's improvised sarong. "Oh."

"Henrik," said Bartle, answering her question, "will sleep on a hammock in the linhay."

"I'm sorry to cause you such trouble," apologized Bonifacia.

"Think nothing of it, my dear. My leg keeps me out of the loft these days. And Henrik's the warrior, always roughing it. I'd venture to say he finds the hammock something of a treat. Isn't that so, Henrik?"

"Just so, Uncle. Far superior to sleeping on the cold ground."

"Aye. Well it's way past my bedtime. I suggest the both of you get some rest."

Bonifacia curtsied and wished them both a pleasant good night. For added measure, she stuck her tongue out at Strella and scampered up the rungs to safety, careful to unhook the ladder from the edge of the loft.

"Delightful girl," laughed Bartle. "Terrible pity. Good night Henrik."

Bonifacia fell fast asleep and did not wake until the smell of fresh baked bread stimulated her appetite. She peered cautiously over the ledge. No one, or no thing, stirred below. Bonifacia did not relish the idea of being left alone in the house with the frightful old shorka. Reaching over to grab the ladder, she quietly made her way to the cottage floor. Strella, to Bonifacia's relief, was absent from her usual mat by the door.

Steam rose from a copper kettle and porridge bubbled from a small black pot hanging from a chimney crane over the embers. Within the brick bread-oven beside the hearth a loaf the color of crème caramel had finished rising, filling the room with its warmth. *Safe.* That's how everything felt.

The door opened with a bang and Bartle strolled in, Strella close upon his heels. The big toad croaked just once and stole over to her customary mat, adopting her habitual wide-eyed and nearly lifeless stance.

"We've been out hunting," beamed Bartle. "Two plump squirrels for the pot." He held them up for Bonifacia to admire.

"Strella hunts?" she asked.

"'Course she does."

"I thought shorka laid eggs."

"Well, both. You don't know squat about shorka, do you?"

"No, I'm afraid not, Uncle."

"No reason you should, I suppose." He knocked the mud from his wooden clogs and left them beside the door. "Most folk keep 'em for the eggs. Takes a lot of know-how and a musical ear to get them to hunt."

"Did you say musical ear?"

"Sure. Everyone fixates on those big beautiful eyes, but shorka love a good tune. Strange thing is, they're all but deaf to ordinary natter. Here, I'll show you." He took a little oval-shaped ocarina from his pocket and lacing two fingers over top gave it a "*toot.*" Strella immediately dropped her head to the floor mat.

"Extraordinary!" exclaimed Bonifacia. "May I try?"

He handed her the instrument. "Hold it like so, but two short breaths this time, one right after the other. Toot, toot."

She blew on the ocarina twice in swift succession and Strella quickly raised herself back up, resuming her usual dog-like pose.

"*Que asombroso!*" Bonifacia cried gleefully.

"Now we've got to reward her. You can't compel a shorka to perform without some form of compensation. That wouldn't be polite." He unlatched a small box fastened to a baldric slung over his shoulder and removed a big topaz-colored beetle the size of a Spanish dollar. Strella croaked eagerly.

"Now, if we were outside I'd toss the poor beastie in the air and that would be the end of it. Inside the house, it goes atop the pedestal by the hearth. That's the custom. You do the honors, Bonifacia." He handed her the enormous insect. Bonifacia grimaced as the creature squirmed to free itself from her tightened fist.

"Mind you step away from that pedestal quick as you can once you let go the beetle."

She knew from the gatekeeper's cottage what would happen next. Following Bartle's directions, she placed the insect atop the pedestal and stepped back just in time to avoid a lashing from Strella's wondrously long tongue. The beetle vanished in the blink of an eye.

"I'm not sure I care for that part of it," admitted Bonifacia. She admired the ocarina before handing it back to Bartle. "Henrik has one just like this."

"'Course he does. I gave it to him as a boy. Younger than you at the time. Taught him all I could about training shorka to hunt."

"But he doesn't seem to care much for them," said Bonifacia. "Doesn't even like their eggs."

"My fault, I guess," replied Bartle. "I made the mistake of giving him a whelpling to train for himself. Should 'av known he wasn't ready for the responsibility. Too young."

"Why? What happened?" asked Bonifacia.

"There was an accident. Henrik grew very attached to the shorka. Named her Josephina, as I recall. Made a pet of her." Bartle sighed. "It doesn't do to become too familiar with creatures in training. Henrik was over confident. One day he took his shorka out into the mire to go hunting on his own. I can't say for certain, 'cause I wasn't there, but I think he got a trifle nervous when it came down to it. He got confused and couldn't master the notes on the ocarina. He lost control of Josephina. At the same time his music drew the wild shorka to him. I told you, they're natural cannibals. Poor Josephina was eaten by the others right in front of Henrik. He wouldn't go near them after that. Not for a very long time. Henrik's got a talent for hunting shorka, but his heart isn't in it."

The awful story reminded Bonifacia that Henrik had to put down his horse partly on her account and she felt all the worse for it.

"Where is Henrik?" she asked.

"Gone to visit some friends. Now, sit you down and let's have some breakfast. Henrik tells me you don't much care for shorka eggs. There's plenty of porridge in the pot. The bread and tea is ready and we can have that with fresh melat. How 'bout a drop of cold milk? Would you like that?"

"Milk?" exclaimed Bonifacia. She glanced uneasily at Strella. "Where does the milk come from?"

"From a cow, you silly girl. Where else?" Bonifacia blushed. "Eat up and afterward we'll have ourselves a gander round my little empire."

Bartle found Bonifacia an ancient-looking pair of wooden sabot that almost matched her shoe size. "They belonged to Henrik and his father before him as young lads, near enough your own age. Nothing better for walkin' the river banks," said Bartle.

Her clothes were still wet on the line, so she departed the cottage together with Bartle in her oversized shirt, kitchen sarong and wooden shoes. Behind the main house, Bonifacia could see the linhay where Henrik's hammock lay strung between two uprights. Aside from a granary that looked a little like a Black Forest cuckoo clock, Bartle kept two kitchen plots split by a shallow brook. A few of the herbs and vegetables that grew in the garden looked familiar to Bonifacia, like silver sage, Brussels sprouts and aubergine. Others had a more primeval appearance with broad fuzzy leaves and conical flowers.

A small manger did indeed contain a single brown cow of a sort Bonifacia had only seen in picture books, but a cow nonetheless. It glanced dispassionately at them while chewing on a pillow of hay laid across a timber trough.

They traversed the brook by way of a narrow footbridge. A simple split-rail fence like the one Henrik had lifted her over marked the outer limits of the steading. Although they were headed in the opposite direction, Bonifacia was curious. "Did you build that awful contraption across the river?" she asked.

"The boatswain's chair? Naw. That was a gift you might say, from a Weshnut that owed me a favor."

"A Weshnut? What's a Weshnut?"

"One of the sea folk beyond the mountains."

"Oh," said Bonifacia. "Funny sort of name."

They followed the trail through tall grass and patches of colorful loosestrife until the cottage was well beyond view. With the morning sun still at their backs they turned onto an adjoining track that followed a further branch of the stream to their right. Dragonflies with iridescent trunks and translucent wings trimmed in silver skipped on the air along side them, while crested blackbirds berated Bonifacia and Bartle with shrill mechanical voices from their quivering perches atop the towering cattails. Plumed sedge and dense tussock masked from view the nearby rush of swiftly flowing water. Although she could not see it, from the clamor Bonifacia knew the river could not be more than a yard or two beyond her reach.

The track was spongy underfoot and cut with shallow rills of orange water that made her grateful for the sabots. On they walked until the trail veered sharply right again, cutting through a clearing of open bog separated from the bank by a line of tangled willows. The marsh meadow was unremarkable except for bunches of hound's ear profuse with tender blue blossoms and low-lying huckleberry. The clearing provided Bonifacia with her first unobstructed view of the distant horizon.

She could see now that Bartle's well-concealed sanctuary was in reality an island gripped within the powerful flows of an implacable river, like a ship gone aground in the middle reaches. They stood upon the stuck prow, the river diverting off into two raging steams around them. Far off on the horizon a chain of craggy snow capped mountains stretched as far as the eye could see, home to the headwaters of the river.

"How beautiful they are," exclaimed Bonifacia.

Bartle looked up, shielding his bushy white brows with one hand. "Yes indeed."

"Do the mountains have a name, Uncle Bartle?"

He sniggered. "Everyone calls them somethin' different. Depends on your point of view, I guess. To some, they are the Og'yre's Teeth or Purple Mountains. To others, the Fire Hills or Snowy Tops. The Kaladwen called them the *Grith Mathrain*—the Giant's Spine. Ulfair maps mostly name them The Untold Mountains. The same goes for the bigger peaks. Everyone's got a different name for them." He pointed. "See that big wide one with the top sheared 'way?" "That's Broken Mountain. Least that's what my ol' da always called it."

Bonifacia had a sudden image of Bartle standing on the very same spot as a young boy, lithe and eager, his father pointing out to him the severed peak. "And what about the river? Does it have a name?"

"'Course it does. All rivers have a name. It's called the *Chigraw*, a twisting on the old tongue. Means cold waters."

Bonifacia scanned the near horizon. Her eyes were drawn to a fenced enclosure on the far side of the fen. It contained a number of tiny cabins. "Who lives there?" she asked. "They remind me a little of the *cavas* back home that we use to store the harvest."

"There's no yield in those. That's where I keep m' shorka." Bonifacia's eyes darted apprehensively around the open bog. "Don't worry darlin'. There's none runnin' about this island, not unless someone has gone and let them out of their pen. I catch the little beggars in the swamp marsh on the other side of the river and bring 'em across by boat. Here's the perfect spot to train them. Good open ground. No distractions, no prying eyes. And if one of them somehow manages to escape, it don't get very far." He laughed. "Would you care to see them?"

Bonifacia could tell from the look on Bartle's face that he was very eager to show off his precious beasts, but Bonifacia wasn't quite so keen. "Perhaps another time, Uncle. Shouldn't we be getting back? Henrik might be waiting for us." He was clearly disappointed, but led the way back to the cottage.

Henrik was indeed waiting for them when they returned, sitting in a chair near the hearth with his feet up on one end of the table. "Mind your manners," chastised Bartle. Henrik pulled his legs down quickly. "What news is there from down river?" he asked, while feeding a fresh beetle to Strella from the pedestal.

"The countryside is buzzing with word of the lord arbiter's return. They say he is in the company of the Duke of Menom and that our troubles will soon be over."

"The lord arbiter?!" exclaimed Bonifacia. "They mean Peter, don't they? Thank the Lord! He's alive!" It didn't take long for Bonifacia's mood to shift quickly from delight to anger. "But I keep telling you people, Peter is not your lord arbiter! And this duke whatever, he's responsible for murdering Captain Gothrain in cold blood. I guess he's snatched poor Peter away too. Doesn't anyone care about that?"

Bartle and Henrik cast each other furtive glances. "I daresay Queen Xhôn cares," replied Henrik, "but there's precious little she can do about it. The duke raids Kaladar with impunity while the Imperial Army vacillates. Fewer people these days trust the news out of Piernot. Borganin will advertise whatever he pleases."

"Well what can be done?" demanded Bonifacia.

"About your friend Peter? Nothing," said Henrik.

Bonifacia sank despondently into a chair by the fire. "This is madness. How are we to get home?" she wailed. "We don't belong here. Mother must be in a state by now."

"We must get you to Piernot," pronounced Henrik. "That's the only possibility. The queen will know what needs to be done. It was she that brought you here, intentionally or not." Henrik and Bartle regarded one another, a wordless conversation taking place between them. "But there is one small problem," continued Henrik. "My friends tell me the Ornish have seized the pike road between here and the capital. To reach Piernot, we must travel by way of the foothills."

"Henrik!" exclaimed Bartle. "Don't be absurd."

"It's the only way Uncle."

"The girl is safe here and welcome to stay as long as she likes. What you're suggesting isn't worth the risk."

Henrik smiled. "A generous offer Uncle, but we must let Bonifacia decide for herself." He turned his eyes to her. "Uncle Bartle's not wrong, you know. There are potential hazards. Still, it's doable if we take care and stick to the lower elevations."

Bonifacia sat on the edge of her chair, weighing out her options. Take the road to Piernot and risk capture by the Duke of Menom, do nothing and never see Galicia again, or, try to reach Piernot through the foothills with their unnamed and unspecified perils. There was no easy answer. Her mother would say, 'better to fall from the window than the roof.'

She sighed deeply. "*Grazas* Uncle, but I think I must find Peter somehow and be on our way." She glanced again at Henrik. "If Henrik is willing, we'll go by the foothills to Piernot."

Bartle looked momentarily disappointed, but forced a smile. "Well then, nuthin' else for it. I must do what I can to see you properly organized for your journey."

Chapter 7

Menom

Peter awoke with a start. *'Huh?...'* He was back in his own bedroom at the *pazo* in Galicia! Open-mouthed, he gazed around the room in astonishment. 'It was all a dream?' *But how could it have been?* He shivered involuntarily. *It seemed so real.* An overwhelming sense of happiness and relief came flooding over him. Pulling himself from bed with a laugh, he lit a candle, dressed quickly, and scooted over to his cousin's room. 'Bonnie, wake up!' he shouted and let himself in. He stood over her as she lay in bed, the taper draping his frame in pale yellow light.

'Peter! You scared me half to death. What's happening?' she asked. 'Why are you dressed?'

'We must wake your mother. We need to tell her, Bonnie—*immediately!*'

She rubbed the sleep from her eyes. 'Tell her what, Peter? It's the middle of the night.'

'*Everything.* No holding back this time.'

Bonifacia climbed out of bed and donned her dressing gown. 'I'm not sure I understand.'

'Don't you see?' exclaimed Peter. 'The ruin in the hollow... it's connected to something big, but nothing like you, or I, or anyone else could ever imagine.'

She chewed her lip, more worried about her cousin's present state of mind than any ill doings in the meadow. 'All right, Peter. Let's go wake mother.'

With that, Peter turned on his heels and rushed away down the corridor, Bonifacia one step behind. He stopped in front of her mother's bedroom door and knocked repeatedly.

'Aunt Generosa, it's Peter. I must speak with you. It's important.' No answer came from within. He knocked again, and then reached out to try the door handle. But the door opened of its own accord and there, standing before him, loomed the towering figure of Captain Menhar, a menacing smile etched across his ugly face...

"Hush," said a feminine voice. "I think he's coming round."

For the life of him, Peter could not manage to focus his eyes. The room and everyone in it was a complete and utter blur. "Who are you?" he asked. "I can't make out your face."

"A side effect of the poison. It should wear off soon," replied a soft reassuring voice. You've come through the worst of it. Sleep some more. I will be here when you awake."

Peter needed no encouragement. He felt as if he'd been run over by a four-in-hand. In a moment he was again fast asleep. If he dreamed once more, he did not remember it. He awoke sometime later, knowing full well that it would not be in his own bed at the *pazo*. He opened his eyes and tried his best to pull himself up onto his elbows.

"Lady Aflyn!" came an excited voice, different from the one he'd first heard. "He stirs."

"Move aside Beshwan." Peter could discern movement at the foot of his bed, but it was still cloaked in heavy shadow. He closed his eyes tightly and then opened them again, wincing from the sharp pain that lingered at the base of his skull. The veil slowly lifted from his eyes and he was able to see a young woman, not much older than myself, seated in a high spindle-backed chair, gazing intently at him, her delicate hands folded neatly upon her lap.

This was Peter's first occasion to see a Gwellem woman close up. He had prepared himself for the worst, picturing otherwise pretty girls with great shaggy eyebrows and a hairy nose to boot. Only this girl was beautiful to behold in every respect, and yes, she had great long brows like the rest of her men folk, but they fell in two luxurious tresses interwoven with filigree strands of gold and tiny teardrop pearls.

"I am Lady Aflyn," she announced, with a genteel nod of her head.

Peter cleared his throat, "My name is Peter. Peter López de Soto," he replied. "I'm pleased to meet you."

"I am pleased to meet you too, Peter. This is my handmaid, Beshwan," she said, gesturing toward a girl, older by some years, seated in the opposite corner. Unlike her mistress, Beshwan had fashioned her brows in simple plaits wrapped in a bun and tied with ribbon over each ear.

"How do you do," he replied.

Blushing, the handmaid clasped a hand to her mouth, failing to suppress an annoying giggle.

"That will do, Beshwan," said Aflyn, gently chiding the handmaid. "How old are you?" she asked, turning to Peter.

"Fifteen," he replied.

"That's odd," said Aflyn. "I supposed the lord arbiter to be much older than that. I'm only sixteen and one half myself."

Peter decided not to make an issue of this "lord arbiter" business. "What has happened?" he asked.

"Oh dear me," she said, "you would like to know, wouldn't you. Where is my head? Beshwan," she said, turning her attention, "run and tell Father that our guest has awakened."

Beshwan regarded her mistress with hesitation. "But, my lady…"

"Go on and do as I say. He's in no condition to harm me now is he? Father will want to know he's recovered."

Beshwan rose from her chair, curtsied and whirled out of the room, making sure to leave the door wide open.

Aflyn turned to Peter, smiled and said, "Now where were we? Yes, of course, you wish to be brought up to date on all that has happened. How much do you remember?"

"I remember receiving a dart to the shoulder." He rubbed the spot, still tender to the touch. A peek under his shirt revealed a bruise the size of an English crown. Then the awful memory came flooding back. "I remember a man, a fellow from Palkvo's court…" he had trouble finishing.

"Lord Palkvo is my father," interjected Aflyn. "That was Tibor, the man who tried to kill you."

"Kill *me?*" cried Peter. "I thought he was aiming for the duke and caught me by mistake.

"It was no mistake," replied Aflyn. "He was aiming for you."

"But why?" he exclaimed. "Why would anyone do such a thing?" He was shocked beyond belief.

"Tibor understood you were planning to endorse Lord Borganin for the imperial mantle. He thought he could prevent it by murdering you off."

"How do you know all this?" he demanded.

She shrugged. "A conspiracy of one is very uncommon. Others were found who sympathized with Tibor and have admitted the truth. The duke was furious." She looked into Peter's eyes, perhaps hoping for a reaction. "His plans for you are put off for the time being. You are very lucky you know."

"Lucky?!" This was the second time someone had said as much. "Is the duke still here?" he asked.

"No, he has ridden off, but left word that you are to join him at court as soon as you are able to travel. Father will escort you to Menom."

"He must think me very valuable to ask your father to waste his time on such an errand."

"Oh, he does indeed."

There was a slight commotion at the door. Palkvo entered with a look of relief upon his face. "Ah, I see the lord arbiter has returned to the land of the living. I am sorry for this incident." Peter wasn't at all convinced that he was.

"I suppose I have you and the Lady Aflyn to thank for my recovery," he replied.

"Thank you," said Palkvo, "but most of the credit must go to the Bakan, Joshkar."

"Joshkar?"

"It would appear that he has many hidden talents. I suppose Menhar knew this when he chose him to watch over you. It was an antidote of Joshkar's devising that pulled you through. Don't ask me how he knew what to use, but he did."

"Where is Joshkar now?" asked Peter.

"Resting. He has hardly left your side these five days."

"Five days!" he exclaimed.

"Yes little lord. Such a stir you have caused. Are you well enough now to travel?"

"Father!" interjected Aflyn. "He has only just awakened."

Palkvo smiled at his daughter with evident affection. "Yes, of course, my dear. As always, I am too impatient. A Palkvo trait. Take as much time as you need, Lord de Soto." He dipped his head ever so slightly and departed.

"Your father does not like me," said Peter.

"Nonsense. It is the duke he does not care for."

"All the same, I am a bother to him."

"There may be some truth to that." They studied each other in silence. "Oh. I have something that belongs to you," said Aflyn. She reached down to remove an object from the hand-bag that lay on the floor beside her chair. It was the little enameled wolf.

"Why, yes. So much has happened. I'd forgotten all about it."

"I had one of our guildsmen fashion a chain for it. I hope you don't mind. A pocket is no place for a treasure such as this." She handed it back to him. He admired the chain and then slipped the pendant around his neck.

"That was thoughtful of you," he said, clasping the miniature wolf to his chest. "My aunt would have been terribly cross with me if I'd lost it."

"Your aunt?" she replied. "You'll have to explain that to me."

Of course it made no sense to her. "Another time perhaps." He pondered the girl sitting before him. "Where is your mother?" he asked.

"My mother was taken with the marasmus when I was nine," she said. "She dwells in the great hall of my ancestors."

"I'm sorry to hear that," he replied. "It must have been awful for you. I never knew my mother. She died giving birth to me."

"How sad," said Aflyn. "I mean, to have never known your mother."

"Others have been very kind to me, particularly my Aunt Generosa."

"The one who gave you the wolf?"

He blushed. "Yes. The one who *gave* me the wolf."

Aflyn smiled, which caused her brows to shift just a little. "I must go," she said. "Beshwan will take care of you until Josh-kar returns." She stood up, curtsied with studied perfection and left the room."

Beshwan stared tight-lipped at Peter from her chair in the corner of the room.

"What's wrong with you?" he asked the handmaid pointedly. "Why do you keep giggling so?"

She stood up and curtsied before answering, "Beg your pardon, m' lord. Your brows. You haven't any."

He rubbed his forehead self-consciously. That wasn't exactly true, except in a relative sense. "Surely you people aren't born with such prodigious eyebrows," he rejoined.

"No sir. Not exactly. But it's darn uncommon for someone your age not to have 'em. It's…um…well, a little freakish, if you'll pardon me."

Freakish?! Outspoken girl! "Well," he replied, "you'll just have to get used to the idea. This is normal where I come from."

"Yes, m' lord." She curtsied once again and sat back down.

Freakish? My old boots! Freakish is a shipload of folk who think a fifteen-year-old boy can be their confounded lord arbiter. He wanted out of this madhouse, and badly, but how? The doorway home seemed further and further away with each passing day.

A servant arrived with a tray of food and drink. He could not bring himself to eat, but sipped at a goblet of tart red juice flavored with a sprig of spearmint. Joshkar came to his room a little while later, bowing very formally as he entered.

"Don't do that!" groaned Peter, irritably. "More than anyone, you make me feel ridiculous."

Joshkar shrugged his shoulders. "Very well, I will respect your wishes when no one else is present."

"And while we're at it, call me 'Peter.' None of this lord arbiter rubbish." The bowman nodded without protest. "I understand you saved my life," he added.

"I was only doing what Captain Menhar and His Grace, the Duke, would have me do."

"Yes, I'll bet that's the reason. Come over here." Joshkar looked at Peter uncertainly. "Come here," he commanded. "I won't bite you." Joshkar stepped toward the bed and Peter ensnared him in the biggest bear hug his frail arms could marshal. "*Grazas,*" he whispered. "Thank you Joshkar."

Only after he eased his grip was Joshkar able to shake himself away. "You're welcome," he muttered, red with embarrassment.

"Lord Palkvo was quite surprised by your curative abilities. I must admit, I am too. I took you for a geographer," said Peter, half teasingly.

"People are generally very self-sufficient where I come from."

"But you haven't explained to me how a Bakan comes to be in the service of Orn?"

"I was the third of three boys. No place for me at home when I came of age. Bakans in general have a strong connection to the bow. We're often recruited for service in the ranks of archers, especially those in my shoes."

"I see. It's not all that different where I come from," remarked Peter. "The first son inherits the land or the family business, the second takes a commission in the military and the third enters the clergy. I'm the first, and only, son."

"And what will you inherit?" asked Joshkar. "Property or the family business?"

"If I ever get back, the family business."

"And that is?"

"Biscuits."

The Bakan's brows rose far up on his forehead. "Biscuits?!"

"Yes. I know it sounds ludicrous, but my father is a biscuit manufacturer and a very wealthy one. There is a war going on back home. Troops from all over the empire are fighting the Boers in southern Africa. My father supplies hardtack biscuits to the army and navy. Not just for South Africa, but India, Egypt and the Sudan as well."

This was apparently more than Joshkar could take.

"Biscuits?" He began to laugh and could not bring himself to stop.

"What are you laughing at? It's not very funny really. Next year Father means to start me on learning the business in earnest."

"Forgive me. It's a respectable occupation. It's just hard to imagine the lord arbiter imperial as heir to a vast biscuit empire."

"Go ahead, make fun if you want. You haven't heard the worst of it. My great-great-great grandfather, Manuel López— the one you Gwellem make such a fuss over—worked in the kitchen of a local monastery before you heaped titles on him and sent him home with a pocket full of treasure."

"I knew he was a rogue, but a scullery boy?"

"That's what my father once told me. I think now he must have been a very cunning and resourceful individual."

Joshkar chuckled. "No doubt." He gathered himself and changed the subject. "As soon as you are able, we ride to Menom."

"So I gather...Joshkar? Am I in serious trouble?"

He gazed at Peter, his face all somber and grave. "You will be fine," he assured, "so long as you keep your head about you. Say as little as you are able, deliver what you must, and bide your time. Your day will come young biscuit king."

Biscuit king—forever after Joshkar's pet name for Peter.

Three days following his conversation with Joshkar, Peter gathered on horseback with his escort in the courtyard of Lord Palkvo's manor. He was provided with a fine palfrey and Joshkar a charger of his own so that he might ride at Peter's side. Aflyn was there to see her father off. She passed by Peter's horse, curtsied, and bade him a safe journey. He, in return, wished her continued good health and happiness, and asked if she would like him to bring anything back from the big city. The truth be told, he made the offer more for his own encouragement than hers.

Aflyn smiled politely. Beshwan giggled as always. "Perhaps," she said. "If you were to return with a honey cake I would not reject it. There's a baker's shop near the wharf. You can tell it from the bee's nest carved upon the lintel. My mother used to bring me cakes from there when I was little."

"Then I shall see to it," declared Peter, as their column departed. They passed through the debouche and out onto the drive that led away from the estate. It was a long ride to Menom from Lord Palkvo's manor, mostly along well-traveled roads dotted with innumerable hamlets. Joshkar proved a willing tutor, helping Peter put to good use the many hours spent in the saddle. At his urging he kept his eyes open, making a concerted effort to learn about the communities and people they passed along the way.

"Our destination," said Joshkar, "lies abreast the River Talsis. The port at Menom has eclipsed Piernot and is now second only to Tagra on the Hemsto coast. You'll see for yourself the duke's grand building scheme. He's engaged thousands of skilled artisans from across the empire to adorn the palace and government buildings. The great families aren't immune to the duke's fiery ambition. They compete to outdo one another, erecting stone towers all over the city each more ostentatious than the next."

"That's all very interesting," remarked Peter. "But what about the others, Joshkar? The Ulfair? You've told me next to nothing about them, or the so-called 'wizards.' What manner of beings are they? And the portals?! My life has been turned upside down on account of these...*people?*—I don't really know what to call them—and yet all I get is more riddles when I make any inquiry. Shall I ever see an Ulfair?" He was all-eager and impatient to understand the forces with which he was confronted.

Joshkar looked at him with an expression of utter exasperation, as one might regard a puppy whose effusive explorations are beginning to wear thin. "That is because they *are* a riddle," he replied. "Their origins are shrouded in myth and legend. Nothing said about them can be said with any certainty.

"All I can say, is what I have told you before. The Ulfair arrived through the portals and established the empire. As far as I know, the portals through which they, and the one through which you yourself passed, were built by the wizards. Wizards are a strange and elusive lot, their numbers fade with each passing year. When the last of them are gone, the portals likewise will lapse into history."

Dashwan had said as much before he died. Peter kept on him. "But why were the portals built in the first place? For the convenience of the Ulfair? And how do they function?" These seemed to Peter increasingly vital questions.

"Ah. So many questions. Alas, I have no answers for you on that account. You will have to find yourself a wizard to interrogate."

Find myself a wizard?! His list of needs was growing and any hope of ever returning home diminishing in equal measure. Peter needed to find the Wolf Queen, his cousin Bonifacia, and now—a wizard. Given his circumstances, he hadn't the vaguest notion how he might find any one of them.

"I don't suppose you have some ideas on how I might accomplish that?" he persisted.

"No, I do not," laughed Joshkar, "but I am sure you will find a way in time."

Peter rode on in silence, catching snippets of the scurrilous conversation between two soldiers riding closely behind. They traveled at an almost leisurely pace, camping each night, halting periodically to feed the horses or to break for a cold repast. Lord Palkvo was not, in the main, a man for bivouacking by the side of the road. Peter's bottom ached from days in the saddle, so he was very glad indeed when the column reined in their horses at a commodious inn from which wafted the heavenly scent of roasting meats and apple cider.

His stomach grumbled for all to hear, but food would have to wait just a while longer. The Gwellem in Lord Palkvo's company were, by and large, a devout bunch. Having missed moonrise while on the march, they formed concentric prayer circles in the center of the yard before settling in their rooms. Locked arm in arm like a scrimmage before the start of play, Palkvo's party offered up a brief prayer to the "Eternal Architect" of the universe. Peter chose to participate in his own fashion, asking Jesus and Mary for their help and guidance.

He shared a room with Joshkar and four soldiers who had scarcely claimed their bunks before running off to the tavern below. "Come," said Joshkar. "I expect the food will be excellent and Lord Palkvo in the mood for some entertainment."

Peter followed Joshkar down the stairs and into the dimly lit hall that served as both a dining room and public house. The inn was obviously a popular place as it was crammed from wall to wall with soldiers, journeymen, merchants, farmers and nobles either coming away or en route to Menom, all of them making the loudest imaginable din. The smell of roast and cider was thick in the air and Peter's stomach grumbled loud enough to beat a banshee.

The hall came to a sudden standstill, the uproar evaporating into leaden silence. Heads turned to look his way. Peter felt the blood drain from his face, and wished for the first time that he had longer brows.

It was Palkvo that broke the awkward silence. Rising from his seat, he addressed the room. "Friends," he said, "good people of Orn. The lord arbiter rides to an audience with the duke. A toast! A toast to peace and prosperity!"

There was a moment of uncertainty. Mugs lifted into the air and the words repeated. "To peace and prosperity!" they replied. To Peter's great relief the hall swiftly resumed its former humor. Palkvo waved for them to join him at his table.

Peter found a place on the bench beside Palkvo and his servant, Amran. Joshkar on a bench opposite. "Thank you," he said.

"Thank me?" said Palkvo. "For what? Lying to these good people?" He leaned over to whisper in Peter's ear. "Your presence in Menom is a virtual guarantee that war will come, *and very soon*. They think you are their last hope for peace, but it is the other way round."

Peter grew cross. "Why don't you kill me then, and be done with it?!"

Palkvo glared at him between half closed lids. "Because my house and all that I hold dear would be forfeit. It is for *her* sake that I stay my dagger. I am forced to choose between my daughter and my people." He twisted his jaw in anger and despair.

Peter looked over to Joshkar. Palkvo caught his eye. "Your bowman can tell his master whatever he pleases," barked Palkvo. "Borganin knows very well what I think. He cares only that I do as I am told."

"Is there no way out of this?" moaned Peter. "I want no part of it."

"There is a way," replied Palkvo. "You can denounce Borganin's grab for the imperial mantle and the Padishah of Stônar's groping influence."

Peter looked at him in puzzlement. Could it be that easy? He stood up suddenly and shouted at the top of his lungs, "Good people…" He'd barely got the words out when Amran, Palkvo and Joshkar grabbed hold of him in unison and hauled him back down.

"You little idiot!" shouted Palkvo.

"Why? Didn't you just say that all I had to do was denounce Lord Borganin?"

Palkvo held one hand to his forehead and let out a deep breath. "I appreciate the sentiment, de Soto, but you are no more free to do as you please than I."

"I don't understand you people," blurted Peter in growing vexation and confusion. "You say a war is in the offing, that you do not desire it, but are equally powerless to prevent it. Is there nothing to be done?"

"It's like a tempest on the horizon," explained Amran. "You can see it coming, make preparations to some extent, but plead or pray as much as you want, the storm *will* come."

"Storms are of God's making, wars are not," retorted Peter.

Palkvo inspected the lines on the palm of his hand. He had nothing more to say. They ordered food and refreshment and ate their meal, discussing only minor points related to their stay in Menom before retiring to their rooms for the night.

After a leisurely breakfast they got back on the road the following morning. A succession of burgeoning towns suggested the provincial capital could not be far off. Owing to the greater volume of traffic, the highway leading to Menom henceforth comprised two tracks in either direction, separated by a wide ditch-style median. Since the fields flanking the highway were either fenced off or bore crops, those seeking rest or repair had little choice but to avail themselves of the ditch. The median stretched toward the horizon like a grubby ribbon crammed full of refuse, tents, and sidelined transport, small herds of livestock and beasts of burden grazing on the trampled grass amid the blur of scattered cookfires.

Peter, in the company of soldiers, was readily recognized. Folk would stop and point, whispering, "The lord arbiter. There goes the lord arbiter."

After enduring several hours of this, he took Joshkar by the elbow, "I should like to purchase a very large hat at the next opportunity. Anything to hide my brows. Only I have no money."

"They will recognize you with or without one," he laughed. "Word of your arrival precedes you. Lord Borganin has made certain of that. It does not serve his purpose to keep you secret."

The closer they came to Menom, the more Peter began to doubt his chances of coming through this experience unscathed. He found himself wondering (not for the first or last time) if his notion of heaven held valid so far from home.

"Tell me, Joshkar, about the god to whom you pray. I wonder if he (or is it a she?) is anything like ours."

"I may be many things, but I am no holy brother," he replied.

"You will do," he insisted.

"Do you enjoy the old sagas, young biscuit king? Before the Ulfair, there were many gods, always in pairs like Talsis and Bos."

"The rivers?" he prompted.

"Yes, husband and wife, brother and sister, sometimes two sisters or two brothers, like the moons Creto and Porfan. They did not always get along. It was the Ulfair who taught us to see things differently, to place our faith in The Eternal Architect who sets all things in motion. Over time the old gods departed."

"But you still pray to the two moons?"

"No," he snorted, "not *to* them. But the act of praying *at* the rising of the moons is so deeply ingrained in us that the holy brothers and sisters let the practice stand. It is to the supreme architect of the universe that we now bend our prayers."

"But what do you say when you pray? I've strained my ears to understand, but can't follow."

"No doubt. The words are usually spoken in the old tongue. It is a simple prayer of gratitude for having been blessed with yet another opportunity to touch the World and the lives of others. Life is brief and one must make the most of it." He smiled at Peter, rather condescendingly.

Shortly before noon their company crested a steep rise. Before them lay a broad patchwork of farms bordered on the horizon by a ribbon of teal—the River Talsis. To their right, visible, but still some distance off, soared the walls and white towers of Menom. From this point forward the highway was transformed. Soldiers stationed at various milestones asserted, at long last, some semblance of order and the road kept in excellent repair.

An officer of the Ducal Guard laid their column over at one of these mileposts, taking down a report of their passage and forwarding it by swift mounted courier to Menom. The rider set off at a harrowing gallop down a narrow track that paralleled the main road reserved especially for this purpose. Peter felt more than ever like the Christmas goose, his sense of impending doom building with each step closer to their destination.

Before long, the great city came into larger focus, the shops and warehouses along the quays of the faubourg bristling with the yards and masts of a hundred ships, the city's impressive outer walls dwarfed by a multitude of exquisite belvedere towers, colorful banners fluttering against the blue sky.

The large amount of traffic into Menom necessitated the construction of an outer barbican and barracks just in advance of the city. Behind it stretched a long stone bridge over a dry riverbed that fronted the main gate. They were greeted by the captain of the guard who politely, but firmly, directed everyone to dismount and stable their horses.

"No one bearing arms is permitted to enter the city unless on duty," he instructed. Beds were provided for Peter's escort in a bunkhouse beside the stables. Palkvo, Amran, Joshkar and Peter were directed to wait until a ducal escort arrived to convey them to the guest palace.

"The guest palace? Did you hear that?" muttered Palkvo in disgust. "It isn't enough he has his own palace. He's got to have a *guest palace* as well. Borganin already imagines himself the Prince Imperial."

Their escort arrived a short while later, a troop of horse to accompany a four-in-hand coach with a chestnut and roan in the lead and two dark bays at the wheels. They took seats inside the carriage and soon found themselves whisking through the city gates and down the cobbled avenues of Menom, the coachman's horn winding at every turn and intersection.

Peter beamed at the passing sights despite himself. Menom was an astonishingly vibrant city—the streets and walks teeming with journeymen, building supplies slumped in corves across their broad shoulders. Fishmongers, the morning's catch hanging from hooks in shop windows. Elegant merchants. Tin and copper smiths' freshly minted wares laid out on tables, gleaming in the afternoon sun. Chapmen, water sellers. Ladies out for a bit of shopping, handmaids in tow. Doughty men with their sleeves rolled up toting heavy loads in barrows, and grocers, their produce displayed in neat rows with painstaking care.

They passed through a tall wrought iron gate and the carriage clattered to a noisy halt inside the courtyard of the guest palace. A coachman opened the door and invited Lord Palkvo and his party to dismount. Their escort rode off and the gates closed behind them, leaving them in the hands of the chief domestic. The old man introduced himself as Harmond. With the assistance of the palace staff, he showed them to their rooms.

"Supper is at half past five," he intoned.

"Will His Grace be joining us this evening?" asked Palkvo.

"I'm afraid not," replied Harmond. "He asked that you make yourselves at home. Arrangements have been made to see that you are suitably attired for court. The tailors will see to you tomorrow after breakfast."

"I see," said Palkvo, although Peter did not. Lord Palkvo had provided for his needs in that regard very early on. He was more than satisfied with his present attire.

"Perhaps the lord arbiter would care to take in the view from the tower?" suggested the chief domestic. "It offers a spectacular view of the city and river."

"That's very kind of you," replied Peter. "I believe I'd like that."

"Good," said Harmond. "As soon as you've settled into your rooms you may ring for an attendant and he will show you to me."

At that, Joshkar piped in. "The lord arbiter is not to go wandering about the palace or anywhere else outside of my company."

Harmond looked at him with an expression of wide-eyed surprise. "Of course not. That is a given, Master Bowman."

Apparently Peter's chances for ever escaping were now considered so remote that he was given a room well separated from his benevolent jailer, Joshkar.

"You heard what I said to the domestic," said Joshkar when he saw the room arrangement. "You will not go wandering about without me."

"If you insist," said Peter.

"I do insist," he replied. "Have you forgotten that there has already been one attempt upon your life?"

"So you are my bodyguard now and not my turnkey?"

By the look on his face Peter's words had cut him deeply. It surprised him, quite frankly. Their conversations had drawn them closer, but Peter was never quite certain of how far their friendship extended.

"Since that first day, it has always been my task to watch over you," replied Joshkar.

Chapter 8

The Old Kaladwen Highway

"Here, put this on," said Bartle, handing Bonifacia a floppy hat made of butternut felt. He took a step back. "That will do in a pinch to hide those uncommon brows. Sorry there isn't more we can do about your clothes. You may stick out for a bit. Henrik's friends may have something better for you."

"It's time we were off, Uncle," said Henrik. "Grab your belongings, Bonifacia. Let's get going."

She picked up the canvas haversack filled with food and other sundry items for their journey and strapped it over her shoulder. Together they headed out the door of the cottage, Bonifacia pausing to give the shorka sitting near the entrance a guarded pat on the head. "*Adeus* Strella."

They followed Bartle through the garden, past the little brook and over to the side of the island facing the mountains. Taking the narrow track through the reeds and hassock, they hit upon the river. A canoe lay hidden amongst the rushes.

"The Chigraw can be a mite testy at times," warned Bartle. The churning water beyond the bank looked very rough indeed.

"Have you no contraption like the chair across the other branch?" asked Bonifacia.

"Did, but it were washed away years ago," said Bartle. "I'll get in first, then you, and Henrik last. Stay in the center of the boat and don't move about. If it should tip for any reason, grab hold of one of the ropes and don't let go."

They sat the canoe in the water. Bartle picked up one of the two paddles and climbed into the stern. "Okay Bonifacia, get in. Henrik give her a hand."

Bonifacia crawled unsteadily toward the middle of the canoe and sat kneeling with her back to Bartle. Henrik climbed forward and pressed the boat away from shore with the edge of his paddle. Like a shot, the boat was caught in the grip of the river's powerful current and holus-bolus quit the grassy shore. Bartle and Henrik paddled furiously to steer the canoe through the turbulent water, past perilous outcroppings that threatened to smash them to bits and dark swirling eddies intent on pulling them under. The little boat lurched dangerously from side to side as it tore along, the violent foaming river drenching them all with a cold spray that dripped down their brows and into their eyes. "Hold on!" shouted Bartle over the din of the rapids.

The tip of the island shot by on their left and Bonifacia, gripping the gunwales tightly, turned her head to see if she could spot the point where the two branches of the river merged from their headlong dash around the isle. The little boat bounced along like an angry badger and although her heart was racing, Bonifacia unaccountably found herself laughing with delight.

Exhausted and breathless, Bartle and Henrik pulled the boat past the center point of the river and into calmer waters skirting the far shore. Selecting a suitable place to bring the boat in, they paddled with all the strength left in their arms, the canoe sliding onto the pebbly beach.

All three stumbled from the boat, their hands resting on their knees to catch their breath, Bonifacia still laughing loudly. "That was ripping good fun!" she cried.

"Fun? I don't understand," said Henrik, still short of breath. "You balked at riding the boatswain's chair, but think that was fun?"

"I don't much care to hang from a line alone in the dark. This was different. You were paddling next to me." She glanced at the swift churning water. "How will you get back to the island, Uncle Bartle?"

"Same as always," he replied. "I'll portage back up river and let the current take me across." She frowned. "Don't you worry," he assured her. "I've done this a thousand times or more. If it makes you feel better, you can help me carry the canoe back to the launch before you head off."

Bonifacia nodded in agreement, but when the boat was lifted off the ground and up over their heads, she found she was too short by far to lend a hand. "No worries. You can check the path ahead," suggested Bartle. "Make sure the route is clear for us." This, at least, gave Bonifacia a sense of contributing to the effort. It was a long hike to the launch point, necessitating several rest stops along the way, during which Bartle talked enthusiastically about getting his shorka ready for market.

When they reached the launch, Bartle and Henrik laid the canoe in the sand and then stood facing one another. Bartle embraced his nephew, giving the tress of both his brows a loving tug. The kindly old Gwellem then knelt down in front of Bonifacia. Having no brows to tug on, he gave her instead a little pinch above the cheeks.

"You do as Henrik says, okay? And write me a letter when you get to meet the queen. If she doesn't already own a shorka, tell her your Uncle Bartle has the finest in the empire." Bonifacia's eyes began to water.

"Yes Uncle."

"Look here," he said, "I've got something special for you." He reached into his jacket pocket and pulled out a silver orb, about the size of a hen's egg. "Take this and keep it safe. If you come across a wizard you can trust, you may give it to him and tell him who it came from."

"What is it?" asked Bonifacia, examining its smooth polished surface.

"Nothing in the wrong hands and more than I can explain. Wizards have little use for coin. Think of this as something you can bargain with."

Bonifacia buried the curious object in a side pocket of her satchel.

"Okay, away with the two of you. I can look after myself from here." He kissed Bonifacia on the forehead.

"*Grazas,* Uncle." She embraced Bartle one last time and with a sullen face, followed Henrik up and over the brae and off into the woods.

The track from the riverbank soon narrowed to little more than a slot between trees. "You must know this country very well," remarked Bonifacia.

"I suppose," said Henrik, without slackening his pace.

"Will we actually cross over the mountains? I'd like to have a look at the ocean before I leave."

"I'm not planning on it. A lot depends on who or what we encounter along the way. Now hush. We've a great deal of ground to cover and I need to focus on our path."

"*Vale,*" said Bonifacia, sulkily.

On they walked through the rest of the morning and right on through to the gloaming of the day. Bonifacia was footsore and cranky after her long march. "Are you sure we're not lost?" she asked. "It's getting awfully dark."

"No, we're not lost," glowered Henrik. "It's just taking much longer than I anticipated on account of your short legs." Bonifacia wrinkled her nose at him. "We should make camp," he continued. "If we start out early tomorrow we can reach the cottage before mid morning."

"Thank heavens," replied Bonifacia. "My feet couldn't take much more of this. I need new shoes."

So Bonifacia and Henrik settled in a pleasant tree lined dell for the night, enjoying soup cooked up over the campfire with chunks of hearty bread for dipping. After supper, Henrik squatted beside the fire and played a tune on the ocarina.

"That's lovely," said Bonifacia. "Can you teach me how to play it?"

He shuffled next to her. "You must first master how to hold it and breathe the notes properly," instructed Henrik. "Watch here." He demonstrated and then passed her the instrument.

Holding the ocarina felt a little like holding a frightened turtle to her lips. She did her best to mimic Henrik, running her finger tips down the short scale and then up again, blowing each note with care.

"Not half bad," he exclaimed, genuinely surprised by her ability.

"It's not the first time I've played an ocarina," she admitted. "Uncle Bartle taught me a few notes for Strella while you went off to visit your friends."

"Ah," said Henrik. "And did the old girl obey your commands?"

"Uh huh," she said proudly.

"I'm impressed." He took the ocarina from her and demonstrated the first few bars of the tune he had been playing. "Now you try." He handed it back.

An hour flowed quickly by and with practice Bonifacia had mastered both the ocarina and the tune. "You have a remarkable ear to learn so very quickly," said Henrik.

"I play the piano at home," replied Bonifacia, as if that quite accounted for it.

"A *piano?* Is that like an ocarina?" asked Henrik.

Bonifacia had never needed to explain a piano before. "Not exactly. It's more like a big wood box with a row of keys on the outside and little hammers inside that strike at different strings as you play."

"Perhaps you will show me sometime," said Henrik. "I can't quite picture it." She yawned despite the pleasant time she was having. He smiled. "It's late. We should get some sleep."

They gathered together a makeshift mattress of evergreen needles and laid themselves out on the forest floor. In a matter of moments they were deep in slumber.

In the morning, Henrik rekindled the fire to shake off the damp. They took tea and biscuits and set out again. Beyond the ravine the ground opened up considerably in a series of alternating glens and downs, affording a clear view of the distant mist enshrouded mountains. Goat-like creatures roamed the pastures, oblivious to their passage.

"Not many folk about," commented Bonifacia.

"No, not many. We've come in the backdoor, so to speak. The cottage is just over that next hill."

They crossed over the knoll and Bonifacia could see smoke rising from a chimney pot. The grange occupied the green between two low hills. A young woman was working the garden in front of the cottage and was quick to spot their silhouettes coming up over the crest. She shielded her eyes with one hand and called out. A man joined her from behind the house, standing closely by her side until Bonifacia and Henrik arrived.

Henrik reached out and gripped the fellow by the ends of his brows, tugging them gently, as she'd seen Bartle do. Then he stretched over to kiss the young woman on both cheeks.

"It's good to see you again Henrik. We heard from Brejan you might be coming this way."

Henrik looked down at Bonifacia. "This," he said by way of introduction, "is Bonifacia Espasande. If you've spoken with Brejan then you know she is kin to the lord arbiter imperial."

The reference to Peter took her by surprise. The man bowed and the woman curtsied. Bonifacia blushed and curtsied in return. Such formalities seemed absurd so far removed from anywhere. "This is my good friend Tomner, Tom for short, and his wife Lianne," said Henrik.

"Pleased to meet you," said Bonifacia.

"And how 'bout Little Tomner?" asked Henrik. Tom and Lianne's heads swiveled in unison toward the cottage. Bonifacia then noticed the cradle sitting under the shade of the front stoop. "Belated congratulations, by the way."

"May I?" asked Bonifacia. She had yet to see a Gwellem baby.

"Of course," said the proud parents, leading them up to the house.

They pulled aside the mantilla covering the cradle so that Bonifacia could peer at the infant. It looked like any human newborn except for the well-developed fawn colored eyebrows. Bonifacia had to fight back the urge to laugh. Newborn Gwellem looked like little old men. Big bristling brows made them look like *angry* little old men.

"What a beautiful baby," she said.

Tom and Lianne beamed.

"He's the spitting image of your father," remarked Henrik.

"Yes, I suppose he is," said Tom. "Come, you must be parched after your journey. We'll fix you some refreshment."

Bonifacia and Henrik sat at the dining table while their hosts prepared tumblers of freshly squeezed fruit juice flavored with spearmint.

"How are things for you both?" asked Henrik.

"As well as can be. 'Course Little Tom there has changed the pattern some."

"I can well imagine," said Henrik.

"I heard from Brejan about your situation. 'Twas he that warned us of your coming. Said you were thinking to take the foothill track to Piernot. Is that so?" asked Tom.

Henrik only nodded.

"I wouldn't advise it. You'd have better luck cutting a deal with the Ornish."

Henrik turned dark. "You don't mean that Tom."

Tom didn't flinch. "You know Menom has moved against the queen's forces at Piernot?"

"The duke is a poltroon," replied Henrik. "He doesn't have it in him to face the Imperial Army on the open field of battle."

"With the Padishah of Stônar by his side, he does."

"The Imperial Council will never let that happen. It's all bluff and bluster."

"The council has lost all meaning. Its time is past," retorted Tom.

"Strong words for a country shepherd."

Tom rested his tumbler on the table. "Look Henrik, I'm not trying to argue with you. I just don't want to see you hurt. From what I hear, you're lucky to be alive after your run in with the duke's men. Just think about it."

Henrik smiled. "Very well my old friend, I'll think about it. There may be a better way."

"Good," said Tom. "Let's forget it for now and do some catching up. How's that eccentric old uncle of yours?"

Tom had chores to do about the homestead and Henrik went off to keep him company, while Bonifacia made herself comfortable in the garden, helping Lianne with her own chores.

"That's very kind of you, m' lady," said Lianne, passing Bonifacia a large tuber freshly pulled from the ground. She loaded it into a cart beside the garden.

"It's nothing," said Bonifacia. "It's wonderful actually to have a bit of normal work to do. 'Helps to keep my mind off other things."

"Those clothes aren't exactly suitable," remarked Lianne.

"They're all I've got, except for an oversized shirt from Uncle Bartle."

"Come then," said Lianne. "We can cut down to size a thing or two of mine."

"Would you?" said Bonifacia. "I'd be ever so grateful."

Lianne gave her a big friendly smile. "Of course."

Lianne fished a few discarded items from a trunk and they spent the early afternoon rotating between altering clothes and fawning over Little Tom. Bonifacia helped Lianne prepare a stew for supper. The meat was a bit pungent for Bonifacia's taste, but the meal nonetheless hearty and satisfying.

The sun disappeared over the horizon casting a purple blanket over the open meadow. The first of the evening stars surfaced in the blue-black sky. Bonifacia sat on the stoop and listened to Lianne hum softly to Little Tom as the insects began a twilight concert of their own. *So peaceful, so far removed from the troubles of the world.* Tom took out his ocarina, as did Henrik, and together they played a sweet duet to accompany the moonrise.

With apologies for the lack of proper accommodation, Tom and Lianne stuffed two paillasse and laid them out on the stoop for Bonifacia and Henrik to arrange their blankets on.

"Good night," said Tom and Lianne. "We'll see you in the morning. Pleasant dreams."

Bonifacia had no problem falling asleep. She dreamed of the patio garden back home in Galicia, sitting at breakfast sipping chocolate. Her mother reading the latest news from Madrid. Peter at her side, devising silly patterns with the food on his plate to make her laugh.

"Bonifacia," someone whispered.

She awoke to find a dark figure looming over her and made to scream, but was stifled by a firm hand across her mouth.

"Hush. It's me, Henrik."

She nodded and he removed her hand.

"What?…"

Before she had time to finish her question, Henrik cut her off. "We've got to get out of here. Get your things together. Be very quiet. Like a mouse. Understand?"

She didn't really, but could feel the sense of urgency in his voice. Carrying her shoes in one hand, she put her bag together and followed Henrik down the stoop and away from the cottage, their shadows stretching off in the glow of the moons' light.

When they were out of sight of the house, they dusted off their feet and put on their shoes. "Henrik," asked Bonifacia. "What's wrong?"

"Tom plans to turn us in," he said sullenly.

She was shocked beyond words.

"I've known him all my life Bonifacia. I can read him like a parchment. He's gone over."

"But surely Tom would never betray you?" she insisted. "He's your friend."

"I can't blame him really. He's got a good life, a nice farm, a beautiful wife, a new baby. He's bought the duke's propaganda that changing horses is the ticket to peace and plenty. Tom doesn't want to lose what he's got."

"I thought from your conversation with Tom this afternoon that you'd changed your mind too," admitted Bonifacia. "That we should turn ourselves in and plead our case before the duke."

"I was just going along. That's madness. Tom will rue the day he sided with Orn against his own people."

"Oh, Henrik, I'm so sorry," said Bonifacia.

He shrugged. "Tom doesn't mean for us to get hurt. He really thinks the duke will treat us well. I just don't see eye to eye with him on that. Well, the bottom line is we can't take the route I originally intended. Tom knows me too well. We've got to put some distance between ourselves and the farm before sunrise. We'll be safer once we reach the foothills. It's far too open here."

Off they charged in the direction of the mountains, Bonifacia doing her best to stay awake and keep up with Henrik's big strides. The walking was easy enough in the clear moons' light over gently rolling hills, cropped low to the ground by the ruminant creatures that seemed to roam everywhere. But after a few hours of hard paced walking, Bonifacia was struggling to pick up her feet and falling further behind.

"Bonifacia, you must try to keep up," said Henrik, urging her on. "The sun will be overhead soon and we must get ourselves at least as far as the forest eaves."

She trudged up to him, panting for breath. "Henrik, just I can't. I'm worn out."

He stood looking down at her, his hands on his hips. "Very well. Hand me your bag." He strapped it to his own, then, quite unexpectedly, scooped her up in his arms. Without another word, he set out toward the mountains.

Bonifacia was terribly shocked to be so rudely handled, but was physically and mentally beyond the point of complaining. In a moment she was fast asleep, lulled by the rhythm of his footsteps.

She awoke some hours later in the shadow of a great pine, sunlight piercing through gaps in the forest canopy. Birds flitted and chirruped in the treetops. Henrik lay where he had collapsed from exhaustion, his legs and feet spread before him, his mouth hanging open. He hadn't even taken time to remove his pack. Bonifacia smiled and let him sleep, then turned on her side and slept some more.

"Wake up sleepy head," said Henrik, prodding her gently. "Have a bite to eat and a wash up. There's a stream over yonder."

Bonifacia stirred slowly. Her back hurt from resting on the hard ground, but she was grateful for having slept. She did what Henrik directed, but in reverse order, washing first in the cold water and then having something to eat.

"Do you know where we are?" she asked.

"This time I have to admit, I am a bit lost. But I know where we are in a general sense."

"That's reassuring," said Bonifacia.

"Your legs up to a little more walking?"

She stretched them out along the ground. "Yes, I think so. And how about you? You must have carried me for miles."

"I don't know how far a *mile* is, but yes, you owe me for that one, your ladyship."

She looked at him with growing admiration. "Henrik, would you please call me *Bonnie*. I'm tired of hearing you say 'Bonifacia.' I miss the sound of it."

"Bonnie. All right, *Bonnie,* get your things together and let's get started."

Off they went charging deeper into the foothill forest, skirting bogs, outcroppings, and precipitous combes where a single false step could end in misfortune. Higher and higher they climbed, following the slots carved out by woodland creatures, avoiding patches of tanglewood and other obstacles. Here and there, leaping the sodden banks of passing streams or pioneering switchbacks to the top of a particularly steep rise.

Bonifacia was amazed to find her legs, in fact, growing stronger with each passing day, all the heavy trekking becoming less and less a hardship.

Each night, they camped under the trees and Henrik taught her a new tune on the ocarina. Some were old Gwellem folk songs. Others, lullabies, jigs and even straightforward shorka commands. They had names like, "The Innkeeper's Reel,"

"Child's Lament," and the one that made Bonifacia laugh, "Brows like Moire Silk."

"When I get a chance," offered Henrik, "I'll fashion you an ocarina of your own and we can play duets together."

"Oh, I'd like that very much. I loved the tune that you and Tom played together. Thank you, Henrik." She examined the bulbous instrument more closely. "What happened to your parents?" she asked spontaneously. "You never speak of them."

He lowered his eyes. "They were killed by Og'yre. I was a just a tot. We lived beside the farm that Tom and Lianne now occupy."

"Dashwan said something about Og'yre. Who or what are 'Og'yre'?" she asked.

"Creatures that inhabit the mountain peaks."

"You mean *those* mountain peaks. The ones right above us?" She pointed toward the near horizon.

"Yes, I'm afraid so."

"The same creatures that killed your parents?"

"Uh huh."

"Is that why Uncle Bartle and Tom were against us coming this way?"

"We'll do what we can to steer clear of them. The Weshnut keep a pretty firm grip on the Og'yre. They haven't made real trouble for Gwellem in a long while."

"I heard Uncle Bartle mention the Weshnut. He said it was a Weshnut that built that contraption across the river."

"That's right. I'd forgotten that."

"If these Og'yre are as savage as you say, how do the Weshnut manage to control them?"

"A business transaction of sorts. I'm not very clear on the details. Weshnut don't mix with other Gwellem. Strange bunch. A lot of funny ideas about the world. Are you afraid to go up there, Bonnie? Into the mountains?"

"Yes, a little," she replied.

"Good. A little fear is healthy. Keeps you on your toes. That's what I say." He tugged on his right ear while examining her face. "You know, it's not too late to turn back. This way we stand a chance of reaching the queen. The other way I can pretty much guarantee you'll be taken by the duke, like your cousin, Peter. But as I said before, the choice is yours to make."

"I've already made my choice," reiterated Bonifacia. "Don't ask me again."

"All right. I won't."

"Henrik? Why are you doing this for me? It seems an awful lot to ask."

"The empress sent for you, didn't she? Just doin' my job."

"Yes, but…"

"No *buts* about it. Soldiers do what's asked of them. That's their lot in life." He walked off to prepare his bed, effectively ending the conversation.

During the night, the temperature dropped and the wind picked up without warning. Henrik roused himself to gather an extra layer of cedar boughs and together they huddled beneath it for warmth. Very soon, however, the looming storm scattered their meager covering. The fine blonde hairs on Bonifacia's arms prickled in the heavily charged air. Yellow leaves discarded on the forest floor toppled end over end carried along by great whistling gusts then went suddenly spiraling skyward like a flock of frightened gulls. Branches dashed against one another, clattering noisily. The trees began to creak and groan as they bent against the mounting gale. In the space of a an hour the green weald transformed from a tranquil refuge to a gray tract that looked and felt as if it were about to crack wide open.

"Quickly, grab your things," shouted Henrik. "It's going to rain any minute and we've got to find ourselves some proper shelter."

They pressed their way through the forest up a series of stope-like ridges, aiming toward a point where the ridgeline suggested the best prospect of a dry crevice. Thunder clapped behind them and the wind drove ever harder against their backs. The first desultory drops of rain began to fall, quickly turning the ground to a slippery farrago that interfered with their progress.

Somewhere along the way Bonifacia got separated from Henrik. Her first instinct was to panic, but she forced the urge aside. *Be sensible,* she told herself. *Exploring separately improves our chances of finding shelter.*

She scanned the rock face. An exceptionally dark rent caught her eye and she clambered toward it. Obtaining it, she realized she had no light or lamp with which to reconnoiter. *Stupid girl. Should have thought to bring a light.*

The rain began to fall in steady torrents. Thinking she could determine the cave's suitability, she got down on her hands and knees and crawled forward into the narrow crevasse. She was part way in when a bolt of lightning struck the trees behind her. For a split second it lit the tiny cavern, enough time for Bonifacia to jump with a scream, striking her head against the hard ceiling. She pulled herself out of the cramped cave as quickly as she could.

Henrik was at her side a moment later. "What happened?" he shouted above the howling wind and driving rain. "I heard you scream."

"In there," cried Bonifacia. "I saw a man! A little man in a red hat and a long beard!" She rubbed the top of her sore head, grateful for the heavy felt hat that Bartle had given her.

Henrik instinctively went for the sword at his side, but looked straight into the face of the pelting rain and dropped the idea.

"Whoever he is, he's going to have to share with us."

He got down on his knees, pulled off his pack and crawled part way into the fissure as Bonifacia had done. Reaching into his bag he drew out a taper and a porcelain box containing a few precious embers that came roaring back to life when he blew on them. The crevice walls danced in the lambent glow of the lighted candle.

Henrik squeezed himself around and beckoned Bonifacia inside. "There's no one in here," he shouted.

Bonifacia scuttled her way into the cave, pulling her satchel behind her. Water dripped from the brim of her hat. She pulled it from her head and tossed it at her feet. "I saw him clear as day," she said, looking about the cave. "See there!" She pointed to a pile of dry kindling that Henrik had knocked over on his way into the shelter.

"Well, your little friend isn't here now, but if this belonged to him, I thank him for it."

"You can't light a fire in here," protested Bonifacia. "We'll suffocate!"

Henrik held up the taper to inspect the inside of the hollow, then reached behind his head running his hand against the very back wall. "Soot," he said, showing his blackened fingers to

Bonifacia. He reached back again. "I can feel cold air on my hand. There must be a crack in the ceiling."

"Then that's how the little man got out without our seeing."

"He'd have to be a very little man indeed," replied Henrik skeptically.

"He wasn't one of your Og'yre, was he?" questioned Bonifacia.

"Little man, red hat, long beard? I shouldn't think so." Bonifacia let out a sigh of relief. "One thing's for certain," added Henrik. "We're not the first to light a fire in here. I'd like to warm my feet and take some breakfast until this storm lets up."

"Are you in the habit of getting things backward?" she asked.

"I don't follow?" said Henrik, puzzled.

Bonifacia pulled the makings of a meal from her pack. "Never mind," she said.

Another flash of lightening illuminated the crevasse for a brief second, followed almost instantly by the rumble of nearby thunder. Outside, the storm lashed the hillside. "Come to think of it," said Henrik, "we may as well spend the day here. After a gale like this the ridge will be crisscrossed with streams and loose rock. Better to give everything a chance to settle."

"What if he comes back?" she asked.

"Your little man?" He kicked the hilt of his sword toward her.

"That's not funny," she said.

"I'm sorry," said Henrik sitting up. "That was cruel. I just don't see that it's worth worrying about."

"I suppose you're right," replied Bonifacia. "Where do we go from here? I mean, after the storm is over."

"We leave the foothills behind and head straight up into the mountains. I'm hoping to strike the old highway. Tom would never think I'd try that route."

"How can there be a highway up there? It doesn't look possible."

"I've seen a short section of it. There used to be a city on the slopes of Broken Mountain. The road ran from it to the headwaters of the River Talsis. Taking it would just about get us to Piernot."

"If that's true, it sounds as good a plan as any," declared Bonifacia.

They ate their breakfast, dried and warmed their feet, slept again and generally waited for the storm to dissipate, which did not occur until very late afternoon. They emerged from their cave like a pair of waking bears.

"How quiet it seems," said Bonifacia. "And so much devastation." The heavy rains had brought disfiguring flash floods down the mountainsides, together with enormous boulders that left smashed trees in their wake, great gouges in the hillside, and a vast moraine on the valley floor far below.

"The proverbial quiet after the storm," said Henrik.

"I will certainly say my prayers tonight," said Bonifacia. "I'm glad for the shelter of that cave."

They strolled about, exploring the neighborhood of their temporary home, using the time productively to scrounge for what little dry wood they could find and whatever nature had to offer in the way of comestibles. The storm, in particular, brought large quantities of sweet marron to the ground that would otherwise have been beyond reach. "These will make fine roasting," proclaimed Henrik.

Darkness fell upon the hillside forest with astonishing rapidity. Bonifacia and Henrik crawled back into their cave and made themselves as comfortable as they could for the night. They sat quietly, listening to the crackle and pop of burning firewood until moonlight crept up to the entrance of their improvised dwelling.

"Tell me about Creto and Porfan," said Bonifacia, breaking the silence. "That's what you call your moons, isn't it? There must be batches of stories about them. Are they made of green cheese like our Moon?"

"Green cheese?!" laughed Henrik. "I shouldn't think so. But you're right. There are a great many stories about them. Some of them are very odd indeed."

"Tell me one. A favorite."

"Hmm. It's been a long time. Let's see if I can remember it the way my mum told me...In the beginning, the Great Light was always shining. There was never any darkness in the World and people lived without fear in a land of perpetual day.

"Then, the Great Light in the sky lost her crown, or corona as some say, and went off in search of it. For the very first time night fell upon one side of the World as the Sun went circling round the globe to find her missing crown. In those days, there were no moons in the sky to shed even the tiniest drop of light when the Sun went away. The people were thrust into complete and utter darkness. They huddled together in their cottages in dismay, learning fear for the first time.

"At the end of one new day, the Sun went around the other side of the World in search of her lost crown, as had become her habit, and was surprised to find a great icy ball in the sky with a handsome long tail trailing off to the stars. 'Have you seen my crown?' she asked the Comet.

"'What does it look like?' he replied.

"She described it as best she could.

"'I don't think so,' said the Comet. 'Maybe you can draw a picture of it for me?'

"So she drew a picture of her crown for the Comet.

"'Your drawing is too far away for me to see clearly. Bring it closer,' said the Comet.

"She naively brought it closer to him, which gave the Comet the chance to grab hold of her. He forced himself upon her and after a while went away satisfied, smugly wagging his long icy tail behind him."

Henrik looked upon Bonifacia's transfixed face in the firelight. "Hmm. Maybe this story wasn't such a good idea."

"Didn't you say your mother told you this story as a boy? Go ahead. Finish."

He had his doubts about the wisdom of doing so, but continued anyway. "In the end the Sun found her crown, but soon gave birth to the twin moons Creto and Porfan. Creto and Porfan were wayward children from the very start that kept running off to play at games. The Sun did her best to raise them like herself, but they were too much like their father and their flame kept going out.

"The children of the Great Light, Creto and Porfan, have ever since engaged in an eternal game of tag, a sign in the night sky that their mother, the Sun, will soon come chasing after them. They retain enough of their mother's light that the night is not as it once was, and people have consequently cast away most of their fear of the dark."

"A charming story," remarked Bonifacia. "Except for that bit about the comet forcing itself on the sun."

"It's just a story," he reminded her. "Now go to sleep. If the weather is cooperative, we should make up for lost time tomorrow."

She said a silent prayer as she had promised and curled up to sleep beside the fire.

The morning dawned clear and bright, full of new promise. Despite the landslides, rocks and fallen silva caused by the previous day's storm, the birds once again sang in the trees. Bonifacia pondered their ability to weather such a tempest. "It's rather miraculous, isn't it? I wonder where they go during big storms."

"Perhaps there's a little man who keeps them sheltered in a cave."

"Stop your teasing," she chided.

"Then don't set yourself up by asking such silly questions," countered Henrik.

They hoisted their bags and set off up the kame. "Watch your step," said Henrik. "There's a lot of loose debris."

They picked their way round the fallen trees and landslides, slowly making their way to the top of the first rise. Once they got that far, Henrik pointed toward the next ridge and they headed off again. Higher and higher they went, until they were so high up that they were nearly clear of the highest line of trees. Bonifacia stood panting next to Henrik, who was near as winded from their strenuous effort. They stood at the very juncture of the foothills and the mountains, gazing out toward the far horizon. "Just look at that view!" exclaimed Bonifacia. "It's spectacular!"

From their vantage point, they could see well beyond the foothills, past the River Chigraw and a hundred leagues beyond into the heart of the great weald of Kaladar and Orn. Bonifacia turned herself about to face the towering peaks that began almost at her feet, looming straight up into the clouds. "My gosh!" Heading away from where they stood in either direction stretched an endless line of jagged snow capped mountains.

"As picturesque as all this may be," said Henrik, "we're here to find the old road to take us on to Piernot." He pointed in the direction of the River Talsis. "That way, I think."

Since the days of ancient Kaladar centuries of wind, rain and snow had taken their toll on the great range, causing it to crack and shear away in places. Colossal shards of stone from the toppled mountainsides lay strewn across their intended path, like fallen titans. "You don't honestly believe there's a road under all this mess, do you?" asked Bonifacia, skeptically.

"Only one way to find out," he replied. He walked forward and kept going until Bonifacia had no choice but to follow. Cautiously they picked their way across the piles of rock and scree, doing their best not to tumble and break a bone or smash their heads. It was exhausting work that left them bruised and battered.

After climbing around one particularly large and intimidating rock, Bonifacia was stunned to see the indications of a cobblestone avenue projecting out from under it. Of course the road was in sad repair, scraps of brake and grass protruding between the polygonal blocks, but all in all a fairly level way. It skirted the foot of the mountains for several hundred yards and then disappeared again beneath more fallen rocks.

"What did I tell you?" said Henrik, "the old Kaladwen road."

"It must have been a fine highway in its time," remarked Bonifacia. "I remember seeing Roman roads much like this in Ourense."

"Strange names," said Henrik, "but I'll take your word for it. If your Roman friends were anything like the Kaladwen of old, they were a people to be reckoned with." He adjusted his pack and carried on down the broken highway, clearly delighted to be walking in his ancestors' steps. Bonifacia, for her part, enjoyed the chance just to walk free of impediments, even for a short distance. In a small way, discovering the road meant that they were actually making progress.

Close in to the mountains, twilight came early, prompting them to seek shelter for the night. The best they could find was a shallow corrie in the lee of a mountain. Henrik was loath to light a fire, fearing it might draw undue attention, but hard rock makes a poor berth in many respects and Bonifacia began to shiver uncontrollably as the temperature dropped steadily through the night. Worried for her well-being, Henrik chanced a modest fire.

If anyone noticed, it went unremarked by Henrik and Bonifacia, for they survived the night unmolested. Bonifacia awoke, her face drawn and tired from a long cold, sleepless evening.

"That was foolish," admitted Henrik. "We should have prepared better than that."

"Live and learn," said Bonifacia, trying to put a cheery face on what might have been a disaster. "Thank you for the fire."

"Let's hope this day's road is less difficult," said Henrik.

"I'm all for that," replied Bonifacia.

They took their time over breakfast and headed out again, taking it very slowly. Following the broken line of the old road they crawled up and over, or down and around various obstacles as they encountered them. The most frightening hazard turned out not to be sharp rocks or loose stones, but mountain streams and small waterfalls that cut athwart their path. Fortunately, these were generally shallow crossings, but they made for especially treacherous footing. Bonifacia and Henrik took more than one soaking in the frigid mountain waters.

"Somewhere down below, these streams merge into the Chigraw," remarked Henrik.

"The water is certainly cold enough," replied Bonifacia, remembering Bartle's words.

It wasn't all hard going. They reached a stretch of the old road that went on for a league or more before coming to an impasse. As they picked their way around, Bonifacia said, "Look, up there. What's that?"

Henrik turned his head to see where she was pointing. On a shelf above them stood the remains of an old building, its lichen-covered walls almost indistinguishable from the rock face behind. "Stay here. I'll scout it out." Henrik scampered up the ridge and disappeared from sight. Bonifacia waited anxiously beside the road, her neck craned up toward the point where she'd last fixed eyes on him.

In a few minutes time he returned, climbing back down the same way he'd gone up. "It looks like it may have been a way station of some sort. Not very big but the walls are solid. A small part of the slate roof is still intact. I'd say this is our home for the evening."

"Do you think it's safe?"

"Sure. We should be able to build a decent fire inside without it being seen. And if we can find ourselves some seasoned wood there won't be much smoke to speak of."

Bonifacia agreed and they set about scouring the area for firewood. It was a long haul from where the few remaining trees were and up to the abandoned way station, so she emptied her haversack to carry bits of dry twigs and kindling up the slope. "There's some sort of inscription carved into the lintel above the door," said Bonifacia, studying it.

"I hadn't noticed," said Henrik. He brushed away the dirt and debris that covered the heavy stone. "It's in the old tongue...*Gethrela Mien Corthwelan Sor.*"

"How sweet it sounds," said Bonifacia. "Like music or a swift flowing stream."

"You think?"

"What does it mean?" she asked.

"Storage Hut One Hundred Six."

Bonifacia put a hand to her mouth and started to laugh, Henrik along with her.

Most of the roof was gone, but there was enough slate covering the back end of the building to offer a bit of shelter. They cleared the floor for a place to sleep and set a small fire for supper and to offer a little warmth as nightfall began to settle on the mountain.

"That's more like it," said Henrik, stretching his arms in the air. "I'm looking forward to a good night's sleep."

Bonifacia was utterly exhausted and drifted off as soon as her head touched the bower she had arranged for herself. She slept soundly and did not awaken until the first glimmerings of a pale dawn. She rolled over to find Henrik sitting bolt upright and mindful of something.

"Wha...?"

"Hush," whispered Henrik, cutting her off.

"What did I...?"

"Be quiet!" he repeated, pressing an urgent finger to his lips. He stood up and slowly drew his sword, then motioned for her to follow him. They tiptoed together toward the door and peered cautiously down the hillside to the road below. Only a stone's throw away stood five repulsive-looking creatures lounging about the roadway, one carrying a lighted torch.

They stood taller than the average man by a head, even standing on heavily bowed legs. Their gray skin shone waxy in the pale morning light, tufts of wiry hair protruding from ears set like two ogee arches on either side of their twisted faces. Large muscular arms hung from black leather gambesons, gripping menacing cudgels and halberds with claw-like tenacity.

Bonifacia gasped.

"Og'yre," said Henrik under his breath.

She turned the word over on her tongue, puzzling it out. "Og'yre…" The name sounded so very familiar. *Og'yre. Ogre.* "Not *Og'yre*—Ogre! They're Ogres!" exclaimed Bonifacia, with the force of sudden realization. "Why didn't you say so in the first place?"

"Quiet down. They'll hear you."

The creatures seemed unaware of their presence, as if taking time out from a routine patrol.

"Ogres don't really exist," said Bonifacia, nonplused.

"Maybe not in your world," replied Henrik.

Bonifacia watched as the Og'yre lollygaged about the road, debating some matter of significance only to themselves. One of the creatures wandered away from the others and her heart sank as the beast found something unusual at the side of the road. Unable to accept the idea that she'd done anything so foolish, she instinctively glanced toward the rear of the way station to see if her bag was sitting there, but of course it wasn't.

She watched in silent horror as the Og'yre lifted her haversack for the others to see. It snorted loudly and sniffed the air. As if on cue, all five Og'yre turned their misshapen heads upward to where they both stood.

"Run," commanded Henrik. "Run, now!"

Chapter 9

Rebellion

Peter climbed the tower that rose above the duke's guest palace with Joshkar coming up behind. It was a long climb, but as the chief domestic had promised, well worth the effort, for it afforded a spectacular view of the city and surrounding country. From its largely decorative battlements they were able to take in the city from all directions.

Menom was laid out on the sides of a gentle ridge that dipped down from the broad plateau over which they had traveled to form the near bank of the River Talsis. The city's founders evidently viewed the Keartlands as the most likely approach for an invading army, constructing two lines of protective wall to front the river, while only a single high wall abutting a dry ditch protected the city from the landward direction.

The ducal palace, not surprisingly, constituted the predominant edifice within those walls, sitting atop the crest, surpassing all other structures for height and beauty, like the queen of morels. The guest palace stood farther down the slope so that it was necessary for Peter to crane his neck to gaze upon its splendor, even from his superior vantage point.

Clustered all around the ducal palace, the towers, mushroom domes and cupolas of the great families reached for the sky in the way that plants compete for access to the sun, many structures so new they were still sheathed in scaffolding. The outer limits of the city and the streets immediately beside the river housed the shops, homes, inns, warehouses and taverns of the general populace, modest and practical, with the notable exception of several distinguished guild houses.

"Where are the churches, the great cathedrals?" asked Peter "I would expect to see them in a city such as this."

"Gone," replied Joshkar. "Razed during the Great Renewal."

"All of them? Gone?"

"Many years after the Ulfair arrived and word of the Eternal Architect had taken root, a movement began that led to the start of the prayer circles. Look down there," he said, pointing. "Do you see the many open plazas where people congregate to pray at moonrise?"

"Yes."

"That is where the temples once stood, their blocks and pillars now adorn the palaces and manors you see about you. If you ever get to Piernot you may yet see one or two of the old cathedrals. The few that remain are mere shells, shadows of their former glory."

"And the priests? What happened to the priests, your holy men?"

"You mean the brothers and sisters. There are fewer of them than in the old days, but you can still find them if you wish, mostly as spiritual advisors to the great families. Some are itinerant, moving from circle to circle offering their services to those in need."

Religious studies were never Peter's strong point. The Great Renewal Joshkar spoke of brought to mind his lessons at St. Stanislaus on church history. Father O'Neill's admirable, but ultimately futile attempt to instill in Peter's "empty head" an appreciation for the great calamity brought about by Henry VIII's "lamentable dissolution of the monasteries," failed to trump his all-consuming interest in the latest cricket scores. Peter could no more draw a comparison between the Great Renewal and the Protestant Reformation than recite the Magna Carta.

He gazed over the parapet. The land across the river, the Keartlands, looked an empty grassland, a few lonely tracks leading off into the interior. The River Talsis, as wide as the Thames or Danube, glinted a deep sea green in the afternoon sun. The docks were crowded with sailing ships, barges and a bevy of smaller boats unloading their heavy cargoes of quarried stone, fish, grain and other products to sustain the burgeoning city. "All the traffic is headed down river," said Joshkar. "Piernot, the only other major harbor up river, is under blockade."

"She's out there somewhere," said Peter, putting aside all of it for the moment. "*Bonnie.*" The wind picked up just then and the ducal banner fluttered on the flagstaff above their heads. "I wish I could stay up here forever, Joshkar."

He regarded his charge with a mix of pity and mild frustration. "There is just the one narrow stairwell up and we are safely beyond the reach of archers. I could probably fend off a besieging army for a week, but we would likely starve or die of thirst before long."

"That won't be necessary, but thanks for the offer."

"Come young biscuit king, some good food will take your mind off things."

It was soon apparent that Peter was to be treated as a prince, albeit a captive one, while in Menom. He could not have anticipated it. The evening meal was exceedingly good and his room decidedly on the sumptuous side. There was a great game being played out here, of that he had no doubt. He took Joshkar's advice and played along. At least in the short-term, he was having a rather remarkable time.

The next morning three tailors and a half-dozen seamstresses arrived to take their measurements. By late evening, Peter had a complete wardrobe of elaborate court apparel, including silk stockings and a pearl-edged turban.

"I look like Little Lord Fauntleroy," he moaned. "Only I don't suppose I will ever teach the duke the meaning of compassion."

"I don't know this 'little lord' you speak of, but you're right, you look ridiculous. And so do I," added Joshkar, frowning at his own image in the looking glass.

The arrival of their new clothes coincided with a warning from Harmond, the chief domestic, that they were to attend His Grace, the Duke, the following morning. They were directed to the courtyard where the troop of cavalry and the four-in-hand were waiting to whisk them to the ducal palace. The big iron gates cranked open and off they went at a brisk trot down the cobbled streets and up the hill for the short ride to the palace. Unlike the guest palace, whose paved courtyard lay just behind the gates, it was necessary to approach the ducal palace down a broad avenue set amid an expansive lawn and garden populated by deer and flocks of colorful peafowl.

"Who are they?" asked Peter, as their carriage rolled to a halt. A company of soldiers resplendent in red and black uniforms paraded off to one side of the porte-corchère. Joshkar leaned forward to look out the window.

"The padishah's men," he sneered. "Soldiers of Stônar."

"Oh," was all Peter could think to say.

"You are to come with me," directed a member of the palace staff as they dismounted the carriage. He led them through an outer wing, down carpeted corridors lined with artworks, statuary and sumptuous urns. Their escort paused before a set of tall doors, opened them and ushered them in. "Wait here," he instructed. "Don't touch anything." He departed, closing the doors behind them.

The room was opulent in the extreme. One wall was covered in brightly painted panels set with murals of hunting scenes. Peter was startled to see a depiction of the toad-like creature the cowled gatekeeper kept beside his cottage door, caught in the act of snatching a bird in flight with its enormous tongue, two hunters laughing uproariously at its side. The opposite wall was lined with tall rounded windows framed in heavy brocade drapery. An exquisite marquetry table ran down the center of the room, set with three gilded candelabras and a crystal bowl filled with glass fruit. At the end of the room, atop a velvet-covered dais, sat a single ornate high-back chair.

Joshkar took up a formal stance off to one side while Peter wandered about. He was startled by the doors suddenly swinging wide and the duke striding in unannounced, two courtiers at his heels. He looked to Joshkar, who bowed deeply and Peter, following suit, stammered, "Your grace."

Snapping his fingers, the duke gestured for both of them to rise, and then proceeded to inspect Peter from head to toe. Borganin looked the epitome of the Sun King, bedecked in blue and gold silks, a pair of jeweled slippers and a matching ribbon threaded through his splendid long brows.

"Where is the wolf?" he asked impatiently.

"The wolf, my lord?"

He rolled his eyes. "The wolf, you idiot boy. The witch's token of office."

Peter unfastened his tunic, revealing the object hanging from a chain fashioned especially for him by Lady Aflyn. "Wear it outside your jacket," he commanded.

Once again, he did just as he was told, rebuttoning his clothes and leaving the little ornate pendant to hang across his chest.

"Now take a seat over there." Borganin nodded toward the big gilded chair at the end of the table. "When the envoy comes in do not even think to open your mouth. Not a word to him. Do you understand me? Not a word"

He felt the urge to spit in Borganin's face. Instead, he obediently sat in the chair at the end of the table, looking every inch a maharajah. "You," said Borganin to Joshkar. "Stand by his side." Joshkar bowed deferentially and came over to stand next to Peter. Although Peter knew he had no right to expect much from Joshkar, he was mollified by his presence.

"Do not move," instructed Borganin. "I will be back shortly with our guest. The rest of you, take those objects off the table. I want the envoy to have an unobstructed view of the lord arbiter." He spun about and left the room, taking his courtiers and table furnishings with him.

Moments later the doors opened and a court herald pompously announced, "His Excellency Minister Noran Tassmat of Stônar and His Grace the Duke of Menom, Master of Orn and the Upper Talsis."

Peter made to rise, but Joshkar quietly urged him back in his seat. The ambassador and the duke strode forward, positioning themselves just opposite both of them at the end of the long table. They bowed before Peter, which caused him to blink in surprise. He wisely kept his thoughts to himself.

"Lord Arbiter," began Borganin, "I have the honor and privilege of presenting to you Minister Noran Tassmat, special envoy of His Most Serene Highness Balkur Hamut IV, Padishah of Stônar."

The ambassador was a giant of a man with a square jaw and almond shaped eyes. His head was completely shaven except, of course, for his long brows, which were woven through with tiny bells. He wore a long coat cut much like the one he'd seen Dashwan wearing, but red and black in color, similar to the company of Stônar guardsmen outside the palace.

He approached Peter on his own. Skirting the long table, the ambassador stopped at the foot of his chair, eyed the little enameled wolf that hung upon his chest and then brazenly reached forward to grasp it in one hand. Peter was so completely taken off guard, he gasped aloud. Tassmat bent slowly over him, bringing his face so close to Peter's he could feel the man's breath upon him. It was all Peter could do not to gag on the pungent odor of aromatic herbs packed into the lining of the ambassador's collar. Tassmat scrutinized both the wolf and Peter, with particular attention to his brows. Then just as suddenly, he let go the pendant and stood back up. Taking one step backward he bowed courteously.

Nervous sweat trickled down the nape of Peter's neck. He returned the unexpected salute with a nod of his head. Tassmat whirled about and walked back to stand at Borganin's side. With another courteous bow to the duke, he took his leave. The doors to the great hall closed behind him.

There was momentary silence and then the duke clapped his hands together in triumph, a great smile lighting up his handsome face. "Splendid!" he cried. "Splendid! Give the lord arbiter a second bowl of pudding for dessert tonight. He has earned it!" Borganin laughed heartily and departed, leaving Joshkar and Peter in the hands of his chief domestic.

Peter, for his part, was nonplused. "Joshkar, what just went on here?"

The bowman did not answer. "Let's get out of these ridiculous costumes," barked Joshkar. "I think we've done our part here." Peter got up from his throne, following Joshkar back to the carriage where they waited for their mounted escort to reform. Joshkar seemed disinclined to talk until they got back to the guest palace.

They met again high above the city in the quiet isolation of the tower. "Now tell me," insisted Peter, "what was that all about?"

"Look down there, toward the river," replied Joshkar. Peter glanced over the parapet. "Do you see the galley crossing over to the Keartlands."

"Yes, I see it."

"That will be Minister Tassmat on his way back to Stônar."

"What of it?"

"Come, young biscuit king. Use your head."

"Don't toy with me, Joshkar. I am not the lord arbiter, nor am I a king. All these doings are beyond me."

He looked thoughtfully at Peter. "The minister is bringing word to His Most Serene Highness that His Lordship, the Duke of Menom, has won the endorsement of the lord arbiter in his dispute with the empress. Events will be set in motion that cannot now be undone."

"What sort of events? What do you mean?"

"It is plain, the duke will inform the members of the Imperial Council that he has signed a trade agreement with the padishah. Moreover, he will tell them the lord arbiter imperial endorses his position. He will then advise the council that the padishah has dispatched his armies to enforce their treaty rights and that they will soon be marching side-by-side with those of Orn to depose the empress. He will recommend to the council that they fall in step and recognize his leadership."

Peter was speechless. Joshkar was talking about all-out war. He was furious at having been so manipulated. "You knew what was about to happen. Why didn't you say something?"

"And what would you have done, my lord arbiter?"

"I don't know, but I might have done something. At least if I'd understood what was going on…"

"There's nothing you, or I, or anyone else could have done that would have changed this outcome. Lord Borganin will have his way. If not by this absurd charade, then by some other means. You just made it a little easier for him."

"It makes me ill to have aided him in the slightest," protested Peter. "I detest the man and I don't much care for being part of his excuse for going to war. This is madness. Look at me. I'm only fifteen!"

"So you keep reminding me." His voice took on a new tone. "Peter, some good may yet come of this, although you might find it hard to see right now. You still have your head. You have your title." He placed a reassuring hand on Peter's shoulder. "Listen to me. I am no one. What happens to me is of no consequence. But with you there is a chance. A small chance I'll admit, but at least a chance that someday you may be able to use your newfound influence for the better."

"I'd just as soon go home, thank you."

"I think we've had that discussion," he replied with a smile. "Just now I'd like to do the same." He struggled to find his next words. "Peter?"

Joshkar's expression was so intense it startled him. "What is it?" he asked.

"Do you see this ring?" He held out his left hand for Peter to examine. "If anything should happen to me, will you see that it is delivered safely to my brother in Bakus Sura? The ring was a gift from him when I left home."

"Don't talk nonsense."

"Just promise me that you'll take the ring to my brother."

"What's your brother's name?"

"Karline. Karline, of the house Othmond."

Peter could not bring myself to argue. "*De acordo*," he replied. "I will take the ring to your brother, if it comes to that. But in return I want your promise that you will not desert me. Not now. Not ever."

"Clearly, I've already done that," he replied.

His primary service to the duke complete, Peter was unceremoniously delivered back into the hands of Lord Palkvo, who had been anxiously biding his time in Menom. It did not take long for word to reach Palkvo concerning Peter's formal "endorsement" of the duke. Although he could not possibly have doubted that Peter was a mere puppet in the entire affair, disdain for Peter was nevertheless written all across Palkvo's face. He complained bitterly to Harmond. "Why am I to be saddled once again with this off-worlder? I'm not the brat's father!"

"Lord Borganin has a great deal to contend with right now. You are already familiar with the boy," explained the chief domestic. "He has allowed the bowman, Joshkar, to remain in your employ as recompense."

"Recompense? I suppose I must feed and house the bowman as well?" The chief domestic shrugged apologetically. "Damn the man!" Palkvo turned to face Peter. "I don't want any trouble from you, de Soto. Stay out of my way. If you have any sense you'll arrange to get yourself some decent armor before we head off. Borganin can damn well pay for it. I certainly won't." He stormed away.

"Armor?" blurted Peter. "Why would he say that? Why should *I* need armor?"

"Lord Palkvo, of course, will be accompanying the duke on campaign," explained Harmond. "I would be pleased to arrange a trip to the armorer for you."

"Are you daft? I don't need any armor!"

"It has been a very long time since I have been in battle, of course," continued Harmond paying Peter no heed, "but I would recommend a light breast plate and perhaps some greaves. A sconce at the very least."

"Joshkar," cried Peter, "say something sensible. Tell the man I have no need for armor. I'm not going to war!"

He just looked at Peter rather sullenly. "He's right. You should go see the armorer."

"Not you too?"

"No one expects you to fight, but you may come in harm's way. Battles are difficult things to predict," explained Joshkar.

"My God!" he cried. "You really mean it?"

"I'm afraid so," said Joshkar. "Lord Borganin isn't about to let you out of his sight, not for some time yet. And it serves him well to have you riding at his side."

Peter slumped into a nearby chair. "This just gets better and better."

Harmond had the tailors cut a set of proper campaign clothes for Peter and arranged for his visit to the ducal armories. The chief armorer was a heavyset fellow with a bushy red beard that bobbed up and down when he laughed, which was often. He regarded Peter as a special challenge.

"Ah," said the armorer. "Obviously light weight but enough to deflect an indirect blow, and stylish. The duke will expect something stylish. Perhaps a corium habergeon dyed maroon with inlayed steel pauldron, and levelar tasse? Yes I think so, and leather gauntlets. A conical casque with nose guard. Nothing too heavy or awkward. That should do. No! What am I thinking? A nose guard? Fool. The people must be able to see his brave little face. No nose guard. And one more thing. A gorget, but on a chain with the imperial wolf emblazoned on it. That's the touch!" His eyes beamed with excitement. "Do you think you'll need a shield, my lord?" he added as an afterthought.

"No, I *don't* think I will need a shield," he replied grumpily.

The armorer stood back a step to conceptualize his overall design, smiling at his own brilliance, although Peter had yet to don a stitch of armor. "I will have your suit ready by the end of the week," he said, and hustled them out of his workshop.

Peter craned his neck up and down the busy street. "I promised Lady Aflyn I'd bring her a honey cake from Menom. Do you think we could find the baker she mentioned? Somewhere near the wharf."

Joshkar indulged him and together they went off in search of the bakery. It was actually a great excuse to do some exploring. They caused quite a stir as they walked about the narrow streets, sticking their heads into a variety of shops. Eventually, they found the bakery with the hive carved above the lintel. The baker that greeted them knew precisely which cakes he was referring to. "An excellent choice, your excellency. Our signature creation." The baker brought out a tray for them to inspect.

"How long will one of these last?" asked Peter.

"I can wrap them specially, but they will harden over time and the honey will crystallize eventually. I would say they should be eaten within the week if you want to enjoy them at their best. Otherwise just warm them in the oven for a short time. They'll regain much of their freshness."

Joshkar paid for two small cakes as Peter had no pocket money of his own. When they returned to the guest palace Peter put one cake aside for Aflyn and joined Harmond and Joshkar for a clandestine nibble on the other later that evening. They met in a cozy annex off of the chief domestic's quarters. Peter soon discovered that he rather enjoyed old Harmond's company. The man was gentle at heart and had seen a great deal of court during his lifetime. His anecdotes were both fascinating and enlightening.

"This is truly delicious," said Harmond, the tuft of his goateed chin sprinkled with golden crumbs. "Some more cider anyone?"

Joshkar nodded enthusiastically and Harmond topped off his mug. "How long have you been working at the palace?" asked Peter.

"Hmm, let me see," he stroked his chin, knocking some of the crumbs to the table. "Must be thirty seven, no thirty eight years this coming autumn. I've only been chief domestic these last twelve, mind'. I was in the army before all that."

"I could have guessed," replied Joshkar. "Which battalion?"

"The 1st Battalion, Second Cohort of Orn Archers," said Harmond with evident pride. We were almost all of us recruited from Bakus Mara."

"Hah!" said Joshkar, thumping the table with the flat of his hand. "I thought I detected a bit of an accent."

"True," said Harmond somewhat apologetically. "I've been away from home for so many years it has faded almost to the point of being unrecognizable. Much easier to pick it out when I'm in relaxed company. You're from Bakus Sura, aren't you?"

"No disguising that," said Joshkar. "How'd you come to change employment?"

"I saved the duke's life during the last war with Stônar," replied the old man. "Not this duke, of course, his father. Years later, I injured my shoulder. Couldn't string a bow after that if my life depended on it, so they offered me a job here." He grinned cheerfully.

"Have you never wanted to go back to Bakus Mara?" asked Peter.

"Oh, I've been back, half a dozen times," he replied. "I was married you know? Dear Salva. More than twenty years," he reminisced. "Gone these past six. Anyhow, here I am, king of the castle, so to speak. And how 'bout yourself?" he asked Joshkar. "What's left for you in Bakus Sura?"

"Not much. My eldest brother, Karline, keeps the family farm. Real nice wife and kids. I've another brother, Felshok. Full of himself. Haven't seen him in years. He's on the Duke of Camstol's staff, doing I don't know what."

"No woman?" prompted Harmond.

"None that I can call my own. Who'd have me on a master bowman's pay?"

Peter listened to all this with peculiar fascination. He was only fifteen, after all. Old Harmond took notice and harumphed discreetly, prompting Joshkar to change the direction of the conversation. Talk eventually shifted to Peter and questions about the world he came from—*Earth*.

"How do you come to live in a different realm than the land of your father's people?" asked Joshkar. "*Eng-land*, did you call it?"

"My grandfather sided with Charles VII, a Carlist pretender to the Spanish throne. He was on the losing side and fled to England after the war, together with his family—all, that is, but my father's eldest sister.

"I was born in England, but Spain is a kind of second home. The regent is a foreigner too, an Austrian, the Archduchess María-Cristina of Habsburg-Lorraine. Spain isn't much like England, to tell the truth. It's an old empire that struggles to keep up with the times (well, that's what my father says). He says Spain earned her drubbing at the hands of the Americans." He paused long enough to stuff another morsel of honey cake in his mouth. "The Americans," he added, "have taken Spain's best colonies for themselves."

Harmond nodded sagely. "Something like that will happen here if Stônar gets a leg over."

Peter went on to describe how Queen Victoria, much like Empress Xhôn, reigned over a vast empire on which it was said 'the sun never sets.' "She is a pious and clever widow" he underscored, "who relies on the advice of her prime minister. Even so, conflicts with neighbors and uprisings abroad are just about an everyday occurrence."

"And, what are the cities like in England?" asked Joshkar. "Now that you've seen it, is there any place so grand as Menom?"

They supposed Peter would struggle to come up with anything comparable. Joshkar and Harmond regarded him with skeptical expressions as he described modern conveniences like locomotives, electric lights, the telephone, gramophone, and the horseless motor carriage. While this was all very interesting, they were more attentive to his tales of modern warfare, listening with particular fascination to his descriptions of iron battleships and weapons of near limitless destruction, all things Peter had gleaned from the pages of the London papers.

When it came his turn to probe them, he took the opportunity to ask Harmond if he thought it just short of peculiar that he should be so easily acclaimed lord arbiter, when clearly he was not the same individual that had previously provided service to the empire. Peter was sure Harmond would be the voice of reason that he had been desperately seeking.

But Harmond shrugged his shoulders indifferently. "A small matter in the scheme of things," he said. There was a cultural divide here that Peter could never fathom, a pervasive blindness that reached deep into the core of these people.

They talked over their honey cake and cider for hours into the night, managing to fend off, however briefly, the coming day. When Joshkar at last made excuses to retire for the night, Peter was already nodding off and poor Harmond's eyes were red as strawberry tarts.

The next few days, all of Menom prepared to mark the duke's departure. By whatever means, Peter could not tell, the general populace appeared to understand that this confrontation with the Imperial Army was going to be climactic. While the troops were being organized and prepared, the citizenry primed itself for an exuberant send off.

Peter received a new bay mare for the campaign, which he was allowed to ride within the stable enclosure and the courtyard of the guest palace. He named her "Bonnie," and spoiled the animal terribly with turnips that Harmond pinched for him from the palace kitchen. His armor eventually arrived, together with a package from the duke.

"What do you suppose is in it?" asked Peter, indicating the as yet unopened package.

Joshkar picked it up and shook it next to his ear. Peter smiled at the universality of some instincts. Taking a blade from his boot, the bowman slit the cord tied around the package. Inside was a handsome mantelet and matching saddlecloth beautifully embroidered with the running wolf. "Symbols of office, like that ornament around your neck."

The wolf was much more than an "ornament," but Peter refrained from making an issue of it with Joshkar. He examined the duke's gifts. "They are certainly beautiful," he remarked. "Does His Lordship expect me to thank him for them?"

"No," replied Joshkar. "He expects you to wear these fine trappings in public, so that when you ride next to him the world can see that Menom marches against the empress with a clear conscience."

Peter blushed with anger. "How much of this does he expect me to put up with?"

Joshkar's face told him everything he needed to know. In a few minutes he had him in his new uniform. "You look splendid. Every inch the warrior prince," he proclaimed, adjusting the mantelet at Peter's shoulder.

"You're enjoying this far too much," he accused.

Joshkar regarded Peter with something like pride. "Much better than that abominable court costume. Come see."

He gazed at himself in the looking glass. "I look absurd."

"On the contrary, you look like you were born to it," he retorted. "The uniform suits you. Are you comfortable?"

"Surprisingly well," he had to admit.

"The fat smith knows his trade," quipped Joshkar. "Let's go for a ride and see how well you manage that habergeon and helmet from atop your horse."

It seemed a reasonable suggestion. If Peter had no choice but to wear a suit of armor in public, he at least wanted to look like he could handle it. He had Bonnie saddled up with her new regalia and was half way round the courtyard when he noticed that the mounted troop had paused momentarily from their duties to watch him ride. He had rather expected they would have a good laugh at his expense, but far from it, they saluted respectfully as he passed.

Peter felt a sudden rush at this simple act of deference and was dumbstruck by his own behavior. What was at the heart of it? Ego? Vanity? A growing sense of self-importance? And based on what? Having stumbled like an oaf through a portal in time and space. The thrill quickly turned to shame and embarrassment. He hung his head and dismounted.

"What's wrong?" asked Joshkar.

"Nothing," he muttered. "Nothing at all."

Harmond brought them word later that day that the duke was gathering his army on the plain above the city. In a few days' time there would be a grand review. In the meantime, they were to report to Amran, Lord Palkvo's personal steward, and make the necessary arrangements to join the campaign.

Peter could deal with Amran, the archetype of administrative efficiency. He seemed to have no personal opinion of him, one way or the other. Batmen and stewards for the officers, grooms, scullion boys, cooks, wainwrights, ferriers, rations for the troops, provender for the animals, even herders for livestock, all masterfully organized and arranged for by Amran in advance of their march.

"Lord Palkvo will command a full cohort of cavalry for the campaign. You will ride with one of the independent troops. Pack your saddlebags tonight with the bare necessities you will need for the march," he instructed, "and have your valise ready in the courtyard by mid-morning for the baggage train. Third Cestus Cosimlara is expecting you. He is out on the wold with the rest. Mind you don't get lost along the way."

Peter and Joshkar took their leave of old Harmond and then went out to join the third cestus on the plain before the landward wall of Menom. Riding out through the bustling city gate, Peter was struck immediately by the remarkable transformation wrought upon the landscape. A vast army was mustered on the field the other side of the dry ditch. Long lines of tents, the dust from pounding hooves and hobnail boots, and smoke from innumerable cookfires grayed out the horizon.

"Where is the barbican that stood over there?" Joshkar asked a passing soldier. "There was a tower and barracks the other side of the ditch when we arrived."

"Taken down," said the soldier, "to make way for the grand review."

Joshkar's astonishment was equaled by Peter's. They rode over the stone bridge and went in search of Lord Palkvo's standard. There were so many troops, carts and camp followers on the field that it took a great deal of time and effort to locate their lines. Palkvo and Amran were still in the city, but Palkvo's captain, Sefint, pointed them in the direction of Third Cestus Cosimlara's burgee-tipped pennon. The cestus was sitting beside a cookfire with a few of his men when they arrived. He clambered to his feet to greet them with a formal salute.

Cosimlara, as it turned out, was himself a mere boy in uniform, perhaps three or four years older than Peter, and hailing from a junior line of one of the great families. Plainly nervous in their presence he was, nevertheless, very gracious and anxious to make them feel welcome.

Knowing nothing of Joshkar and Peter, he presumed they shared his enthusiasm for the rebellion. Cosimlara prattled on about the coming battle and his eagerness to see an end to the much-despised Ulfair dynasty. "Tomorrow will be a memorable day," he declared, "but nothing to compare to the day Piernot falls to the noble houses of Borganin and Palkvo. We will take back what is rightfully ours."

"Hear! Hear!" replied his men. Cosimlara might have thought his guests would stand up and applaud his fiery words. But Joshkar and Peter just sat with their tin-metal teacups, gazing at the poor boy in sullen silence.

He cleared his throat. "Right. Come, let me show you to your tent."

The remainder of the evening was spent cleaning weapons, polishing tack and grooming the horses to perfection in readiness for the morning's review. It promised to be a spectacle unlike anything witnessed by the good citizens of Menom and Orn in a generation.

The assembled host rose early the next morning, ate breakfast, decamped and prepared for the big event in hushed anticipation. Joshkar was helping Peter put on his armor when a rider from the city arrived. "His Grace, the Duke of Menom, desires your attendance, my lord."

"What? Now?" asked Peter.

"Yes, my lord. "You are to accompany me. You may bring Master Bowman Joshkar with you, if you so desire."

Another surprise. "If *I* so desire?"

"Don't take the duke too literally," whispered Joshkar. "These are words for the sake of appearance, today of all days."

"What do you suppose he's up to this time?" asked Peter.

Joshkar replied with his usual shrug.

Turning again to the messenger Peter replied, "Thank you. We will need a few minutes to obtain our mounts."

Cosimlara was all disappointment. He imagined himself riding at the side of the lord arbiter in the review. Peter apologized for being called away and assured him that his men looked splendid. He offered to point them out specifically to the duke given the opportunity, which cheered the fellow considerably.

They rode back to the city as troops on the field took to horse and began to muster in line. One of the companies they passed along the route were bowmen dressed in corium armor and maroon cloaks.

"Joshkar. Aren't those your comrades?" Peter could never shake the memory of their uniforms from the day they helped ambush poor Dashwan and the rest of their party. Joshkar surely recognized them too, but stared stubbornly ahead.

"Huy!" shouted a voice from amongst their ranks. "Joshkar!" The man whistled between his teeth. "Don't you look a pretty sight. Have you forgotten your old pals so soon?"

Joshkar swiveled his head around to face the man. "Aye, I remember you, Benfac. You still owe me a quarter guilder." The archers hooted and stamped their feet.

The city by this time was awash in bunting and rose petals. An enormous ducal banner (which incidentally did double-duty as the flag of Orn) hung from the city wall side-by-side with the colors of the house of Borganin. Thousands of people streamed noisily atop the ramparts and along the base of the outer wall to cheer the troops or catch a glimpse of a loved one on the field. The occasion was marked with all the heightened passion and exuberance of a Scotland versus England football match.

Inside the walls Peter and Joshkar were met by an aide to the duke who took charge of their mounts and steered them toward a private stairwell leading up to a bartizan overlooking the field. Members of the Ducal Guard let the pair pass without so much as a glance. They climbed the stairs to find the duke, a few key members of his staff and other sundry dignitaries, surveying the army assembled on the plain. Peter had expected to meet up with Borganin's chief lieutenant at a military review of this magnitude, but was relieved to see that Captain Menhar was nowhere in sight.

The duke had ordered the embrasure atop the parapet removed for this special event so the citizenry and soldiers on the field had a clear and unobstructed view of his nibs. "Ah, I see the lord arbiter has joined us. Come! Come! You must not miss this," exclaimed Borganin upon catching sight of Peter. He was in a rare jubilant mood.

Peter was jostled to the front of the pack. From somewhere a wooden mounting block was conjured as a kind of dais and he was prodded to step onto it, giving the assembled masses, whose attention was temporarily fixed upon the duke, a chance to observe the lord arbiter. There was a simultaneous murmur from the crowd.

Peter flushed with embarrassment, his knees quivering like raspberry jelly. *So, so many people gawking just at me!* He felt sure he'd die right then and there. But his thoughts turned suddenly to anger. Clearly, his only purpose was to lend credence to the lie that the duke's scheme was sanctioned by a higher authority. Borganin personally adjusted Peter's mantelet so that his imperial livery was given the widest possible audience. He cringed at Borganin's touch and the overpowering stench of his lavender cologne.

Along the ramparts trumpets blared in unison, thankfully turning the weight of all those eyes away from Peter. "It begins," whispered Borganin under his breath. A roar went up from the assembled throng. Off to their left Peter could hear, *and feel,* the reverberation of massed kettledrums and horns belonging to the Ducal Guard.

For the next hour they stood atop the bartizan acknowledging the passing army. There was mounted cavalry armed with pennant-tipped lances and alternating cohorts of infantry outfitted with long spears, bows, halberds or axes, all marching in lockstep behind their standards. Palkvo saluted smartly as he rode past at the head of his division. Peter could just pick out the tiny figure of Third Cestus Cosimlara and his fine little troop as they wended their way along. He did not bother to point them out to the duke, despite his promise. Next came the company of Stônar guards that he'd seen at the ducal palace in their striking red and black uniforms. No one was left out. Even a small contingent of Weshnut sailors and a team of dog handlers.

The review ended with several massive war machines of wood and iron pulled by teams of strange lumbering beasts of burden, their long tusks nearly brushing the ground. The army reassembled on the wold beyond the dry riverbed and turned to face its commander-in-chief. The crowd's attention naturally returned to the bartizan, and Peter found himself suddenly swept off the mounting block and back out of sight with a single dismissive sweep of the duke's arm. It happened so quickly, he nearly tumbled to the floor. Borganin stepped forward to address the assembled populace.

"Good people of Menom and Orn, fellow Gwellem…" He spoke with a surprising powerful voice that carried well beyond the walls of the provincial capital. "This is a momentous day. Today we march, friends and former adversaries, arm-in-arm to dislodge the yoke imposed on us by the off-worlders—occupiers and interlopers who for too many centuries have tyrannized and oppressed our people." His words were greeted with thunderous applause and shouts of unconditional support. Listening to his speech, Peter could not help but wonder how the citizens of this strikingly affluent city could feel hard done by. The lord arbiter whom they'd saluted not moments before, moreover, was himself an off-worlder. Could they not see the contradiction? The duke waited for the ovation to die down before continuing.

"United under a single banner, we embark upon this sacred undertaking with gladdened hearts and strength of purpose knowing that The Eternal Architect will see us through—to establish for ourselves a new era of fairness, peace and prosperity." More cheers. More ovation. His tone turned then suddenly somber. "I will be straight with you. The enemy will not give up without a fight. Some of the brave young Gwellem you see before you here today will not be returning at the end of this historic campaign. But let me assure the wives, parents and offspring of those that are lost in this great and noble endeavor, that their sacrifice will not have been in vain. They will be forever remembered in our hearts and in our thoughts as heroes. Heroes who gave their lives for our shared vision—Gwellem pride and glory at last restored!"

His oration was met with a tumultuous roar of approval from the gathered crowd. It made Peter fearful and sick to his heart. "Fellow Gwellem, remember us at the rising of the moons. Onward to victory! On to Piernot!" With a wave of his hand, the duke turned and whirled off, the people of Menom showering him with heartfelt words of adulation. Peter and Joshkar trotted down the stairs after Borganin, gathering the reins to their horses and quickly mounting up. Joining the duke's personal retinue, they departed through the main gate. Rose petals rained down on their party, scattered from baskets hoisted by teary-eyed inhabitants. "Menom! Menom!" they chanted as they rode past.

Their horses clattered over the stone bridge and out onto the open plain. The duke and his party cantered to the front of the column to the acclaim of his soldiers, while Joshkar and Peter peeled off to find their place in Cosimlara's troop. The assembled army was so large that it took a quarter hour for their cohort to begin moving off, and then another half hour for the walls of Menom to pass away behind them. It was only then that Peter realized the broader implication. He was really and truly going off to war.

Chapter 10

Gemesh

Bonifacia bolted from the doorway, fleeing up the narrow combe behind the ancient way station. As she scrambled over the rocky escarpment she could hear the labored snorts of the Og'yre as they climbed the ridge toward Henrik and the scornful words he used in place of rocks to heap upon them.

She fixed her eyes on an outcropping that offered at least a small chance of a hiding place and clawed her way up toward it. As she did, the clash of iron and steel reverberated up the mountain and she knew with dreadful certainty that Henrik could not long outlast the onslaught of five large and terrible Og'yre ("Ogre"). She turned the word over on her tongue. "There are Ogre on this planet. I'll be meeting up with Puss in Boots next."

Up she climbed, scraping knee and forearms against the ragged rock, struggling to keep her breath. She was two-thirds of the distance to the outcrop when the echoes of the armed struggle below came suddenly to an end. Turning her head to search below, she saw one of the beasts emerge from the direction of the way station and immediately threw herself to the ground.

The Og'yre gripped a halberd in one hand, his powerful chest rising and falling with each breath, nostrils testing the air for her as it scanned the hillside. Bonifacia, lying very, very still, stopped breathing altogether.

The creature, all at once, descried her and came bounding up the hill. With a shriek Bonifacia leaped to her feet, scrambling up the ridge, hoping desperately to reach the outcrop and maybe, just maybe, a place beyond the Og'yre's reach.

She was clambering past a sizeable boulder when she heard a voice go, "Psst!" and nearly jumped out of her skin. Looking

135

back to see who or what had spoken, she spotted the face of the little man she'd seen illuminated by a flash of lightening in a cave some days past. "Young lady," said the little man from a crack in the ground. He beckoned with his stubby fingers for her to join him down below. Instinct held her back. Her mother, she felt with utter certainty, would tell her never to follow strange little men into holes in the ground. But there was the Og'yre making steady progress toward her and the outcropping still well beyond her reach. She studied the earnest face of the little man and decided to risk it.

Waving him aside, she turned about and dropped herself feet first into the confines of the hollow, and none too soon! In a stound, the shadow of the Og'yre loomed over the entrance, blocking the sunlight and thrusting Bonifacia and her companion into darkness. The creature was far too large to fit through the opening, but got down on its belly, thrusting in one enormous hairy arm below the shoulder. The hole that contained them wasn't very deep, hardly more than her own height, but it went back far enough that the two occupants were just beyond the Og'yre's reach. It groped about, blindly hoping to snag one or both of them.

Frustrated, the Og'yre poked its head inside and glared at them from upside down, the stench from its filthy breath filling the shallow cave. Bonifacia crouched back, crushing the little man against the wall. Not willing just yet to accept defeat, the Og'yre withdrew its head and tried stabbing at them with the axe-end of its long halberd, but couldn't quite get the angle on them.

Bonifacia was immediately reminded of her mother's groundskeeper, Carlos, and the time she and Peter narrowly escaped a skewering by the old gaffer, prodding their hiding place behind the hedge with the backend of a garden hoe after they'd trampled one of his new shoots. This, however, was a much more serious matter.

Foiled, the Og'yre howled in rage. Bonifacia breathed a sigh of relief, thinking the worst was over. But the creature wasn't quite through with them. It rolled the great boulder she had scampered round over top the entrance to their shelter, effectively sealing them in. Bonifacia cried out in despair as the cave was plunged into darkness.

She hadn't long to fret, however. The cave was suddenly and unexpectedly illuminated. She turned to face the squab little man in yellow pants, blue jacket and pointed red hat. He pursed his lips and puffed out his cheeks and then held out an oil lamp for her to see.

She couldn't help but smile at this curious figure. "Are you a wizard?" she asked.

"Me?" said the little man. "A wizard? I've been called many things before, but never a wizard. I'm a Gno'man."

"A Gno'man?" repeated Bonifacia, and then the light dawned on her. "A gnome!" she cried. "Like in the fairy stories. Mama would call you a *mouros.*"

"I'm not sure I care for the sound of that," he replied, "but there are certainly many long tales about Gno'men."

"First an ogre, now a gnome. What's your name?" asked Bonifacia.

"Gemesh," he replied, pursing his lips and puffing out his cheeks.

Bonifacia curtsied, "I'm very pleased to meet you Gemesh. My name is Bonifacia. Thank you for rescuing me from that Ogre."

"Ogre? Oh, yes, the *Og'yre.* You're quite welcome."

"Gemesh, I have many more questions for you, but just now I'm very concerned about my friend." She glanced about the hole they were in. "That, and the fact that we seem to be stuck here."

"Yes, I can certainly see your point," said Gemesh. "The Og'yre will be gone by now, and so should we. Will you hold this lamp, please?"

Bonifacia took the lamp from him and watched in complete and utter astonishment as he squeezed his tubby body through the tiniest imaginable crack in the rock and disappeared. "That's simply not possible," she said to herself, yet she'd seen it with her very own eyes.

She stood alone holding the lamp, and waited nervously, wondering if the Gno'man would ever return. A few minutes later, she heard the sound of grinding rock above her head and painful grunts and groans from Gemesh as he strained to pry the boulder away from the entrance to the fissure. He'd got hold of a pry bar from somewhere. Bonifacia backed against the wall, fearful that some of the rock might tumble in on her. The Gno'man eventually triumphed over the great stone and it rolled away, allowing daylight to stream back through the entrance to the hollow.

Bonifacia was momentarily blinded. When her vision returned, she found herself gazing once again upon the trouble-free face of Gemesh, but this time from the inside looking out. *Like the little man carved at the entrance to the tunnel, only much more pleasant,* she said to herself. He slid onto his belly, just as the Og'yre had done and thrust down his arm. "Grab hold," he said.

"What about the lantern?"

"Blow it out and leave it there. Plenty more of those about." With both her hands she grabbed hold of his and he pulled her out with surprising strength.

"You are the most peculiar creature," she said. "but I thank you all the same," said Bonifacia, dusting herself off. "I must see what has become of Henrik. Will you follow me?"

He made a 'why not?' gesture with his shoulders and followed her back down the slope to the way station. Two Og'yre lay dead where Henrik had slain them, but of Henrik and the other three creatures, there was no trace.

Gemesh kicked at one of the dead Og'yre with the toe of his boot. "If your friend is dead, they'll have taken him away for supper. Og'yre have a taste for Gwellem."

Bonifacia's jaw dropped in horror, but before she could say anything more he interrupted, "On the other hand, if he fought well and lived, he's too valuable to them. They'll sell him to the Weshnut."

"Sell him!" exclaimed Bonifacia. "They can't do that!"

"Believe me, they can," said Gemesh. "And will."

"Where have they taken him?"

He looked toward the mountaintops. "Up there, I'd imagine."

"Then what happens to him?"

"They'll take him across Callow Pass to the place where the Weshnut do their trades."

"Take me there," pleaded Bonifacia.

"Pfah!" sputtered Gemesh. "I should say not."

"You seem to know these mountains," she persisted. "I saw you in the cave the night of the storm."

"Maybe so, but I've got better things to do."

Bonifacia was desperate. If it weren't for her, Henrik would never have come to find himself in this predicament. Moreover, she could not imagine making it safely to Piernot without him. There had to be some way to convince the Gno'man to help her rescue Henrik.

"These are dangerous paths even for you," said Bonifacia. "What brings you here? Is this your home?"

The Gno'man pursed his lips and puffed his cheeks. "My home? No. You won't find many Gno'men in these parts. I'm here on business."

"Is that so? What sort of business are you in?"

"I'm a collector of things. The more unusual the better."

Bonifacia thought she had the measure of him. "What would you say if I were to tell you I had something very unusual, something that even a wizard would covet?"

His eyes brightened. "A wizard? Let me see it."

"I would," said Bonifacia, except that it is in my satchel and the Og'yre took it with them."

He looked crestfallen.

"Take me to find my friend and we'll recover the bag. In return, I'll give you the orb."

"But what is it? What does this 'orb' do?"

"You'll have to take me to it first."

Gemesh pawed the ground with one toe as he weighed the risks and potential benefits in his mind. "You're not just playing me? You wouldn't do that, would you?"

"I swear on my grandmother's grave," replied Bonifacia, crossing her heart to seal their covenant. Gemesh had no idea what her gesture meant, but thought it a powerful promise.

"All right," he said. "We have a deal. But I warn you, it won't be easy and there are great risks involved."

"I'm getting quite used to taking risks," she replied. "Let's not waste any time, shall we."

"Very well," said Gemesh. "Follow me."

For more than an hour, Bonifacia and the Gno'man trudged along a nearly indecipherable trail leading high up into the range, stopping twice to drink from the frigid mountain waters. They were well above the tree line by this point with sweeping views over the Chigraw to far-off Orn.

"You don't seem terribly concerned about running into any more Og'yre," she commented.

"Well, there's always a chance of that," admitted Gemesh, "but if we worry on that too much we shan't get to where we're going."

Not exactly reassuring words. "I don't suppose you have any food with you? All my food was in my pack."

"A little farther yet and we'll get to that," said Gemesh, rather vaguely. A little farther turned out to be another two hours of hard slogging up the mountainside. "This way," said Gemesh, at last. Bonifacia followed him up to the desolate rock face, a near vertical slab of pink and gray granite.

"Here?"

"Turn around and close your eyes," instructed Gemesh. "The brotherhood would pluck my toenails if they thought I'd shared our secrets with a boomken Gwellem."

"What's a boomken Gwellem?" asked Bonifacia.

"You are. Or at least, I think you are. Now turn around and close your eyes."

"Is that really necessary?"

"Just do as I say."

She complied, deciding not to argue the Gwellem issue for the time being. She could hear Gemesh grunt as he struggled to budge something heavy. There was the sound of grinding rock and then silence. A tap between her shoulder blades made her jump.

"You can turn around now," said Gemesh.

She spun about and found herself looking straight into a kind of circular shaft drilled into the rock face about two feet above the ground. "Oh my."

"You'll have to crawl on your hands and knees to get through, but it's only a few spans across. I'll start through first and light a lamp."

He popped himself into the opening and crawled off into the darkness. Moments later his pudgy face reappeared framed within the aperture, backlit by the dim glow of a lantern.

"Come in, come in," beckoned Gemesh. She got down on all fours and crawled inside the opening. It was only four or five yards to the other side. Bonifacia immediately felt the temperature drop and her arms go all chicken skin.

Once inside, she kicked her feet around and dropped the short distance to the floor. Setting aside his lantern, Gemesh lowered down to the floor a heavy candlestick chandelier that hung in concentric circles by a rope from the ceiling. He lit the candles and raised the fixture back up. The remaining shadows evaporated from the chamber.

The room was a kind of casemate, crammed with dusty tables, high chests and towering armoires, all in need of major repair, but inconsequential really when compared to what they held. Everywhere she looked the floor and shelves were piled high with knickknacks and odds and sods of remarkable variety: helmets, buckets, rope, shields, farming equipment, saddles, candle sticks, pots, pans, carpets, urns and whatever else, all piled willy-nilly.

"What is this place?"

"In ancient times it was a way station for Gno'men, something like the one down by the old highway. It's been in my family's keeping for many, many years now." There was a large iron wheel fitted with a spinner knob beside the hole they'd crawled through. Taking hold of it, Gemesh cranked shut the outer door, once again concealing the way station from view.

"I didn't see a device like that outside," remarked Bonifacia.

"'Course not," said Gemesh. "If there were, any sort of burglar could get in, couldn't they?"

"It's freezing cold in here," stammered Bonifacia, her teeth beginning to chatter.

"I can fix that. Just a second." He trotted over to the far corner of the room, kicked some useless items to one side and pried open an armoire door that looked as if it hadn't been unfastened in a hundred years. Inside were piles of clothing. He fished out a long fleece-lined coat and helped her to put it on. She immediately felt the warmth flood over her. "Thank you," she said, in all sincerity.

"It helps that you're the same size as a Gno'man," replied Gemesh. "Oh, one more thing." He went back to the armoire, this time fetching a boxy hat of curly white wool, much like the Persians wear, plus a pair of elbow length mittens. "That's sure to keep you warm. You'll need those where we're going."

"And where's that?" she asked.

"Down there." He pointed toward a door at the back of the casemate sitting partly ajar. It blended so well with all the heaps of junk she hadn't even noticed it. "We'll come out close to Callow Pass, but first, let's have something to eat, shall we? I'm famished."

He cleared a space just wide enough for the two of them to sit opposite one another at the end of a long dusty table filled with collected whatnot. "Take a seat," he said. Then with lamp in hand, he dipped out of the room through the partially opened door.

She craned her neck to see where he'd got to, but there was no sign of him down the darkened corridor. *He moves like the wind,* she thought. With Gemesh out of the way, she took the opportunity to poke about the room. A small box on one table was filled with mismatched flatware. An armoire with its doors nearly off the hinges contained shelves of empty colored bottles. It wasn't all junk. A small banded chest lying atop a sideboard fairly brimmed with precious minerals and rough gemstones. She stared at it in wonder until she heard Gemesh muttering to himself down the hall and hastily regained her seat.

Gemesh emerged with an enormous platter balanced on one hand, the lamp still clutched in the other. The platter was piled high with fresh flat bread, cheeses, smoked meat, apples, two glasses and a bottle of cider. He very adroitly lowered the platter onto the table. Bonifacia hadn't eaten since the night before and was so utterly ravenous she couldn't even think of a few polite words to say as she scoffed down her meal.

The food was all very good and she ate far too quickly. When she was finished Bonifacia emitted a thunderous burp that no reasonable person would have believed possible of someone so small in stature. "My goodness," said Bonifacia, cupping a hand to her mouth. "I do apologize."

Gemesh was expressionless, then suddenly belched loud enough to rattle the chandelier. They slapped the table and laughed heartily.

"Oh, I haven't had a proper laugh in so long," cried Bonifacia. "Not since I last played with Peter in the garden."

"Who's Peter?" asked Gemesh.

"Peter is my best friend, and cousin. We came through the portal together."

"Pufftht!" spat Gemesh. "You came here through a portal?! I thought you were a boomken Gwellem?"

"You haven't told me what that means. Actually, I'm not from this world at all. You can see for yourself that I don't have the brows." She self-consciously scrubbed her forehead.

"Well yes, I can see that. I thought you were a felon. Gwellem cut the brows off criminals. It's a form of punishment. So if you're not Gwellem, what are you?"

"I'm a human being," said Bonifacia. That sounded strange. The first time in her life Bonifacia had found it necessary to declare her humanity.

"A *hu–man?*" said Gemesh. "I don't believe I've ever met…wait a minute!" he scratched his right ear. "I remember a number of years ago some chaps came through a portal. They called themselves human, from a world called Terra, as I recall."

"That's right," said Bonifacia. "It's the Galician word for Earth. Terra or Earth, it's all the same."

He looked at her wide-eyed, concern reflected in his face.

"What's wrong?" she asked.

"Those humans were not much better than Og'yre as I remember. The old emperor ordered them all hunted down."

"There are good humans and bad humans," she declared.

"I suppose that's true of everyone," admitted Gemesh. "My brother is very, very bad."

"There you go," said Bonifacia.

Gemesh's eyes suddenly lit up. "Did you by any chance bring something with you from your world?"

"Only my clothes which were in terrible ruin and a well used handkerchief, which I don't suppose you're interested in. I left them with Tom and Lianne." Bonifacia thought about it for a moment. She'd come through the tunnel with a hairpin, but lost it during the harrowing ride through the forest with Henrik. "Well yes, I do have one thing, come to think of it." She reached around her neck to reveal her crucifix for Gemesh to see.

"May I?" asked Gemesh, holding out a chubby little hand.

"I suppose." Bonifacia unfastened the clasp and handed him the tiny gold pendant with the figure of Jesus. He held it as one would some delicate treasure.

"From Earth you say?"

"Yes. Mama bought it in Madrid for my confirmation."

His eyes shone with delight. He handed it back to her.

"Does it mean that much to you?" she asked.

"Oh yes, yes," said Gemesh. "That is an especially unique item."

"What would you do with it if I were to offer it to you?"

His eyes grew wider. He gestured with one hand. "I'd keep it here, of course."

Bonifacia glanced at the great piles of amassed junk scattered about the room and tucked the crucifix safely away. "I've been meaning to ask you…how is it that you are able to squeeze through tiny cracks, the way you did in the hollow? Or is that a secret of the brotherhood too?"

"No secret," said Gemesh. He picked up a narrow pipe no wider than a half dollar from the pile of whatnot on the table and with startling dexterity slipped his arm through it, wiggling his fingers out the other side. Bonifacia let out a gasp and Gemesh pulled his arm back out, smiling proudly.

"How do you do that?" she asked in wonder.

"A Gno'man's bones aren't like other people's bones. They're pliable. 'Course it takes some concentration. Does no good to be surprised. My cousin, Wedder, was killed by a Gwellem who hit him on top the head thinking it would do no harm."

"How awful," said Bonifacia.

Gemesh pursed his lips and puffed his cheeks.

"I'm going to clean this up and pack some food for our journey. Wait here. I'll be back in a jiffy."

Bonifacia wandered about the room, poking through Gemesh's treasure horde until he returned. He held out two tote bags tied to the end of short poles. "One for you and one for me," he said. "Enough food, water and fuel to see us through. Are you warm enough?"

Bonifacia nodded. He lowered the chandelier and snuffed out the candles. "We'll use the lantern as far as it will take us. There are more lanterns and candlenut torches stored throughout the passageway." He fixed the lantern to the end of the pole opposite his tote and hoisted the pole up over one shoulder. Then he closed and locked the door to the way station with a big brass key that hung from his belt and they started off down the dimly lit corridor, looking for all the world like a couple of vagabonds in search of their next meal.

For the first quarter-league or so the corridor looked much like one might find at an inn or a manor house, with many paripinnate doors facing into the hallway. It soon transformed, however, into a tunnel of natural rock juxtaposed with the occasional doorway framed in ashlar. At various junctures and intersections were carved relief sculptures of Gno'men, like eerie replicas of Gemesh emerging from the rock wall. Their form was strikingly similar to those at the portal entrance near the ruin and the gatekeeper's cottage. She remarked as much to Gemesh.

"You didn't think the wizards built the portals on their own, did you? They used to keep us very busy with all their little projects."

"Do you actually know a wizard?" asked Bonifacia.

He pursed his lips and puffed his cheeks. "No. The portals were built a very long time ago. It's just common knowledge, that's all."

Bonifacia at first took the figures to be mere tributes to the original engineers of this great underground labyrinth, but her impression of them changed when she realized how Gemesh was using them. Every so often he would stop to examine one of the stone Gno'men in detail and then abruptly change course. So she began to pay closer attention. One carving might be caught in the act of winking or wagging the little finger on one hand. Another depicted with its tongue stuck prominently behind one cheek or standing with its legs crossed. Clearly these gestures constituted a signpost that only Gno'men could accurately decipher. *Very shrewd,* she thought. *Very shrewd indeed.*

The weariness in her legs and hunger in her belly were the only clear means of marking the passage of time. She tried hard not to complain, to take her cues from Gemesh for when it was time to rest or eat. In some ways, hiking through dense forest and up the sides of rough scree-covered hills with Henrik was easier, for at least there were challenges to occupy the mind and body. Here, Bonifacia had nothing to do or particularly look at except the pale swaying light of the lantern that hung on the end of Gemesh's carrying stick. The effect was both tedious and hypnotic. She often found herself unexpectedly immersed in strange and disturbing lines of thought. The impact was not lessened by Gemesh's tendency to talk to himself, for little if any of that conversation made any sense to her.

"There's a nice spot up ahead," said Gemesh. "I should like to rest there a short while, if you don't mind."

Bonifacia was all for that.

They turned a corner and Bonifacia gasped in wonderment. The tunnel intersected one edge of an enormous crystal geode cavern that sparkled in the lantern light. Sheets of curly helictites, tiny glistening soda straws, dripping stalactites and rippling curtains of calcite speleothems adorned the cavern ceiling, reflected in the crystal clear waters of an underground lake fed by a small waterfall at the far end of the grotto.

Bonifacia lay down her tote bag and stood mesmerized, soaking in the ethereal beauty and exquisite watery silence of the cavern. Gemesh, recognizing perhaps the natural magic of the place, opted not to disturb her. He lit two candlenut torches that were stuck in the ground along the bank, and from behind a line of rocks drew out a long fishing pole. Sitting on top the stump of a broken stalagmite, he cast his line into the water. Bonifacia watched the little Gno'man in his blue woolen coat and pointy red hat fish the cold subterranean waters in quiet contemplation.

Waiting patiently the line went taught after a time and the pole bent low to the rippling surface of the water. "Hee, hee!" cried Gemesh, hauling in his catch. It was a large white fish with iridescent scales and albino eyes. He swatted the flopping creature hard against the ground to end its suffering. "More than enough for two hungry bellies."

He cleaned the fish and set a fire using blocks of dried peat kept in a storage box by the lake. The fish sizzled and popped with tantalizing promise from the fry pan. They ate well, after which Bonifacia curled up in a ball beside the fire and fell fast asleep.

She was awakened some time later by the gentle hand of Gemesh on her shoulder. "Time we moved on," he whispered quietly. A surge of guilt ran through her. She'd rested, eaten and slept while poor Henrik was on his way to be sold to the Weshnut at the hands of the Og'yre, *or worse*. Bonifacia roused herself quickly as Gemesh readied for the next leg of their journey.

It was with a tinge of regret that Bonifacia left behind the beautiful grotto, wondering if she would ever see the likes of it again. Come what may, she knew in her heart that she would never ever forget the image of Gemesh fishing peacefully beside the idyllic subterranean lake.

They walked on and on for hours through the maze of tunnels, coming at last to a Gno'man signpost. It stood beside a doorway cased within dressed blocks of stone. The little stern faced men guarding the entranceway were clad in heavy winter clothing, bundled against the elements.

"We have arrived," announced Gemesh. "The way station at Callow Pass."

She eyed the immutable Gno'men in their thick winter clothes. "It gives me a chill just to look at them," said Bonifacia with an enormous involuntary shiver.

"We are very high up. The weather can be fitful at these altitudes."

"Have we been climbing?" asked Bonifacia, in surprise. "I haven't felt it at all."

"It's hard to tell from inside the mountain." Gemesh unlocked the door to the way station. The narrow chamber was piled high with bits of wasting armor, old cook pots and kitchen implements.

"No one's been in here in a long while," said Gemesh, holding up his lamp. "And not often before that."

A circular crawlspace extended out the opposite end of the casemate, just as it had at Gemesh's way station. A constant trickle of water seeped down the wall from the bottom of the aperture, leaving long strands of slippery rust-brown algae in its wake. The rivulet traveled across the cluttered floor to disappear beneath a rusty cuirass.

"Shall we have a bite to eat and a rest before we go on?" asked Gemesh.

"No thank you," replied Bonifacia. "Perhaps later. I'd like to see what is outside, if you don't mind."

Gemesh shrugged indifferently and began to work the crank for the outside door, but it resisted every effort. "It hasn't been used in a long time," he groaned. "I think it will budge with a little more weight on it." He poked about the room for something he could use. Employing the remains of an old spear for added leverage, he motioned to Bonifacia to lend a hand. Together, they heaved on the haft until the wheel began to slowly turn. Once again, there was the muffled sound of grinding stone. "I can take it from here," said Gemesh. "Leave it to me."

Bonifacia stepped aside. Gemesh removed the spear from the wheel, gritted his teeth and cranked down on it with all his might. A dull gray light slowly poured in from the outside through the entry shaft, accompanied by a swift blast of icy air.

"After you," said Gemesh, once the outer door was opened.

Bonifacia pulled herself up into the circular crawlspace. "Ah, yuk!" she whined. "It's all wet and slimy in here." Gemesh passed her the carrying poles and tote sacks. She crawled away through the opening, dragging them behind.

As cold and damp as the Gno'man tunnels were, it was much, much worse outside. Bonifacia emerged to find herself standing on the edge of a narrow mountain path lashed by a fierce wet wind that threatened to pick her up bodily and pitch her off the ridge. For a moment she felt the same uneasy feeling she had when Henrik pulled her across the river in the bosun's chair. She pressed her back against the mountain and looked down at her filthy hands and knees. The wind shrieked and whistled in her ears, digging its way beneath her clothes, testing the limits of her wooly coat, hat and mittens. She pulled up her collar in an effort to fend it off.

Gemesh popped out of the hole in the rock face and breathed in the frosty air as if it were an invigorating tonic. Even more surprising, the point of his tall red hat hardly flinched in the stiff unrelenting breeze.

"Is it night or is it day?" she asked, shouting to be heard above the howling wind. "I can hardly tell." The peaks were lost amid dense gray clouds that scudded quickly by.

"Daytime," replied Gemesh. "About mid-afternoon. I've got to close up the entrance. Turn around and close your eyes. You know how it's done," he shouted.

Bonifacia fully intended to do the right thing, but curiosity or perhaps self-interest got the better of her. She turned and tiptoed after Gemesh, delaying just long enough to watch him work the hidden mechanism for the outer door.

Her curiosity satisfied, she bolted back to the path like a frightened rabbit and resumed her former pose before Gemesh could catch sight of her. A moment later Gemesh, unaware of her treachery, tapped her on the elbow. He had a rope with him. Where he'd got it from, she had no idea.

"I'm going to tie us together," he said. "It wouldn't do for a little thing like you to get blown off the mountain."

Gemesh was not her vision of an ideal anchor, which made his concern for her all the more poignant. Her perfidy began to eat at her. Gemesh tied the rope about his waist and then Bonifacia's, wisely securing their tote sacks at the hip so as not to act as windsocks that could carry them off.

"Where to now?" asked Bonifacia.

"Over Callow Pass to the outpost where the Weshnut conduct their business with the Og'yre. The pass is guarded, so we'll have to take a detour round. And I should warn you, the trail is a tad steep."

"Couldn't you have built your tunnel a bit closer to the pass?"

"Too much risk of being discovered," he replied.

As they traveled beyond the Gno'man way station, Bonifacia could see the entrance was exceedingly well hidden. A sharp ledge jutting out from above kept the location of the concealed door in perpetual shadow. "Like a Gwellem's eyebrow," she remarked.

The trail Gemesh spoke of was hardly discernable from the mountain. Climbing high above the bench where they emerged, Bonifacia and Gemesh continued up the fractured lichen-covered mountain, the cold wet relentless wind beating down on them. An enormous gust caught hold of Bonifacia's hat, pulled it from her head and tossed it off the mountain, leaving her hair to whip freely about. She looked at Gemesh between half closed lids, still marveling at how his pointy red hat managed to stay so effortlessly atop his head.

For two more hours, they struggled against the elements and the steep mountain, clinging as best they could to the hazardous trail and to one another, until reaching a relatively level stretch of rocky fell. "We can get rid of these ropes now," said Gemesh. "The going should be much easier from here." He drew a knife and cut the cord between them so that part of the rope remained as a belt around their waists holding their totes. The remainder of the rope, he looped around his shoulder.

Gemesh placed a finger to his lips and pointed off to the right, then motioned for Bonifacia to get down on her hands and knees to follow him. Silently, they crept up to the edge of a deep schism. "Down there. Callow pass," whispered Gemesh. They peered together over the edge. A stone's throw below, a narrow road crept between two sheer faces of the rock. In a corrie at one end of the defile several Og'yre sat huddled next to a cookfire.

"Gemesh?" whispered Bonifacia. "Is that what I think it is?" Tied to a spit, roasting over the fire was the unmistakable form of an Og'yre.

"Disgusting isn't it? They eat their own sick and lame when there's nothing else about." Gemesh gestured for her to move back. "Our timing is good," he said. "The wind favors us." Gemesh taped the side of his nose. "Og'yre' have a highly developed sense of smell."

"Why aren't they guarding up here too?" asked Bonifacia, with an anxious glance in the direction of the Og'yre.

Gemesh looked at her in puzzlement. "Because the road is down there," replied the Gno'man, as if that explained everything. He canted his head to one side. "You're not thinking to take them on, are you?"

"No, of course not," she replied, "but you can see for yourself that we could do them some mischief from this vantage point."

"And how long do you think we would have to live after that?"

"I see your point. Where to from here?"

"That way," said Gemesh pointing over the drumlin toward the windward side of the mountain. "This is the border between Kaladar and Kayu Tun, the Weshnut homeland. We can loop around, connecting back with the road much farther down."

"Then let's get on with it," said Bonifacia impatiently.

Gemesh led off, loping close to the ground with Bonifacia running behind. They darted across the fell as quickly as they could, aiming for the lee of some distant rocks, then hugging them closely, they descended the versant on the opposite side of the mountain.

Although it remained dark and overcast, Bonifacia was delighted to see the wind drop off considerably the farther down the mountainside they went. There was also a good deal more scrub brush growing between the rocks, which gave them something to hold onto in places where the footing was precarious.

They made a wide loop below the false summit in this way, eventually emerging behind an outcrop near a switchback in the road. The Og'yre and their campfire were out of sight somewhere high above them now. Bonifacia and Gemesh huddled together behind the outcrop, peering cautiously down the road, planning their next move.

"So where is the outpost from here?" asked Bonifacia.

"Across the road and down the hill to the right. That will take us in behind the post." He pursed his lips and puffed his cheeks. "Things become very ticklish from here on in, very ticklish indeed."

"I've little doubt of that," said Bonifacia.

"Better if we wait here until nightfall," suggested Gemesh. "In the meantime we can do a few things to prepare ourselves."

"Like what?" asked Bonifacia.

Gemesh unfastened his tote and fished out a small ceramic jar. Unscrewing the lid, he offered Bonifacia a quantity of the sticky murrey-colored paste.

"Yuch! That's repugnant," exclaimed Bonifacia. "What am I supposed to do with that?"

"Rub it on your hands and face."

"What for?"

"It confuses the Og'yre. Makes you smell more like one of them."

Wrinkling her nose, she dipped out a quantity of the foul stuff with two fingers. "Don't tell me what's in this. I don't want to know." They applied the compound to their exposed skin and then, at Gemesh's insistence, proceeded to rub dirt and mud over one another's clothing to help disguise their profiles.

"Mother would die if she could see me now," said Bonifacia.

With little else to do until nightfall, they propped their backs against the outcropping and indulged in a cold, but welcome, repast. Bonifacia ate greedily and afterward tucked her head beneath her collar and dozed off under an ashen sky.

By the time she awoke, dusk had settled on the mountainside. They roused themselves and crept silently from behind the outcrop, scampered across the road and over to the fell on the other side. Keeping within the shadows, they slunk down the hill toward the faint lights of the outpost, and then cast themselves into a shallow depression from which to make a closer observation. Bonifacia could see the outline of a large domed structure and several slate-roofed sconces built low to the ground and spread in a semicircle over the uneven plateau.

Most, if not all the inhabitants of the outpost, were congregated on their far left, engaged in a celebration of some sort or other and making a very disagreeable ruckus. "Og'yre aren't big on fortifications," remarked Gemesh. "No fancy perimeter walls, bastions, or anything like that."

"Handy for us. Where do you think they're holding Henrik?" whispered Bonifacia.

Gemesh shrugged, "He could be anywhere down there."

"So?" asked Bonifacia, "what's your plan?"

Even in the gathering dark, Bonifacia could see Gemesh purse his lips and puff his cheeks.

Bonifacia sputtered. "Gemesh! What are you telling me? You brought me all the way here and you don't have a plan?"

"I thought we might work one out together."

"Then you might have said so earlier. I have no experience at this sort of thing. The most I've ever done is play *'hare and hounds'* with Peter in the garden. Surely you must have some notion or other?"

He hesitated. "I don't usually make plans per se when I visit some place. I tend to get the details all muddled up. Much better to follow one's nose, I find."

"Follow one's nose?" repeated Bonifacia. "And where is your nose leading you just now?"

Gemesh gave her a considering look, then bold as brass, stood straight up and commenced walking across the rocky field toward the outpost. Bonifacia gasped, but as the little figure of the Gno'man began to distance himself from her, she forced her quaking legs to do the same and jogged up behind him, her heart pounding in her chest the entire way. To her amazement, they cleared the distance and reached the backside of the closest building without being detected.

"Don't you *ever* do that again!" she chastised, struggling to keep her voice down.

Gemesh either ignored her or did not hear her. His whole manner seemed suddenly transformed, tense, alert, eyes darting vigilantly from side to side. "This way," he said, rushing off.

Bonifacia followed closely behind, doing her best to watch over her shoulder. Gemesh circled around the building, which bore close resemblance to an igloo made of stone. He paused near the front to watch and listen, then motioned for her to keep back. "There are two Og'yre sitting near the entrance," he whispered.

Bonifacia poked her head around him to have a look for herself. They were sitting quietly by lantern light, smoking tobacco pipes and tossing knucklebones in a game of chance. "Let's try somewhere else for now," suggested Gemesh. He craned his neck to look about. "The cookhouse and billets are on our left where all the noise is coming from. I should think most of the Og'yre are over there dining just now—hopefully not on your friend." Bonifacia frowned. He gestured in the opposite direction. "Perhaps we should begin over there?"

It was Bonifacia's turn to shrug. One mad course was as good as another.

They tiptoed back and then over to their far right and the first structure in line. The entrance was unguarded and the door unlocked. Cautiously, they slipped inside and closed the door behind them. Gemesh struck a match and they found themselves amid a room filled with barrels, crates and canvas sacks. "Not here," he said.

They tried the next two buildings with similar results. The one after that brought them right back to where they'd started at the big stone igloo. Moving around to the front, they found the Og'yre guards had departed, but the door left secured. Gemesh scrunched down to examine the lock, "*clucked*" to himself in satisfaction, and then removed from his jacket pocket a slender rod with several uneven teeth at one end. He jiggered the lock and a moment later they were inside.

Gemesh struck up another match revealing a vaulted corridor angled down below the main dome. An oil lamp hung from a bracket on the wall. He put his match to it and beckoned for Bonifacia to follow him down the short flight of steps. Light from the lamp flooded the main dome as they stepped inside.

"What now?" came a weary yet familiar voice. "Bonnie? So help me! Is that you?"

The perimeter of the dome was lined with cells, only one of which was occupied. Henrik stood clinging to the bars, his tunic bloodied and torn. She ran to him, clasping his hand between her tiny fingers. "Henrik! You're alive!"

"What are you doing here?" he asked, both dismayed and delighted to see her. "You should be far away from this place. What a frightful mess you are. Ah, and you stink like Og'yre!" He poked his head to one side, looking between the bars. "Who is this you've brought with you?"

"This is Gemesh," said Bonifacia. "He saved me from the Og'yre."

"A Gno'man! Thieves and outlaws for the most part. I thought they'd all died off."

Gemesh pursed his lips and puffed out his cheeks.

"He's none of those things," protested Bonifacia. "Anyway, we're not here to converse. We're here to rescue you."

"Rescue me? How do you propose to do that?"

Bonifacia turned to Gemesh. "You can fiddle the lock again, can't you?"

"Thieves and outlaws," repeated Gemesh. "Where's my promised compensation?"

"Oh, you see!" said Bonifacia, angrily. "Why did you have to go and hurt his feelings? Where is my bag? Do you know?"

"Over there, by the door," said Henrik, pointing with his chin.

Bonifacia ran across the room and scooped up her haversack from where it lay discarded on a bench near the door. "Gemesh. Let him out. I'll give you your reward."

"Let me see it first."

Bonifacia huffed, and then dug through the pack to find the silver orb Bartle had given her. "There," she said displaying it to him in the palm of one hand. "Will you let him out now, *please.*"

Gemesh turned to the cell and in a matter of moments had Henrik freed.

"That's a handy talent. Thank you, little man," said Henrik. He slumped forward the instant he let go of the bars.

"Henrik!" cried Bonifacia. She passed the orb to Gemesh and rushed to Henrik's side. He pulled himself up, holding one hand to a nasty gash below his ribs. Gemesh pocketed the object with a satisfied smile.

"I'll be fine," said Henrik. "Let's just get out of here."

No sooner had he spoken those words, the door burst open and a host of Og'yre armed with poleaxes, cudgels and flaming torches stormed inside the dome. They ranged themselves around Bonifacia, Henrik and Gemesh.

"My, my, what have we here?" sputtered the biggest of the Og'yre, its hairy ears twitching from side to side. "A prison break? Sharf, that nose of yours will get you far."

The one called Sharf snorted proudly. "I knew I smeeled me a Gno'man."

"And right you were Sharf. A Gno'man in the flesh. Been thirty years since I last seen a Gno'man, maybe longer. Thought they were all dead and gone. All jelly when you cook 'em. No good bones to suck on."

Gemesh pursed his lips and puffed his cheeks.

"Look there Vokran, someone's gone and clipped the poor girl's wings." An Og'yre with one leg shorter than the other toddled over to Bonifacia and poked her eyebrow with a speculative finger.

"*Non me toques!*" she shouted. "Keep your filthy hands off me!"

They all laughed heartily. "Hey! How'd he get out of his cell?" asked another Og'yre, gesturing toward Henrik with the point of his poleaxe.

"The Gno'man," replied Vokran. "They're crafty fellows. Can't hold 'em in an ordinary cell. They can slip between the bars." Gemesh rocked angrily back and forth on the balls of his toes.

"Well, you're a fortunate bunch," continued Vokran. "The dealer will be up from Debs on the morrow, so you won't have long to wait. Either you'll be bought in trade or served up for lunch. One's as good as the other. Sharf, escort the Gwellem to their cells and double the locks. As for the Gno'man, we've got a special place for him."

There was little Henrik and Bonifacia could do under the circumstance. Sharf led them into separate cells on opposite sides of the dome, wrapping a chain and extra padlock about the bars for good measure.

A great windlass was mounted to the floor. One of the Og'yre with a saggy lower lip that drooled as he walked cranked it round several times, in the process sliding a large iron grate in the center of the floor off to one side. "The pit hasn't been used to house Gno'men in many a year. They used to be very frequent guests in my grand-pappy's time. Nice to see old traditions revived, don't you think? In you go," commanded the Og'yre.

Gemesh naturally hesitated, but eventually flung himself down the deep well at the point of several sharp halberds. He landed with a thud and a stifled moan.

"Gemesh! Are you all right?" shouted Bonifacia.

"Yes, yes," came the echoing voice of the Gno'man from far down the well. "Quite all right, thank you."

The iron grate was closed over the trap, sealing Gemesh down below the floor.

"Nighty night," said Vokran. "Sharf, double the guard outside, just in case there are any more of this sort lurkin' about in the night."

"As you say, Vokran." Sharf proffered the big Og'yre a clumsy salute.

The Og'yre departed in fine humor, putting out the lights and plunging the jailhouse into total darkness. Bonifacia spent a hungry and sleepless night curled up on the cold stone floor of the main dome, and Henrik, not for the first time. What bewildered and frankly irritated Bonifacia were the sounds of a Gno'man snoring contentedly from deep within the well at the center of the dome.

After what seemed an eternity, the sound of a key grating in a lock and the clatter of hobnailed boots and weapons bumping down the short stairwell roused Bonifacia. Vokran returned with a smaller band of comrades and a rather exotic-looking individual whom Bonifacia surmised was the so-called "dealer" from Debs.

To her astonishment the Weshnut dealer was a handsome middle-aged woman, a Gwellem, with long dark brows tied in two neat plaits down the sides of her face. Her attire bold yet comely, like a Romany or Greek resistance fighter in one of Dupré's portraits from the War of Independence. She wore a pair of soft boots the color of saffron, a heavily pleated ankle-length white skirt over tight leggings, scarlet waistband festooned with shiny paillettes, and an exquisitely embroidered blue waistcoat over a wide sleeved peasant blouse. Set on a jaunty angle atop a mass of crow-black hair rested a cerulean Phrygian cap with a flamboyant silver tassel.

The Weshnut woman gave Henrik a cursory and largely indifferent glance, while making a beeline for Bonifacia. She paused just beyond the bars to the cell and studied her carefully. "You're the girl Borganin is after," she declared, unable to hide her own surprise. "Why, she's just a child." She turned to face the big Og'yre. "Vokran, get her out of that cell immediately."

"And what about the little man?" he replied.

"What little man?"

Vokran gestured toward the center of the floor. The heavy grate was cranked aside and the Weshnut dealer peered down into the well with the aid of a flaming torch.

"You captured a Gno'man? Remarkable. I suppose you'll be telling me you've netted a wizard next." Bonifacia was brought out of her cell and over to the Weshnut dealer. "What's your name child?"

"Bonifacia, ma'am." She gave a rough curtsy, owing to the soreness in her legs.

The Weshnut turned toward Vokran. "The usual payment—ten barrels for the boy—but four for the Gno'man and one for the girl."

The Og'yre roared in anger. "*Four* for the Gno'man and *one* for the girl?! I ought ta…"

She cut him off. "You ought to what, Vokran? You're lucky the samkan doesn't skin you alive for how you've treated the girl."

"Why? She's just a Gwellem whelp."

"You'd better watch your tongue. Weshnut may be children of The Mother, but we are Gwellem of a sort. Take a closer look, you fool. The girl isn't one of us."

Vokran glowered at Bonifacia in puzzlement. "If you say so. But why only four barrels for the Gno'man?"

"The creature has little more than novelty value. You're not going to tell me you sacrificed even one Og'yre to capture him, are you?"

Vokran's ears twitched from side to side. What could he possibly say? Bonifacia and Gemesh had walked straight into the Og'yre jail of their own accord.

"Are you just going to leave me down here?" echoed Gemesh from below.

The dealer woman took the torch from the Og'yre standing next to her and waved it over the open hole to have a better look at him. "You understand, Master Gno'man, that you were fairly captured within the borders of the Weshnut homeland? It has been thirty years or more that I know of since such an occurrence, but the old conventions still hold. You can stay down in that stinking hole until you rot away, or you can swear a binding oath of service to the samkan for nine years. The choice is yours to make."

Aggravated mutters radiated from the pit. "How 'bout three years?"

"Nine," repeated the Weshnut dealer. "Close the grate."

"All right! All right," cried Gemesh. "Nine years. I'll swear to it. Just get me out of here."

The Weshnut dealer motioned to one of the Og'yre and a rope ladder was brought over for Gemesh to climb out. "Keep a weapon trained on him until the oath is administered," commanded the dealer. She walked over to the cell holding Henrik, as Gemesh's hat and head poked above the floor. "It is obvious you can fight or you wouldn't be here to even answer this question," she said to Henrik. "From where do you hail and what is your profession?"

"From Kaladar," he replied. "I am an akritar in the service of Her Imperial Majesty."

"An akritar? You of all people should have known better than to cross the border without authority."

"We weren't across the border," countered Henrik. "We were traveling the old Kaladwen highway."

"Is that true Vokran? Did you snatch him on the Kaladar side?"

The big Og'yre snorted. "Your maps are worthless. He was trespassing on Og'yre territory. Cost two of my men to take that Gwellem."

She made no effort to dispute Vokran. "Which of your men did he kill?" asked the dealer.

"Kriv and Rofta."

She turned to Henrik. "I'm impressed. You *are* a fighter. What's your name and house?"

"Henrik. My house is none of your damn business."

She smiled at him. "Vokran, it would appear we have no legal claim on the boy. He's yours to do with as you please, but I'll give you twenty-five barrels for him, if you'll see your way to selling him."

"You mustn't!" chimed in Bonifacia. "It's not his fault. He was taking me to the queen at Piernot. We had no choice. The turnpike was barred."

"The Empress Xhôn?" replied the Weshnut dealer. "I guess you haven't heard the news. The empress is dead and Piernot has fallen."

"That can't be!" exclaimed Bonifacia.

"You must be mistaken," echoed Henrik, doubt and anguish creeping into his voice.

"I'm afraid it's true. The Duke of Menom has taken the city. He will have himself proclaimed emperor soon enough, but do not worry Bonifacia, you are now under the protection of the samkan." She turned to face the Og'yre. "Well, Vokran. Do we have a deal or not? Twenty-five barrels for the boy. That's nearly three times the usual fee."

Vokran smacked his lips. "Yes. We have a deal."

"Oh, Henrik. Gemesh. *Sintoo!*" cried Bonifacia. "I'm so sorry."

"That will do," said the dealer. "Vokran, load the akritar into the wain. Make sure he is well chained."

"But it doesn't make any sense! Why are you doing this?" protested Bonifacia. "They've done nothing!"

"I think I've made myself perfectly clear. The Gno'man knew the penalty for trespass when he wandered over the mountains and the akritar understood no less the risk he was taking when he ventured beyond the foothills." She turned to face both Peter and Gemesh. "Is that not so? Answer me, both of you."

They nodded sullenly.

"No!" cried Bonifacia. "Henrik! Gemesh!"

Henrik glared at the Weshnut in defiance. Gemesh pursed his lips and puffed out his cheeks.

Bonifacia wiped back the tears that came unbidden. "I heard what you said to Gemesh. What will happen to Henrik?" demanded Bonifacia.

"The akritar?" The Weshnut dealer regarded him indifferently. "He will be restored to health and then transferred to one of the fleet divisions as a training thrall."

"What's that?" asked Bonifacia. "What's a training thrall?"

It was Henrik that answered. "A practice enemy, Bonnie. Someone trained to fight to the death aboard a ship. It's how the Weshnut hone their navy."

"To the death?!" exclaimed Bonifacia.

Chapter 11

The Padishah's Deceit

Shifting a large army from place to place is nothing short of a Herculean task. Peter was frankly fascinated by the entire process and had to admit to a certain amount of excitement over the whole business. Of course, there were certain hardships and inconveniences involved. He particularly yearned for the simple pleasure of an indoor flush.

Most of the soldiers from Orn, even the young ones, were a good deal older than himself, although there were many young boys amongst the musicians, camp followers and baggage train laborers. Soldiers on campaign are not the least circumspect about the color of their language or the nature of their conversations. Peter heard a great deal around campfires or in the saddle that he did not understand.

Joshkar and Peter got on reasonably well with the men of Cosimlara's troop. Most of them were junior aristocrats or liegemen removed from estates and palaces for service. Their collective and near universal enthusiasm for the campaign to oust the Ulfair was evident from the start, although many differed on the specifics. Some enlisted out of simple fealty. Others for the chance to make a name for themselves, earn some money, or have a bit of fun. Still others, like Borganin, to right old wrongs—"to unseat the occupiers," as they put it.

Much of what Peter heard reminded him a great deal of Basil and Freddy, two young cousins on his mother's side, who shipped off to South Africa so full of enthusiasm and patriotic zeal. *How brilliant they looked in their uniforms!* Freddy, sad to say, was captured at Magersfontein in December '99 and died from some form of enteric disease while cooped up in a Boer prison.

The Ornish advance on Piernot was by the most direct route possible, following the shoreline highway between Menom and the imperial capital along the River Talsis. It cannot have been a secret to the empress.

Mid-afternoon on their third day of march a great cloud of dust appeared along the ridgeline to their right. The army halted and a tempest of speculative chatter rippled through the ranks. *Was it the enemy?* After several minutes of nervous anticipation waiting for orders to swing about, a messenger rode the length of the column with news that the ruler of Taixûs, Prince Waythur of the house of Demkin, had joined their cause. "Huzzah! Huzzah!" shouted the army as Waythur's troops formed a parallel column on their right flank.

Borganin, it appeared, had gambled well. With Taixûs on their side and the forces of Stônar not far behind, Empress Xhôn's position began to look increasingly untenable. The Ornish army again took up the advance, more confident and self-assured than ever.

Peter had imagined that with the addition of Taixan cohorts the sheer inertia of so vast a force would speed them along like some terrible juggernaut, but it was quite the opposite. The advance slowed to a dreadful crawl. The troops from Taixûs had traveled light to catch up with the advancing army and were short on shelter and supplies. They had to stop several times to coordinate an exchange of goods. There were also many tributaries that flowed down into the Talsis and it became necessary to engineer additional crossings or share passage across them where the former was not possible. Precious time was also spent trying to keep the two columns in line, lest one get ahead of the other and present an opportune target to the enemy. Fortunately, it did not rain. Even Peter could tell that with so many men and supplies sharing the same track, they would soon find themselves mired up to their necks in a downpour.

Borganin had conspired to prop Peter up as the lord arbiter imperial for his own nefarious purposes. He clearly never intended for the office to actually hold any substance, but Peter was increasingly drawn to the conclusion that Joshkar had it right. The average Tom could not see through the ruse and respected his rank and title as though it were real. This was a startling revelation. Borganin was far too busy organizing his war to be bothered about Peter. "The Lord Arbiter Imperial" was consequently allowed an astonishing degree of liberty to do as he pleased. For the most part, Peter chose to use this freedom to hang about the command tent in the company of Joshkar, learning what he could about unfolding events. He became the proverbial fly on the wall.

Seeing a messenger ride into camp one afternoon, he hastened to the command tent to learn what was up. Slipping inside, Peter mixed as inconspicuously as he could with his fellow officers who either sat or stood around a table covered with campaign maps and reports. Prince Waythur sat in a folding chair coolly sipping from an embossed silver goblet. The courier brought the latest news from Menom.

"Meflis has voted to join us," announced Borganin, reading over the dispatch.

This news was cause for much jubilation. "Three cheers for Meflis and Prince Tolar!" they all cried.

Borganin let his staff have their moment. "However…" he continued. "Bakus Mara and Hemsto have declared themselves against us. Confound the shortsighted fools!"

"We don't need them! Who cares?!" shouted back Borganin's officers.

"There's more news still. Camstol has declared Bakus Sura a neutral party to this conflict. No great surprise there. The house of Forst has always lacked backbone."

"To blazes with all of them! Any word on our ally from Stônar?" interjected Prince Waythur. He had good reason to be concerned.

"Yes, a little," replied Borganin. "Our agents report the Weshnut have provided Stônar's vanguard passage across the Talsis. Prince Tolar has assured the padishah he will facilitate the movement of the Stônar army through Meflis so that it may join us. I suppose, Waythur, you will have to do the same."

"Very enterprising of the Weshnut," quipped Waythur. "Does your report detail the size of Balkur Hamut's force? You understand, I shall have to send troops back to guard the border with Bakus Mara unless Stônar can be counted on to restrain my good neighbor."

"No, it does not, but I'm certain the padishah will move in considerable force. He'll have to with the Hemstot at his back, if only as a precaution. But I can assure you, Prince Waythur, you need not worry about Bakus Mara. The Duke of Bhat will not be bothering Taixûs with the padishah's army bearing down upon him."

"Well," said Waythur. "I suppose there is some good news in all that, but it does not appreciably change our present circumstance, does it? We will not see these allies by our side for at least a fortnight or longer. They will have to confront Bhat in Bakus Mara and keep a close eye on the grand principal at the same time. So…" He leaned far back in his chair. "Do we wait for reinforcements from Meflis and Stônar to launch our attack on Piernot or do we press on? How is your Captain Menhar holding up without us, Borganin?"

All the names and places being discussed were still very confusing to Peter, but that one name caught his attention.

Borganin took the prince's question as a challenge. "Captain Menhar is a warrior without equal. Despite overwhelming odds he has managed to keep the witch pinned down and her army bottled up between the mountains and the city. But let's be clear, Prince Waythur. He cannot keep this up forever. He hasn't the strength to take Piernot on his own or to defeat the Imperial Army on the open field of battle. He awaits our arrival with remarkable forbearance. Each day we tarry the armies of Kaladar and the empire intensify their preparations against us." Borganin paused to scan the faces of the assembled officers. "We cannot afford delay. I say we move on Piernot immediately."

There was a moment of awkward silence. A captain from Taixûs spoke up. "Is it not precisely because of those preparations that we should wait upon our allies, my lord? Why work up a sweat when we could walk straight over them with the strength of our combined forces?"

Peter heard a voice whisper to him, "Lord Borganin does not wish to share the spoils of his impending victory with the padishah, or anyone else if it can be helped. Why should he delay?"

"Did you not hear me?" thundered Borganin. "Kaladar is on the defensive and reeling from the losses Menhar has already inflicted upon them. A quick stroke is all that is needed to finish them off. Panic and confusion are our best allies. "What say you Prince Waythur?"

The prince sat quietly, slowly turning the silver chalice around and around in his hand. All eyes were on him. "I say we move on Piernot."

"Huzzah!" cried the officers in unison. "To Piernot! To Piernot!"

The Ornish and Taixan allies crossed the border with Kaladar and kept on marching until they were no more than five or six leagues from the walls of Piernot. Peter was enjoying a meal around the campfire when the murderous Captain Menhar rode by accompanied by a small guard. It was hard for Menhar to miss Peter, dressed as he was. He did not bother to stop. He managed, however, to cast a cursory glance in his direction and laughed loudly. Mocking Peter. It stung him to the bone and rage burned in his heart.

Plans were made that evening to invest the city and to do battle with the Imperial Army. Peter's intention at first was to give these discussions a miss. The thought of standing of his own volition in the same tent as Menhar was altogether too distasteful. But Joshkar convinced him, or rather cajoled him into going.

"Ah, Field Marshal de Soto," said Menhar, as he entered the command tent. Peter scowled at him and stood as far off from Menhar as he could manage.

The senior captains argued back and forth for nearly three hours over the best approach to defeating the enemy, finally making a recommendation to Prince Waythur and Lord Borganin, which was accepted. The strategy adopted called for laying siege to the side of the city furthest from the battlefield, employing only enough siege engines as necessary to force the defenders to divert considerable resources upon a separate front.

Three cohorts of archers and an equal number of spears were detailed to watch the main sally ports. Their dual task was to serve as a feint and prevent reinforcements within the city from joining the Imperial Army encamped on the field facing Borganin's right. The object here was to give the enemy the false impression that seizing the city was the duke's main intent. In fact, the bulk of Borganin's forces were committed to defeating the enemy upon the open plain just outside the city walls. There were no plans per se for capturing Piernot until the latter objective was accomplished.

Knowing that the following days were committed to battle, the prayer circles at moonrise were especially poignant. Peter had, by this time, grown quite accustomed to participating in these curiously congenial and unceremonious expressions of faith. Third Cestus Cosimlara led his troop in prayer and Peter used the occasion to ask The Eternal Architect (to use the vernacular expression), to spare the lives of the truly innocent.

After prayer, Cosimlara approached Peter. "We have been honored by your presence, my lord arbiter. My men and I will freely admit to a certain fondness for you. Tomorrow, however, I understand your place is beside the duke. Wish us well."

It struck Peter as profoundly absurd for this leader of men to be asking a fifteen-year-old boy for his blessing on the eve of battle, but people are people he supposed, and under such circumstances draw confidence from the knowledge that somebody somewhere appreciates their sacrifice. In this instance Peter, for better or worse, represented the approbation of the state, and since the duke was not likely to pay the young cestus and his little troop a personal visit he did what he felt was right, stepping forward to do the honors.

Peter had never expected to actually accompany Third Cestus Cosimlara's men into battle, but it pained him nonetheless to take his leave of them. They seemed good fellows, all in all, and it gnawed at him that any should die in the service of a vainglorious man like Borganin or for the sake of some ill-considered cause.

The tents were taken down in preparation for an early morning departure and the rebel army camped under the open sky. Peter slept poorly, unable to shake off the growing tension he felt in the pit of his stomach. He kept reliving the murder of Dashwan and Captain Gothrain, images he'd hitherto managed to block from his mind.

It was still very dark when Joshkar shook him awake. A light rain during the night soaked Peter's hair and coverlet, chilling him to the bone. "Come. It's time," said Joshkar. They drank tea and ate a bit of hot porridge. In the subdued and heavy atmosphere they were inclined to move slowly. Joshkar helped

Peter on with his armor, taking more than the usual care, while they waited for their horses to be tacked and brought over. Cosimlara was busy readying his men, and so they quietly led their horses away from his camp without fanfare, winding their way through the drizzle and darkness over to the duke's headquarters.

Peter doubted that the Duke of Menom or any other member of his command echelon had slept a wink from the look of them. Borganin was imparting a few motivational words and final instructions to his captains when they arrived. To Peter's great relief, they'd missed the bulk of his hopelessly equivocal oration, at the end of which everyone was instructed to mount up.

One of Borganin's aides took hold of Peter's bridle. "You are to stay close to the standards and avoid being killed." That was the full extent of Peter's orders for the upcoming battle. When all was in readiness he trotted off in column behind the others with Joshkar at his side. He prayed to God that the people up front knew where they were going.

They rode for just under an hour. The queen's captains had, in proper fashion, established pickets before the city. Every so often the early morning stillness was broken by sporadic cries as the enemy's vedettes clashed with the van of the advancing force. Evidently, moving an army into position with any hope of secrecy, even under cover of darkness, was a virtual impossibility.

They came to a halt on a slight rise above the city as the first feeble blush of dawn colored the horizon above the fields and surrounding weald. The light drizzle that had dogged them all morning passed, giving way to a mostly gray and lifeless sky. There before Peter spread the imperial city of Piernot extending along the water's edge and rivaling, to a very real extent, the majestic splendor of the towering peaks far off to their right.

Peter had imagined Piernot, as the imperial capital, to be rather like Menom, a cloud of lace-like parapets and pinnacles, but on a much grander scale. Or perhaps a little like Xanadu, flush with gilded ogee-shaped domes. He could see now that he was patently mistaken. While Menom looked like a cluttered potpourri of slender white morels and fairy rings, Piernot looked ancient to its roots, somehow wise and imperturbable without being oppressive, its well ordered auburn-colored stones and verdigris rooftops lending it the aura of a university town like Oxford or Cambridge.

The august walls of the capital city naturally drew the eye, but on this day, their attention was also held by the host assembled on the field between the city and the foothills. The Imperial Army sprawled across the gap, colorful, large, and menacing.

They dismounted. The horses were led off and tethered in a line behind. Borganin settled himself in a folding chair surrounded by his aides and advisors, issuing last minute orders by mounted courier to his captains on the field below. Peter stood beside Joshkar, watching the duke's army assemble on the plain, separated from the enemy by little more than the length of a football pitch.

It is one thing to read from the safety and comfort of your living room about the fighting in South Africa, or to hear pensioners relive old battles against the Mahdi Army in the Sudan—quite another to watch an actual battle unfold before your very eyes. Peter was not privy to the calculations rendered by the empress and her staff, nor could he claim much expertise as a strategist. He could only stand and watch the events of that terrible day.

Piernot was garrisoned to capacity. The Imperial Army was entrenched upon the plain, the city walls on its right flank, foothills on the left, and the River Talsis at its back. To Peter's eye, the forces guarding Piernot looked to have a sizable advantage over their own, the city well prepared and well fortified, if not outright impregnable. He knew also that their troops were rested in comparison to their own and set to fight upon familiar ground. They held, so to speak, the home team advantage.

For their forward echelon, the queen's captains chose to array an unbroken double rank of archers along their entire front, and another three ranks of long spears and poleaxes directly behind, all very well entrenched. The bulk of their forces, the core of their army, were lightly armed by comparison and arranged in columns by cohort, like a series of dominoes behind the van. And behind those cohorts were ranged lines of mangonel for hurling missiles. Still farther back, almost out of sight, were groups of baggage cars and camp followers. To cap off their defenses, two large bodies of heavily armed cavalry guarded the enemy's flanks, one near the walls of the city, the other situated atop the first line of foothills to Peter's right.

All in all, it was an impressive show of force and to his way of thinking sufficiently intimidating. The plans he'd heard discussed within the command tent the day before seemed obscure to him now, and the arrangement of their own forces more than a little incoherent in comparison. Borganin had troops deployed in a lopsided fashion on two sides of the city and a ragtag line of soldiers off to one side, occupying the middle ground opposite the enemy's main force. Peter began to harbor serious doubts about their own chances of success. *Could Borganin really be so ill prepared?*

He supposed the queen's captains must have assumed the duke would come to his senses, now that he could see what he was up against, and perhaps sue for peace. Joshkar offered some insight on the enemy's thinking. "Watch and learn, young biscuit king. The queen's men are old school. Their experience," he instructed, "leads them to believe that Lord Borganin will take the time and effort to muster his troops in line with their own before hostilities actually commence. They expect he will leave the city alone for the time being and focus his attentions on them."

The battle began almost as he spoke those words, with Borganin's siege engines hurling great blocks of stone and balls of sticky flame against the left side of the city, whatever the enemy's expectations. The appearance of a concerted assault upon the walls of Piernot was bolstered by the arrival of crossbow archers and men equipped with scaling ladders. The Imperial Army in their fortified camp could not have failed to hear those opening salvos, but were essentially blind to what was occurring well apart from them on the far side of the city. For the moment there was little they could do but stand fast and hope that Piernot's garrison could manage well enough without them.

From where Peter stood, he could see the queen's captains conferring while Borganin's army meanwhile drifted casually into line. It must have been very tempting indeed for the enemy to rush the rebels' carelessly ordered van, but that would have entailed the abandonment of their painstakingly organized defensive positions. They did not succumb to the duke's thinly disguised effort to lure them out. Cooler heads prevailed. The Imperial Army opting to hold firm and await further developments.

Once it was clear that the city's defenders had taken seriously the attack upon the left hand wall, Borganin gave the signal for the next phase of his offensive. More siege engines and assault troops were brought to bear, but this time against the right hand curtain wall. This was also a ruse, but an apparently effective one.

Because the city garrison had earlier committed to the defense of the far left wall, the right curtain wall was now lightly defended. Peter could see the queen's captain's gesticulating wildly. If left unchecked, even a half-hearted and disorderly attack upon the right wall presented a serious threat to Piernot.

The enemy's first reaction was to deter this new assault with a quick volley from their archers on the plain. Only a small contingent on their right of line could be properly brought to bear, but not without effect. Peter cringed as the first wave of the duke's men were struck down, sacrificed for the sake of a feint.

Borganin's archers responded with a counter volley of their own, and the battle was well and truly joined. As Borganin's men continued their assault upon the right hand wall, the queen's captains released the heavy cavalry whose duty it was to guard the gap between the city and the right flank of the Imperial Army. It seemed to Peter the logical move.

Borganin's assault troops, understandably, melted away before the enemy's advancing cavalry, abandoning their weapons, ladders and siege engines to save their lives. Encouraged by their success, the queen's horsemen broke ranks in hot pursuit. Borganin, to Peter's surprise, could not have been more pleased. In the blink of an eye the fleeing soldiers were replaced by a penetrating wedge of hardened infantry that had been lying in wait for just this opportunity, their presence on the field carefully concealed during the early morning darkness.

Peter recognized them at once as the company of Stônar guardsmen that had accompanied Minister Tassmat. They plowed their way forward following the base of the wall between the city and the enemy camp, wielding their iron-tipped lances and short swords with enough skill and courage to make a Spartan proud. The astonished cavalry scattered into their own camp sowing chaos. Death and destruction followed in the wake of the fast advancing Stônar Guards.

Peter was very glad for the distance between himself and the battling armies. He could see men falling everywhere. So distant and tiny. The wounded dragging themselves along the ground in a desperate bid to escape.

The guardsmen's audacious maneuver, however, was by no means decisive. The great bulk of the Imperial Army was still very much intact. The queen's captains maintained their composure, calmly and decisively ordering the uncommitted cohorts to turn to their right, enabling them to engage the developing threat. The situation turned suddenly perilous for the padishah's heroic guardsmen. One miscalculation, a moment of hesitation, and their valiant effort was likely wasted.

As fate would have it, the enemy behaved much as Borganin and his best captains anticipated. The enemy's decision to change front and put themselves mostly broadside to the duke's forward van was the prearranged signal to form line and advance. The duke's haphazard lines suddenly coalesced, transforming into a tightly disciplined mass of serried ranks. They advanced in lockstep fashion down upon the exposed enemy flank, with devastating effect. In the absence of a clear target the enemy's mangonels never once got off a single shot, their attenuated front easily overrun.

Borganin called off the pretend assault on the far wall of the city and redeployed those cohorts against the steadily crumbling Imperial Army. At the same time, Weshnut corsairs in the duke's service, ostensibly engaged in a blockade of the city, lowered boats filled with armed warriors to cut off any retreat toward the foothills.

Once unraveled, the end came swiftly, like the turning of a massive tide. Peter could see small groups of imperial soldiers dropping their weapons and thrusting their hands in the air, while the defenders along the crenellated ramparts of the city could only watch in dismay. A few brave souls fought on until the bitter end. The entire affair was over in less than two hours. Although Piernot itself was not yet taken, the Imperial Army was utterly and irretrievably routed.

Borganin's army herded the surviving enemy toward the foothills, well away from the city gates, leaving such appalling carnage heaped upon the field that Peter grew light headed at the sight of it. To make matters worse, the duke ordered all of his entourage to mount up for a "tour" of the battlefield.

Peter opened his mouth to protest, but the look in Borganin's eyes was enough to make him back off. Clearly, the duke wanted the lord arbiter imperial to ride at his side within sight of the city walls. *This war is only half over,* Peter reminded himself. The city still stood. Borganin had either to get Piernot to surrender or take it by force.

So Peter mounted up and rode with the duke and his staff down onto the plain, picking their way through the strewn weapons and corpses. Borganin rode beside Prince Waythur, Menhar and the other battle-weary captains, eliciting from them important details of the fight that he'd been unable to observe from his vantage point upon the rise.

Meanwhile, the less severely injured and wounded from both sides were being carried off the field. The dying were ministered to wherever they had fallen. If one of their own, by a few comrades in arms. If the enemy, by the abject members of the duke's baggage train who were more likely to thieve from those fated to die than offer any reassuring last words. Peter did his best as they rode along to look straight ahead and avoid eye contact with the nightmare swirling all about him. He thought he might spew or tumble from his horse at any moment. The party dared not ride too close to the walls of Piernot, but they were close enough that Peter could look up at the wan faces of the enemy watching their procession from the ramparts in anger and frustration. He prayed to God that Bonifacia was far, far away from this awful scene.

A shout from one of Borganin's officers caught their attention. He pointed in the direction of the city. A postern gate had opened and three men in resplendent armor rode out on horseback under a white flag. "Phaw," sputtered Borganin, his disappointment almost palpable. He was surely hoping it would come down to a fight.

They reined in as they approached, the lead-most horseman removing his helmet in order to speak. Although Peter had been forewarned, the man's appearance still took him by surprise. He gasped aloud. *An Ulfair!* The man's piercing gold eyes blazed at Peter with undisguised contempt. There was no hiding the comparison with wolves. Aside from pupils like knife slits, elongated ears and a lower jaw that protruded just far enough to warrant being called a "muzzle," his face was covered with soft gray fur.

"What is it you want?" growled Borganin impatiently.

"Her Imperial Majesty desires a truce in order that we may recover our dead and wounded."

The corner of Borganin's mouth twitched. "You may ride back and tell your witch that she has until sunrise tomorrow to surrender the city. *We* will take care of your dead and wounded."

The Ulfair captain snarled, revealing two prominent upper canines. "And what of the prisoners?" he asked.

Borganin's eyes narrowed. "You need not concern yourself. I have no intention of wasting precious resources guarding that lot. I will parole them shortly."

The Ulfair officer gestured angrily to his companions. They put spurs to their horses and galloped back to the city.

Satisfied with the magnitude of his victory, the duke steered his mount in the direction of the foothills where his army was busy encamping. The wildly jubilant men of Orn and Taixûs greeted Borganin with a chorus of cheers. Thrusting their left fists in the air above their heads and striking their armor with the blunt edge of their weapons, they cried "Menom! Menom!" some weeping openly for joy. Borganin positively beamed.

"The prisoners," said Borganin, gesturing to Captain Menhar. They rode beyond the camp to the long lines of captives squatting dejectedly in the midday sun. They sat on the side of a rough fell, hands tied behind their backs—loyal soldiers from across the empire: Hemsto, Meflis, Bakus Sura, Bakus Mara, Taixûs, Kaladar and even Orn. Borganin regarded them coldly from atop his saddle.

"Are you going to parole them?" inquired Menhar.

"Are there any Ulfair left alive amongst their captains?" he replied.

"Just one," said Menhar.

"Hang him," instructed Borganin. "Make sure everyone can see."

"Your grace!" cried Lord Palkvo, in disbelief.

Borganin turned to face him. "You have something to add Lord Palkvo?"

Palkvo had time to reconsider his outburst, carefully considering his next words. "If not paroled with the others, would it not be better at least to hold the Ulfair for ransom?"

"Ransom?" scoffed Borganin. "What use is ransom to me? By tomorrow morning the city will be ours. As for parole, that is a courtesy reserved for Gwellem. The rules of war do not apply to off-worlders. Hang him," repeated Borganin. "And brand the others on the neck to help them remember which side they chose to take. Then let them return to where ever they call home, so long as it is not Piernot. They can tell their friends and families they were preserved from death by the Duke of Menom. If any express a desire to join our ranks and are willing to swear their loyalty to me, they may be spared the brand." He sniffed the air. "One more thing while it occurs to me. Separate out the Gwellem officers who still wish to return to Piernot. I want their right hand severed before their release to prevent them from ever again taking up the sword against me, no exceptions. Branding is too good for these traitors."

This last command, a true act of mayhem, caused a murmur of complaint amongst the officers present, but not one of them dared to contradict the duke.

"As you wish, my lord," said Menhar with a satisfied grin.

"Monster!" blurted Peter, unable to contain himself. Joshkar put a hand on his shoulder, but Peter would not be deterred. Many eyes turned to him. He burned red with anger and disgust. "You're a vile, despicable creature," added Peter for good measure.

The duke sneered derisively. "You have much to learn about war, young de Soto. You *will* learn with time. Captain Menhar," he said, dismissing Peter altogether, "see to your army and the prisoners. I presume the Ulfair witch will not surrender Piernot without a fight, so I expect all of you at my tent after prayer this evening to plan our siege of the city. Oh, and Captain Menhar, make sure the boy is present for the execution."

Menhar arranged the hanging in a matter of minutes. The unfortunate Ulfair captain was taken aside and strung from a sturdy oak within eyesight of all the prisoners—a captive audience in the most literal sense.

"A lesson to all would be occupiers and oppressors," intoned Menhar, as the mounting block was removed from beneath the condemned man. Peter was inclined, of course, to avert his eyes, but Joshkar insisted that the best way to ripen his sense of justice was to witness an instance of brutal injustice. Peter, frankly, could have done without the lesson. It was enough to watch the dolabra hew the right hand of one man, let alone twenty-two in succession.

Peter had to admit the duke was right to some extent. After witnessing these initial atrocities, the remaining twenty-three hundred or so prisoners acquiesced to being branded on the neck without very much complaint, pitifully grateful for the opportunity to return to their homes alive and more or less intact. A nearly equal number avoided this terrible punishment altogether by offering to change sides and assist in the effort to storm the very city they'd just fought so hard to defend. Peter wasn't sure he could blame them. He just knew that he was filled with a deep sense of anger, guilt, and resentment.

He was in no mood to attend a prayer circle that evening. Borganin and his supporters, he was certain, would use the occasion to express their gratitude to The Eternal Architect for the day's victory, and he was loath to stand beside even the best-intentioned man in his army after the appalling treatment of prisoners. He had absolutely no interest either in attending the duke's planning session for the morning's renewal of hostilities. Joshkar did all he could to encourage Peter to attend the meeting. "But you must go," he argued. "We need eyes and ears inside the tent and I can't gain entrance without you." Peter could not be swayed. He threw himself on his cot and lay there staring up at the inner folds of his tent.

"Fine. Have it your way," sighed Joshkar. "I will prowl about on your behalf and see what I can learn."

"You do that," retorted Peter, lending as much bitterness to his tone as he could muster. He hated everything about the benighted and twisted world he'd found himself in and felt so homesick it burned in his chest. His only hope for ever returning to Earth lay in the hands of an embattled queen, barricaded behind the walls of the city they were about to besiege. His only true friend and relative in the world, Bonifacia, was lost or—God forbid—*dead*. He tucked his face into the nook of his elbow and cried himself to sleep.

He was awakened by loud shouts in the night coming from within their own camp. Joshkar poked his head through the fly a few moments later. "Get up, Peter. There is news worth hearing." Curious, he slipped off his cot to follow Joshkar over to the duke's command tent. Raised voices emanated from inside. As always, the guards let him pass unhindered, but this time, refused Joshkar entry.

Prince Waythur stood with both hands planted on the table. His face fairly pulsed with anger. "How could you not have known?" he bellowed at Borganin.

The duke responded coolly. "I swear to you Demkin, I had no idea Balkur Hamut would try something like this. I can't believe it's true."

"Believe it, Borganin. You set me up!"

"Nonsense. We are allies."

"Then you will ride with me now and throw that miserable bastard back across the Keartlands."

"What's going on?" Peter whispered to the Ornish officer at his elbow.

The fellow looked at him, a little surprised to see who had asked the question. "The padishah's troops have seized the capital of Taixûs." Peter's jaw must have visibly dropped because he added without being prompted, "If the farmer does not guard the hen house…"

So that was it! Prince Waythur, anxious to share in the spoils at Piernot, had left his back door open to the unscrupulous Padishah of Stônar.

"How can this have happened?" demanded Waythur. "You assured me Balkur Hamut was behind you in this scheme."

"He was. *He is,*" replied Borganin. There is some miscommunication perhaps. Calm yourself, Demkin. We will clear this up and get you back to your palace."

"Miscommunication?! The Stônar flag flies over Balva!"

"I promise you. After we have taken the city, we will get this all straightened out."

"You expect me to continue here?"

"Of course," replied Borganin. "Now it is even more imperative that we seize Piernot. If we walk away from here without taking it, Balkur Hamut will see us both as weak. We can't afford to take that chance, now can we? Besides, the padishah would not dare refuse you back your lands once we've broken the power of the Ulfair. You see, Demkin, you must stay and finish the job."

"Don't make demands on me, Borganin. I'll do as I please."

The duke's demeanor turned ugly. "I will put it to you straight, Prince Waythur. If you leave me here to defeat the Ulfair witch on my own, you will find yourself crushed between Orn and Stônar when I am done. That is a promise."

Waythur glared at Borganin. His response came slowly. "Very well, *Lord Borganin*. We shall take the city, *together*."

Peter slipped out and returned to his own tent, leaving Borganin and Waythur's captains to argue over the finer points of the impending siege. Joshkar was anxious to hear what he had learned.

"Frankly, I was surprised to hear them argue so openly," confided Peter.

"The command tent is hardly a public venue, but I grant your point. The duke does not shy away from public confrontation when he is confident of victory. It only adds to his reputation for success. He's a champion browbeater."

Peter chuckled at that.

"What's so funny?" asked Joshkar.

"The expression you used. Until coming here, I never gave it much thought."

He returned to his tent and went back to sleep, or at least tried to. Orders issued from the command tent set many things in motion during the night. At some point panicked cries and the sound of weapons clashing startled Peter from his sleep. Joshkar motioned for him to stay put and, once again, slipped out to see what was going on. He returned after all the noise subsided.

"So, what's happening?" asked Peter. "Were we attacked?"

"No," said Joshkar. "The Taixans have murdered the Stônar guardsmen that were with us."

"Murdered? Every one of them?"

He nodded grimly. "The duke will be furious."

Chapter 12

The Siege of Piernot

Peter awoke the next morning, convinced that the madness of the preceding day had run its course. Surely the empress would have sense enough to surrender the city without further bloodshed? They'd destroyed the Imperial Army. What purpose could there be in holding the city? He prayed beside his cot in the privacy of his tent, asking God to help her see the wisdom to capitulate. The duke would surely treat the queen with respect, allowing her to retire quietly from public life, while he succeeded to the imperial throne.

Joshkar greeted him looking broody and apprehensive.

"What's wrong?" asked Peter.

He hesitated. "The duke intends to personally take part in the siege of Piernot. He's making history and does not want to be remembered as having watched the event from a chair atop the rise."

"Very gallant of him," replied Peter. "So the queen doesn't intend to surrender after all. More's the pity. Ah well, maybe an arrow will find the duke."

"You don't understand, Peter. You are not released from his standard."

"What are you telling me? I'm expected to ride into the city with him?" Peter's voice quavered. "Why? Why should he care?"

"To teach you a lesson for your outburst yesterday."

"Because of that?"

"There's no getting out of it, Peter. Let's have a bite to eat and get ourselves ready."

The butterflies in his stomach prevented Peter from downing much of his morning's porridge. Joshkar helped him on with his armor as he had many times already, but with added significance. "There's no point in giving you a sword," said Joshkar. "That would only draw unwanted attention. You could never wield it properly anyhow." He rubbed the stubble on his chin. "I have an idea." He went round the outside of the tent, returning with a small kite shaped shield and a hefty dagger. "In retrospect, we should have taken the fat armorer's offer to make you a proper buckler." He hefted the little shield in one hand. "Better than nothing. I don't suppose you know how to handle a blade?" he inquired, before handing over the dagger.

"I've still got my folding knife." Peter pulled it from his pocket. "Let me near Borganin and I'll prove to you how well I can use it."

"So you have the pluck, do you think?"

Peter knew full well he didn't. He had no intention of committing suicide. They dropped that line of conversation.

"All I can say about the buckler," counseled Joshkar, "is that if something undesirable ends up coming your way, hold up your left arm. Hopefully that will prevent it." Peter was suddenly very grateful for the fact that Gwellem had not yet mastered gunpowder.

A low rumble of kettledrums announced that it was time to mount up. The horses were readied and they joined the duke's company, rallying behind his standard. Nothing was said of the murderous events of the evening, the slaughter of a hundred and fifty brave men apparently little more than an unfortunate footnote. They rode in silence, the bulk of the army having taken up their assigned positions during the night. Only the sound of jangling bridles and the occasional nickering horse indicated that something major was afoot. In comparison to the day before, it seemed to Peter an otherwise uncommonly pleasant morning. The sun was shining. A few soft clouds drifted lazily overhead carried on a gentle breeze that lightly lifted the rebel banners.

They made the same rise to observe the opening of hostilities. There was no last minute parley, no final warnings, no diplomatic niceties between adversaries. Borganin did not tarry. The empress made her feelings known by continuing to fly the imperial standard with its running wolf over the battlements of Piernot.

Peter dismounted and looked upon that too familiar flag. He felt a fool dressed as he was, and a traitor to boot, although he owed the Ulfair queen no love or loyalty. "She has brought this upon herself," he muttered, in a vain effort to satisfy his own conscience.

Borganin gazed briefly down upon the isolated city, then turned to Menhar and said simply, "You may begin, Captain."

Menhar nodded in turn to his lieutenant, which set events in motion. Kettledrums reverberated across the plain and the great lumbering siege engines were rolled into position. Only this time it was no feint. The soldiers on those ramparts must have been dismayed to see that fully half the machines deployed against them were seized from their own army the day before. With each *whoosh* of the trebuchet and mangonel massive bundles of rock and rough iron vaulted across the sky to be dashed against the ancient city walls. Peter recoiled from the sound of exploding stone.

The duke stood alone the whole time, his hands clenched tightly behind his back, hardly speaking to anyone. A messenger arrived. He turned toward his entourage after a brief conversation with the man. "Mount up. It is time."

Time for what? wondered Peter. Their horses were brought forward. Bonnie acted uncharacteristically skittish. Peter bounced in the stirrup several times before managing to climb on her back. They rode down to the plain where caustic smoke from the burning city had settled in the low ground stinging their eyes and blurring their vision. At the forward-most mangonel, not a hundred paces from the city wall, they halted. The sound of creaking, straining timbers and tensed fiber blended with the excited shouts of soldiers as they repeatedly loaded and fired the terrifying machine. The ground shook with each volley.

Three ranks of archers, the first rank armed with crossbows, advanced in line to stand with Borganin's party. Peter was close enough to the duke to hear him speak with Menhar and Prince Waythur. "Any moment now," he said. "Wait for it." A tremor ran beneath the feet of their horses causing Bonnie to dance about and several other horses to rear up. The towering city wall moaned deeply, like a grief-stricken old man. At first, Peter thought he'd imagined it, then the entire corner face sagged downward. A gigantic cloud of dust and debris billowed up from the collapsing wall, racing toward them like a typhoon and all at once obscuring the city from view. Peter had just enough time to avert his eyes before it engulfed him and the others in their party. Bonnie was not so fortunate. She darted off in wide-eyed panic, Peter clinging blindly to the pommel.

He blinked several times before the dust settled and was able to fully open his eyes—only to find himself wedged up against Menhar. The captain leered angrily at him. "Watch what you're doing, you sodding little prick!" Raising an iron-cleated boot, he kicked Peter solidly on the right thigh. Bonnie reflexively edged away with a sudden jerk, taking Peter back out of Menhar's reach.

Joshkar, having temporarily lost sight of his charge, booted his horse over to where Peter sat doubled up in the saddle. "Are you all right?" he asked.

"I'm fine," he lied, between clenched teeth. Peter thought for sure Menhar had broken his leg.

The siege engines broke off their assault. The duke's company and the line of archers began to advance slowly forward and Peter urged Bonnie to follow along. They halted closer to the walls where a sizable breach had been formed.

"The sappers have done their job," remarked Borganin.

On a signal from Menhar the front rank of archers let loose with quarrels from their crossbows, followed closely by volleys of fletched arrows from archers at their back. Sharp cries of anguish reached Peter's ears as men behind the breach and atop the parapets were struck down with scythe-like proficiency.

"Buckler!" yelled Joshkar as a hail of arrows poured back down in response. *Tuck, tuck, tuck.* The defenders' arrows thudded into the ground, felling both horses and men on either side of Peter. He raised the little shield above his head, deflecting more than one glancing blow. He might have gone deaf from all the shouting and screaming of those about him in the throes of death, were it not for his own heart beating so loudly all else seemed muted in comparison.

It felt an eternity, but the rain of missiles could not have lasted more than a minute. Bowmen on both sides quickly exhausted their supply of munitions. It was no small miracle, in Peter's estimation, that he survived that maelstrom unscathed.

A colossal din rose behind him as Borganin's army rushed toward the breach. Armed with long ladders, hammers and iron pry bars, they threw themselves with uncanny abandon against the shattered curtain wall. The first to reach the wall carried thick fiber mats above their heads as protection against burning tar and oil, which the defenders sluiced through machicolations beneath the crenellated parapets. The mats did not always work and the injuries inflicted in such cases were horrifying in the extreme.

In time, the rebel troops succeeded in sweeping the defenders away from the gap, and the duke signaled for those in his company to pass within.

Following along, Peter urged his horse over the fallen timbers, debris and corpses, emerging within the outermost ring road of the city. Piernot was in pandemonium. Every corner of the great city reverberated with the clamor of skirmishing soldiers, the cold ring of steel against steel, the howling expressions of fear and lamentation. The swallow-tailed banners of Menom fluttered with solemn significance in the grit-laden air.

Borganin laughed, a deep hearty and conceited laugh that made Peter's blood boil. He fingered the dagger that Joshkar had given him, but was prevented from manifesting his intentions by a desperately aimed arrow. It brushed past Peter's ear and struck the duke squarely behind the right shoulder. He twisted in pain, but did not fall from his horse. It took a moment for the duke's startled staff to recognize what had happened. They raced to his side and moved to help him from his charger.

"No! Not here," he barked angrily. "Find me a decent house to rest in, and a physician." Several officers scuttled away to do his bidding. He leaned over in his saddle to speak with Menhar. Peter was close enough to hear him plainly. "Tell your men they can take what they please. I care not. Menom will be the new capital of my empire. I want this city expunged. Burn it to the ground. Do you hear? Not a stone left standing to say it ever stood. And I want that witch's head. Find her and kill her, Menhar."

Menhar smiled conspiratorially. "As my lord wishes." He nodded an informal salute and rode off to join the troops doing battle farther down the street.

It was a pity about the city, but for the moment Peter could only think of himself. "Joshkar, if they kill the empress, I will never get home! We must do something to stop Menhar."

Joshkar gave Peter a considering look then glanced over at Borganin. "The duke is in no condition to pay us much heed. Follow me and stay close." They turned their mounts and slipped away from Borganin's company. Joshkar was right. In the relative chaos, no one noticed their departure or much cared.

Peter had it in his head that they would steal up on Menhar and do away with him before any harm could befall the queen. But Joshkar had something else in mind because he headed in an entirely opposite direction.

"Where are you going?" cried Peter. "Menhar is that way!"

"Don't argue. Just follow me."

They cut their way at a gallop through knots of skirmishing soldiers and fleeing civilians, doing their damnedest to avoid any entanglement. Down narrow cobbled streets and lanes they flew at breakneck speed, their horses' hooves clattering loudly and dispersing terrified passersby in all directions. Tripping up a long flight of stone steps, they reined in at last at an open square at the center of which stood an imposing and evidently ancient edifice.

"Do you remember I said if you ever get to Piernot you may yet see one or two of the old temples?" said Joshkar. "This is one of them."

Peter gawked at the fantastic old building as they dismounted and tied up their horses. It reminded him a great deal of the Church of La Veracruz in La Venta do Carballiño, with its exquisite tower, like an enormous peacock tail feather, but made entirely of stone. He associated Carballiño with *pulpeiras* and occasional trips to the *fiesta* with Bonifacia. A flash of homesickness burned within his heart and he wondered once again about the fate of his precious cousin.

"I presume you didn't bring me here to go sightseeing," groused Peter, worry feeding his impatience.

"The Household Guard will not surrender willingly. Menhar will need time to regather his forces for an attack on the palace. That gives us time to get there before him."

"Get there before him? How?"

"Through there," said Joshkar, gesturing toward the ancient temple. "There's a passageway that leads underground to a wing of the palace, or at least I hope there is. Before the Great Renewal, the ancient king's of Kaladar would travel through the tunnel to stand before the altar."

"How do you know all this? I thought you were from Bakus Sura?"

"My ancestors were hereditary priests of this temple. When the old ways were ended my family fled to Bakus Sura. The stories have been handed down through many, many generations." He smiled at something unspoken.

"You mean you've never actually seen this tunnel?"

"I've never actually been inside the temple," admitted Joshkar, "but I think I could accurately describe every facet of it to you in detail."

Peter was skeptical, but he certainly didn't have any better ideas. "You'll have to prove that to me. How do we get inside?"

Joshkar didn't hesitate. He walked straight up to the main door, with Peter running to catch up with him. There was a lot of activity and people darting about the square, but none focused on the temple. Despite its prominent location, it had more the look of a monument than a living building, something to be admired by passersby, but never actually approached.

The great bronze studded door was locked. "I don't suppose your ancestors took the key with them?"

Joshkar shot him a derisive glance then walked around the far side of the building with Peter still trailing after him. There was a much smaller, less formal door on the side of the temple. It was locked as well, but Joshkar pried it open with a sturdy blade.

They entered the structure from the direction of a small alcove. The building was dark and silent except for the sound of cooing birds in the rafters and the little bit of washed out light that managed to filter through the grimed-over windows floating high above. Joshkar was crestfallen when they entered the nave. The temple had been stripped bare. So empty in fact that even the gentle scuffing of their heels on the stone floor reverberated off the naked walls and columns.

"There should be a line of seven marble saints and the holy servants of The Eternal Architect right over there." Joshkar pointed off to their left. "And over there, the golden adytum that held Karnum's sacred helmet. The great oak altar carved by Farous from a single tree and the crystal chandelier that rivaled the Great Star for brilliance. They've taken everything." It was the first time Peter had ever seen him close to tears.

"What about the tunnel?" he prompted.

It was enough to rouse Joshkar from his unhappy reverie. He looked about the nave. "Over there. Near where the altar once stood."

He pointed to a gap in the wall framed by waist-high carvings of two wide-eyed shorka. Their gaping mouths and flaring tongues reminding Peter a little of imperial lions. They walked between the towering columns to stand beside them. There was nothing to indicate any sort of entrance. Only a vacant stone wall with a few nicks and holes and a bit of sheared-off ironwork.

"The tunnel's behind there, do you think?"

"I'm sure of it. There was a great tapestry that hung here in my ancestors' time, a depiction of the Sun and the Comet. It covered this entire wall between the shorkas. The kings of old came out of the tunnel from behind it."

"So how do *we* get in?"

"I don't know." He inspected each and every block in the wall for some clue, some anomaly that might hint at the location of the mechanism. When that provided no clear answers, he got down on one knee to examine the left hand shorka in detail. "You check the other one."

Peter did as he asked. "Nothing," he said after several fruitless minutes.

"Me neither." In frustration, Joshkar pulled the knife he'd used to pry the door and traced the tip along the joints between the stonework." Still nothing.

"Are you absolutely certain this is the right place?"

"Yes!" snapped Joshkar, with growing impatience.

"You must be missing something then. Think back on the stories. Some little detail you're leaving out."

He closed his eyes, thinking silently to himself, then shook his head. "I can't think of anything."

Peter was beginning to think the whole business about his family being temple priests was a lot of bilge and balderdash to entertain generations of little Joshkars. They sat cross-legged on the cold floor in front of the empty wall, Joshkar nervously tapping the floor with the hilt of his knife.

"Maybe…?" speculated Peter. He had an idea, but it was a long shot.

"Maybe what?" pressed Joshkar.

"Well, maybe nothing…The portal that Bonnie and I came through. It needed a key. I was joking earlier when I asked you if your ancestors had taken the key with them when they left."

"If I had a key I would have said so, wouldn't I?"

"But the key to the portal didn't look anything like the kind of key we're used to. It was a disk. A sort of funny coin."

Joshkar studied Peter's face for a long moment, racking his brain. Then he slowly held up his hand.

"Your ring!" gasped Peter. "The ring your brother gave you!" Peter was distressed the time Joshkar had shown it to him and hadn't bothered to take a close look. It was a sort of moonstone set in a clasp.

"It's been in the family forever." Joshkar pulled the ring from his finger, then employing the tip of his knife, gingerly pried the stone from its setting. It was milky white and nearly round, cut to resemble a bent over tumblebug. "How did you use your key to get through the portal?" he asked.

"It fit into the palm of a gnome's hand."

"His palm?" Almost in unison, they turned their heads to glance first at the vacant wall and then at the two flanking shorka. Joshkar slipped the empty band back on his finger then scrambling to his feet shouted to Peter, "You take the left one. I'll take the right this time."

Peter gave his assigned shorka a proper once-over, but could see no place for the moonstone to fit comfortably.

"Peter," exclaimed Joshkar. "Come over here. Take a look at the tongue on this one." The shorka's exposed tongue sloped back down the creature's throat and out of sight. He regarded Peter with new found hope. "Do you suppose?"

Peter held his breath as Joshkar gently dropped the moonstone down the shorka's tapering gullet. It fell effortlessly into place and then rolled back out of sight, as if the shorka had swallowed it whole.

There was a heavy rumble behind the wall and they both scrambled out of the way. Part of the wall began to slide back, accompanied by the sound of twisting metal. The door ground to a halt no more than two-thirds of the way open. Age and lack of maintenance had taken its toll on the mechanism.

Joshkar stepped forward to examine the entrance. The door was firmly jammed in place, leaving just enough room for an average man to squeeze through. "Its day has run," said Joshkar. "But you see!" he cried, hardly able to contain his excitement. "The old stories are true."

"Yes, I can see that," replied Peter. "It's very dark in there." Frankly, he didn't enjoy the feeling of déjà vu. "Did you bring anything to light our way?"

"It's not like I planned this part," quipped Joshkar. He ordered Peter to hold tight while he went off in search of a lamp. A short while later, Peter was surprised to hear the sound of horses' hooves *inside* the temple! He craned his neck to have a better look and saw Joshkar tying their animals to a column, a lantern hooked to the pommel of one of the saddles.

"Menhar is burning the city," he explained. "People are fleeing in all directions and everything is for the taking. I couldn't very well leave the horses outside. We'd never see them again." He grabbed the lantern and joined Peter at the entrance to the passage.

"I'll go first," said Joshkar. Holding the lantern before him, he stepped over the threshold and disappeared into the inky darkness. "There's a levered mechanism back here for operating the door, but it's jammed up solid. Hey! The stone from my ring is here too," he chirped, happily. "Sitting in a little pocket indentation. I was afraid I'd lost it."

"Good show," replied Peter.

"Well, come along then. What's keeping you?"

Taking a deep breath Peter passed within, adding one request. "If you feel any sort of vibration coming from the floor or walls, you'll let me know straight away. Won't you?" He planned to bolt right back out if he encountered anything remotely similar.

"You needn't fear. This isn't one of your portals," assured Joshkar. They walked together along the vaulted corridor for perhaps ten or fifteen minutes before encountering a mountain of rubble that blocked their progress. The foundations of a much newer building had apparently breached one side of the passage, causing the ceiling to collapse.

Joshkar climbed to the top and held the lantern to the narrow gap between the summit and the ceiling. "It's clear through," he announced, "but we'll have to crawl on our bellies for a few spans. We've no time or means to dig our way across."

Peter shed a few pieces of less essential armor and crawled his way up and over the debris, emerging only a little worse for wear. It was clear going on the far side. Another ten minutes of steady walking and they arrived at a wall with the same sort of levered mechanism as the temple. "Where do you think we will come out?" he asked. "Assuming it still works."

Joshkar shrugged uncertainly. "One of the older wings of the palace perhaps. No king has passed this way in hundreds of years."

"After you," said Peter.

Joshkar spat into his hands and pulled down hard on the lever. Like its twin in the temple, the heavy door slid obediently toward them and then off to one side, only this time, there was the sound of splintering wood and the clatter of objects hitting the floor on the other side. Peter winced. The passageway had taken them into a library. Evidently bookshelves had been built against the wall covering the tunnel entrance.

Weapons in hand, they stepped over the broken remnants of the bookcase and the jumble of bound volumes strewn across the floor. "Do you suppose anyone heard that?" asked Peter.

"The city is under siege. There's no reason for people to be hanging about the library."

"So where to now?"

Joshkar gestured for him to follow. He had no better sense of the place than Peter. They roamed the empty corridors searching for an exit to the outside, wary all the while of whom they might encounter.

The library, as it turned out, was buried deep within the sprawling palace so it took them a frightfully long time to finally locate a room with a clear view of the outside. From its splendidly framed windows they could see straight across the palace green and over toward the ancient keep.

"We don't have much time," remarked Joshkar, quickly assessing the situation.

Peter had to agree. Beyond the palace grounds great clouds of billowing smoke and flame reached high into the sky. The Household Guard, volunteer militia, and what remained of the city garrison had fallen back to the palace to make a final stand. The situation looked very grim indeed. The palace perimeter walls were designed for privacy, not defense—too low and too slight to long withstand a concerted assault. The defenders stood atop costly furniture hauled from the royal residence to serve as makeshift bulwarks. Behind these wretched barricades milled hundreds of frightened refugees.

"I expect the queen will be somewhere near the old tower," said Joshkar. He scrubbed the back of his neck with one hand. "I'm not sure what sort of reception we will receive. This could be a big mistake, Peter."

"You're not backing out now? Not after all this?" He exclaimed. "You've done famously."

"It's not me I'm worried about." His eyes told Peter all he needed to know.

"We *must* reach her, Joshkar. The queen is the only person I know of who can tell me how to get back through the portal. She may even know where I can find Bonnie."

"Of course," he replied. "There's no point slinking about. Stay close to me." He followed Joshkar out into the palace garden. They strolled straight across the green toward the tower as if they owned the place. Near the perimeter wall captains and lower ranking officers were busy reorganizing remnants of their tattered army into ad hoc battalions for the final defense. There was far too much going on for them to take any notice of their passage.

"Over there," said Joshkar, pointing. A cluster of officers dressed in imperial finery stood near a fluttering standard thrust in the ground. A host of officers and messengers sat atop their mounts, surrounded by a ring of guardsmen.

Peter and Joshkar stood tall and walked briskly toward the assembled company until stopped by a young third cestus of the Household Guard. He took them in with a distinctly puzzled expression, then chose his words carefully. "State your business, my lord."

"We must speak with the empress immediately," replied Peter.

The guardsman was polite but firm. "I'm afraid you've picked a rather bad time, sir. You need only look about. The empress is a bit preoccupied just now."

"This is a matter of great urgency," persisted Peter.

"Forgive me, my lord. By order, only members of the household and general staff may approach. If we survive this day, I suggest you seek an audience with the lord chancellor."

Peter had to admit the man had good reason for being stubborn, but he was not about to give up. He removed his helmet and displayed the wolf that hung from his neck. The fellow's eyes widened at the sight of Peter's stunted brows. He removed the chain from about his neck and handed over the wolf. "Take this to Her Imperial Majesty. Tell her the *lord arbiter imperial* is here and begs an audience."

He inspected the pendant cupped in his hand. There was no way for Peter to know what the fellow thought or knew of the "lord arbiter imperial," good or bad, but his tone indicated he immediately sensed trouble.

"Guards! Keep a close eye on these two. They are not to move from this spot until I return. Not one inch, do you hear." They were immediately surrounded by a ring of very tense guardsmen, fingers poised and ready on the triggers of their crossbows.

Peter and Joshkar spent a few anxious minutes cooling their heels. The cestus returned in the company of an Ulfair gentleman, richly clothed in civilian attire. "I am Lord Chancellor Zamarfin," declared the Ulfair. He looked Peter and Joshkar up and down. "Leave your weapons here and come with me, *quickly.*"

They followed along. A number of heads belonging to senior captains and court officials, both Ulfair and Gwellem, turned to observe their approach. They stepped aside, bringing Peter suddenly face-to-face with a graying Ulfair woman—the empress—Borganin's so-called "witch."

Like all of her kind, Empress Xhôn resembled, in some respects, a wolf. She stood tall and dignified with unsettling green eyes. She was dressed in a magnificent ground length cape edged in delicate black lace. Standing in the company of a queen was something altogether new to Peter. He instinctively got down on one knee, offering his obeisance. Joshkar followed suit.

"A noble gesture," remarked the queen. "But I think perhaps you mock me."

Peter looked up at her, completely taken aback. He could just make out the tips of her long white canines. "Mock, your majesty? I would never do."

"Some of my captains might take issue with you." She gestured toward a wan faced Gwellem with a bandage wrapped round the stump of his right arm. Peter felt sick in the pit of his stomach. "Get up the two of you," she commanded. "Borganin and that cur Menhar will be outside these walls in force within the hour. I have no time to trifle with you. You claim to be the lord arbiter imperial. *Rubbish*. You're just a boy." She opened her hand to display his aunt's pendant. "Tell me, how is it you come to be in possession of this object? It belongs to me. And how did you manage to get inside the palace grounds undetected? Be quick."

"My name is Peter López de Soto, your majesty. I am the great-great-great grandson of Manuel López, the lord arbiter imperial. I came through the portal that you yourself ordered opened. Dashwan would confirm all this, but he was killed by Menhar during our ride to Piernot."

Her gray fur-covered snout twisted slightly. "You are the *great-great-great* grandson of Manuel López?" she repeated.

"Yes, your majesty. I make no claim on the title of lord arbiter. The Duke of Menom forced it upon me against my will. It was part of his scheme to unseat you."

"The old wizard you sent to activate the portal," interjected the lord chancellor. "He messed up the calibrations, the imbecile. Great-great-great grandson," he said, shaking his head in disgust. "The security protocols allowed the boy through. That is obvious. There must have been enough similarity in their genetic sequencing for a match."

"That may account for it," replied the queen. "The portals are failing with age. We should have acted sooner. We left no margin for error."

"Clearly, I was brought here by accident," blurted Peter, forgetting all formalities and proper etiquette. "Please, your majesty. You must help me get back home. The token that was inside the wolf was left behind. I can't open the portal door without it."

Her sharp eyes studied Peter carefully, but she did not answer.

"Does Borganin know what you're up to?" inquired the lord chancellor.

"No," replied Peter. "He was wounded by an arrow and we were able to slip away."

"Our sentries have reported this incident," said the queen, "but you have not answered me. How did you enter the palace grounds undetected?"

"There is a tunnel under the wall," said Peter. This caused a great stir amongst the queen's party.

"You need not fear, your majesty," said Joshkar, speaking for the first time. "Lord Borganin has no knowledge of it. It is of very ancient provenance."

"We came to warn you," added Peter. "The duke has ordered your assassination. And he means to raze the city to the ground."

There was a heavy silence.

"You're certain of this?" asked the queen.

"I was present when he gave the order to Captain Menhar, your majesty. I heard him with my own ears."

The chancellor chimed in. "Borganin is a villain. He will stop at nothing. You must leave the palace at once, your majesty."

She gave the chancellor a stony look. "I will do nothing of the kind Zamarfin. My place is here…to the end if it comes to that."

The lord chancellor opened his mouth as if to argue, but the empress quickly silenced him. "I will not leave Piernot, Lord Chancellor, and that is an end to the discussion."

"Your majesty, forgive me. This tunnel they speak of…I believe it could be of use to us," interjected an Ulfair captain. "We could surprise or perhaps outflank Borganin. That would give us a fighting chance, or at the very least some time to improve our position."

Joshkar responded immediately, quickly disabusing the captain of this idea. "I will not betray my comrades in arms. If the queen wishes to use the passageway to leave the city before it falls, that is fine with me, but I will not be party to any plan that would endanger my comrades."

"Traitor!" bellowed the captain, baring his canines. "Your majesty, give me five minutes alone with these turncoats. I will learn the location of this tunnel."

"Your majesty," replied Joshkar calmly, "I believe this boy emerged from the portal for a purpose, as did his ancestor. You must see it in your heart to aid him, for the good of all our people. That is the only reason I have led him here."

"Preposterous," exclaimed the chancellor. "The young off-worlder came through the portal by accident. He has admitted as much."

"And yet," argued Joshkar, "the lad is to all intents and purposes the lord arbiter imperial, is he not? He carries the uniform and token of office to prove it. Step beyond these palace walls and ask anyone you meet. His authenticity is not a matter of dispute. Even your own Household Guard hesitated in his presence."

"Your majesty," countered the chancellor in growing exasperation, "this Gwellem takes us for fools. Plainly, the boy's standing is nothing less than a charade orchestrated by the Duke of Menom."

Her eyes met Peter's and then turned to Joshkar. "What is your name and regiment?"

"Master Bowman Joshkar, your majesty. From the house of Othmond. 3rd Battalion, Second Cohort of Orn Archers."

"That is a Kaladwen name, but I detect a Bakan accent, do I not, Master Bowman?"

"Bakus Sura, your majesty."

Her eyes widened. "Perhaps you are right, Bowman Joshkar. Perhaps there is more to this than any of us understand."

"Your majesty..." interrupted the chancellor, but she waved him silent.

"Bowman Joshkar, I believe we may be able to help one another." Her tone of voice flowed with greater force and determination. "Chancellor, tend to our defenses. I must return to the keep. I promise you, I will not be long. Oh, and see that someone returns these men their weapons." She turned to face Joshkar and Peter. "Come with me."

The queen made her way toward the old tower at the heart of the palace with long but dignified strides, Peter, Joshkar and a small contingent of the Household Guard in tow. The keep was the only part of the palace built as a deliberate fortress, although it had received many alterations over the centuries that detracted from its original purpose. They entered the great hall through a portcullis that may not have been lowered in generations.

The queen swept ahead of them and seated herself behind a writing desk so large and heavy it looked to have grown right out of the stone floor. "Equerry Korsand," said the queen.

A Gwellem officer with salt and pepper brows and large moustache stepped forward, saluting smartly. "Your majesty?"

"Be so kind as to fetch Cestus Lord Manthar from the wall and bring him here. And bid Princess Aixûs attend me immediately."

"As you wish, your majesty." He disappeared to see her orders carried out.

The queen pulled up a sheet of vellum and taking a pen from a crystal and silver inkstand, began to write, the pen making skritching sounds across the surface of the paper. When she was done, she blotted the parchment and dripped a small quantity of sealing wax onto the bottom of the document. With a practiced hand, she impressed the wax with her signet ring. Then she rolled up the document and slipped it into an embossed leatherwork tube.

Looking over at Peter, she said, "Your friend Joshkar believes The Eternal Architect has a plan for you. If that is true, let it be for the good. Come over here young de Soto."

Peter glanced at the drawn faces of those gathered round, then walked over to stand nervously on one side of the great desk. The queen handed him the cylinder. "This may be my last official act as empress. It names you, Peter López de Soto, *lord arbiter imperial*. Be careful. In the wrong hands that document could do you more harm than good."

Peter suddenly recalled the moment he received his first formal salute in the courtyard of the ducal palace. He'd felt ashamed for enjoying an offer of respect he clearly had no right to. He was speechless. "Your majesty..."

"Don't look at me as if I've given you a great gift, Lord de Soto. After nearly a thousand years it would appear the Empire of the Ulfair is at an end. The title comes with no lands, no grants, nothing at all of any substance except for this small enameled wolf." She handed it back to him. "It is entirely up to you and The Eternal Architect to make something of it. I have merely facilitated the opportunity."

In fact, the empress had completely misread the meaning of Peter's loss for words. His good friend at St. Stanislaus, Fernando, might have been impressed. He was first cousin to the young king of Spain, Luís Fernando de Orleans y Borbón, Infante d'España. Peter, on the other hand, wanted only to find Bonifacia and get home as soon as possible.

He empathized, of course, with the empress and her people, but that's as far as it went. He felt no special responsibility to them and certainly harbored no titular ambitions for the strange world in which he inexplicably found himself. What was he to do?

The image of Headmaster Lynch abruptly entered his head. He had no doubt his school master would be appalled to find that he'd done anything less than honorable in the situation or in any way stained the good name of Beaumont College. Peter bowed to the empress in gratitude and she smiled back at him in return, revealing those long white canines. His heart sank in despair.

From an archway leading into the great hall of the keep emerged a young Ulfair woman in the company of a guardsman.

"Ah, Aixûs, my dear. Come over here," said the empress.

The woman swept across the hall and curtsied elegantly before the queen. She was beautiful in an unusual way, wolf-like to be sure, but somehow reminiscent of the royal cats of Siam.

"This," said the queen, "is my niece, Princess Aixûs, the princess royal. I have only one command for you, *Lord Arbiter*. That is to escort Princess Aixûs and her husband, Cestus Lord Manthar, safely to Bakus Sura."

I should have known there would be a catch! thought Peter. His first reaction was to look over at Joshkar, who was standing to one side with his jaw firmly clenched. Princess Aixûs for her part looked sincerely distraught. "But your majesty..." she stammered.

It was at that point that the young Ulfair cestus, Lord Manthar, entered the hall. He kneeled before the queen, dipped his head submissively then rose to stand beside his wife.

"Dearest Aixûs," continued the queen, "you are all that I have left in this world. I made up my mind the moment I learned where this soldier calls home. I do not believe it is mere chance or coincidence that has brought these individuals into our midst at this late hour. There is some guiding hand at work here. I dare not name it. The soldier, Joshkar, hails from Bakus Sura. His Grace, the Duke of Camstol, will grant you protection if it is asked of him. I know it." She turned to refocus those mesmerizing eyes on Peter. "And, *Lord de Soto*...Bakus Sura, if I am not mistaken, is home to the old wizard that works the portal. You will need to make your way there in any case."

Peter's eyes widened with renewed interest.

She stood up from behind the desk and stepped toward him. "You see, your plea has not fallen on deaf ears. You must reach Bakus Sura. Find the wizard. His name is Thomajun. He is reclusive, but there is a man in Targun named Nyadic, a tinker, who can lead you to him. Show him the wolf and tell him of your predicament. Thomajun may be able to return you to your home world. I cannot promise it."

The urgent beat of drums echoed through the portcullus, summoning the last remnants of the Imperial Army to the walls and barricades. Peter gazed at the empress and felt the ebb of history pass beyond the room.

The queen turned to Joshkar. "How many can you safely take with you?"

"We have only two horses awaiting us outside the walls, your majesty. The more we bring out, the more difficult becomes our task."

"I understand," she said, disappointment written across her face. "Equerry Korsand, choose one other. You will accompany Princess Aixûs, Lord Manthar, the lord arbiter imperial and Master Bowman Joshkar to Bakus Sura. There is no time to spare. All of you will depart this instant."

Her tone was emphatic, brooking no argument. Using a tiny key attached to a chain at her wrist, she opened a drawer behind the bureau. From it the queen removed a bag of what Peter presumed was coin and gestured for Manthar to take it. Then she removed her signet ring and pressed it into the open palm of Princess Aixûs.

"I cannot," said the princess, tears welling in her eyes.

"Who better?" said the queen and empress. They embraced and pressed noses, as is the custom of the Ulfair. "Take good care of your wife, Lord Manthar."

He bowed deeply.

"Now be off, all of you. The lord chancellor will think I have deserted him. *And be safe.*" She turned to leave.

Peter had one more question before he could depart in good conscience. "Your majesty!" he shouted after her. "Have you heard anything of my cousin, Bonifacia?"

She turned to stare at him in momentary confusion. The din of war was growing outside the keep, competing for her attention. There was a drawn out moment of silence between them. Her eyes softened. "Fare well *Lord Arbiter*," was all she said and rushed away with her complement of officers and courtiers.

Was she trying to spare my feelings? Or did she just not know? wondered Peter. His mind was in turmoil. For a moment he thought to run after her.

Their little party glanced awkwardly at one another, as if taking stock. Joshkar took the initiative by leading them all out of the keep. Soldiers were massing at the walls and barricades, urged on by the incessant beat of military drums. A group of volunteers began herding the multitude of civilians who had taken refuge toward the tower and a few sturdier parts of the palace. Peter worried for a time that they might get caught up in the gathering mayhem.

"This way, quickly," urged Joshkar, at a near run.

They entered the palace through the same glass door that they'd come out of. Joshkar paused in the outer hallway, clearly disoriented. He turned to Equerry Korsand. "Can you take us back to the library? The fastest way?"

A reasonable decision, thought Peter. No need to blindly wander the corridors of the palace annex as they had done earlier, not with a knowledgeable guide at their service. The equerry nodded and they changed leads, rushing down the deserted corridors.

The library lay just as they had left it. "What have you done?!" cried Princess Aixûs, clearly distressed by the sight of the many ruined books strewn about the floor.

"It was unavoidable," replied Joshkar, without elaboration. He gestured toward the tunnel door. "We must hurry."

"*No. Wait!*" replied the princess, seizing him by the arm. "*Please,*" she pleaded. "Just a moment. I beg you."

He was averse to be so delayed, but nodded his grudging approval. She smiled gratefully and crossed over to the far side of the library, where she ran her hand along several lines of shelved books until she found the volume she was after, a particularly thick tome. The princess passed it to Master Guardsman Gortan with a whisper. The handsome Gwellem blushed to be so singled out in public. Satisfied, she stood a little taller. "All right then. What are we waiting for?"

Safely through the door, Joshkar retrieved the lantern they'd brought from the temple. It cast a thin veil of light a short way down the passage. "There is a constriction up ahead that we'll have to crawl over," he warned, "but it is passable. One other thing before we go on…" He looked Equerry Korsand, Lord Manthar and Master Guardsman Gortan in the eyes. "You keep your swords sheathed unless you have no other choice. Is that absolutely understood?"

It took the equerry a moment to chew over this demand, coming as it was from someone who was both his enemy and of substantially inferior rank. Korsand grew red in the face, and for an instant Peter thought they might actually come to blows.

"Very well," he said.

Peter breathed a bit easier. Joshkar looked to Manthar and Gortan for similar confirmation. They nodded, halfheartedly.

Off they all went down the narrow corridor, uncertainty and doubt filling Peter's heart. Part of him had hoped that he would find Bonifacia in the queen's company and that after being reunited she would send them home through a nearby portal (together with an apology for the inconvenience) and that would be the end to their little adventure. A child's dream, he now realized. A perilous journey still lay ahead. He might never return home or see his dear cousin again.

When they reached the site of the tunnel collapse, he wondered if they might hear some complaint from Princess Aixûs, but she crawled on her belly over the rubble in determined silence. After that, it was a simple matter to reach the door that led to the temple nave.

All but Gortan emerged after squeezing, one by one, through the shattered door greeted by the sound of hooves clattering nervously on the marble floor. Gortan, a splendid bear of a man, struggled but eventually made it through the narrow gap.

Korsand looked guardedly about the abandoned temple. "What now?"

Joshkar pointed to the guardsman. "Gortan, isn't it?"

"Yes?"

"Remove your livery and come with me. I have a task for you and I don't need a walking target at my side."

Korsand interrupted their exchange. "Stay where you are Master Guardsman Gortan!"

"Bless the Eternal! We don't have time for this," exclaimed Joshkar.

But Korsand was plainly unimpressed. He stroked the corner of his moustache. "How do we know we can trust you?"

Joshkar was beginning to fume. "It's a bit late for that, don't you think?"

"Of course you can trust him," put in Peter, coming to the defense of his friend.

"We should stick together," asserted Korsand, standing his ground.

"Look, we need to find your charges something to hide their faces. It will be faster with two of us. The lord arbiter sticks out like a sore thumb. I can't use him for this."

Princess Aixûs had stood aside from the conversation, but decided it was time to weigh in. "Equerry Korsand," she interjected, "you are quite right. We *should* stick together, but I believe Master Bowman Joshkar has a point. It will be exceedingly difficult for Lord Manthar and I to escape the city without some form of disguise. Besides, he is leaving the boy as security, is he not?"

Korsand gave Peter a questioning look. "That's true, your highness. The boy will stay with us. Very well, Bowman Joshkar, but be quick about it."

The guardsman and Joshkar slipped away, leaving Peter alone with Korsand and the others. Princess Aixûs bided her time by strolling about the interior of temple, studying the fall of its columns and balconies. "I've often wanted to visit this place," she remarked. "Even empty and forgotten, it is beautiful, is it not?"

"I have studied these temples," replied her husband. The first real words Peter had heard from his mouth. "They created specious divisions between people and The Eternal Architect. Excuses for a false hierarchy of worship and communion."

Princess Aixûs looked at him with a touch of pity. "Maybe so. I still find it beautiful."

The great main door rattled loudly. All heads swiveled toward it in unison.

"That can't be Joshkar," said Peter. "We broke the lock on the side door to get in. He wouldn't try it a second time."

There was absolutely nothing at hand in that vast cavernous building that could be used to effectively bar the side door. It was only a matter of time before the temple was breached. "Your highness, get back in the tunnel," whispered Korsand.

She dashed across the floor and squeezed sideways through the narrow opening. From where he stood on the other side of the nave there was no chance Lord Manthar could do the same in time. Korsand motioned for him to hide behind a column as best he could.

"They'll see the horses," reminded Peter.

The equerry was stone faced.

It didn't take long. Although they couldn't see the alcove from where they stood, they could hear the door open and the voices of several men.

"Horses?!" cried one of the men in surprise. The sound of a sword being unsheathed echoed through the nave. Four soldiers in the uniforms of Orn entered the temple, their necks craned forward like nervous geese, bows nocked and at the ready. The man in front carried a torch in one hand and his drawn sword in the other.

Peter didn't bother to hide himself, nor did Korsand. The soldiers were taken aback when they saw the two of them standing firm footed, albeit as far away from the tunnel entrance was they could to draw off the intruders' attention. The soldier with the torch looked especially startled, and more than a little confused. He eyed Peter's uniform warily. "M' lord?" he ventured.

"You recognize who I am?" asked Peter, using the same voice he'd used to successfully bluff his way into the duke's command tent so many times over.

"The lord arbiter imperial?" he said speculatively.

"Very good. What business have you here?"

The men never lowered their weapons. "We have orders to burn this building down, m' lord." He indicated the arrows in their quivers and Peter noticed now that some of the arrows below the points had been wrapped in cloth and dipped in oil tar.

His knees grew weak. "I'm countermanding those orders. This building is to be left intact."

The soldier with the torch canted his head to one side. "Our orders came from Captain Menhar not ten minutes ago. How is he not aware of this?" He looked over at Korsand. "What uniform is that?"

Peter had to think fast. "He is my aide. Can you not see that?"

But the soldier had good instincts. He gestured with his chin for the man on his left to circle round to Peter's flank. As he did so, Peter spotted Joshkar and Gortan silently entering the nave behind them.

"I'm sorry, m' lord," said the man with the torch. "We have our orders from Captain Menhar. It would be best if you and your *aide* left immediately." He motioned for one of his men to come forward and instructed him to light the oil dipped cloth on his arrow.

"Why must you burn this building?" interposed Joshkar in a voice loud enough to echo through the temple. He startled the man with the torch and his two closest companions. They instinctively turned to face him.

"I said, why must you burn this building?" his voice quaking with rage. "It has stood for a thousand years, built by the ancient kings of Kaladar. This temple has nothing to do with the Ulfair. Nothing at all."

"We have our orders," repeated the Ornish soldier. His head swiveled between Joshkar and the guardsman on one side, Peter and Korsand on the other.

"Go ahead, Vistach." The man named Vistach, lowered the tip of his nocked arrow into the torch held by his commander, setting it aflame. He tilted his bow up toward the rafters and was about to let fly his arrow when Joshkar threw his dagger across the room, striking the man between the shoulder blades. He released the bow as he fell. The arrow skittled across the stone floor, striking harmlessly against the far wall.

Unable to see what had just happened, Lord Manthar leaned forward enough for the man still circling around to spot him. "Ulfair!" he shouted, and let loose his arrow. It raced across the intervening space and glanced off the column, narrowly missing Manthar. Princess Aixûs, who had been watching all of this from the dark shadows behind the tunnel door, let out a scream. That was enough to distract the soldier for a moment. Manthar charged forward and cut the fellow down before he had time to nock a second arrow.

Joshkar was not so fortunate. One of the two soldiers with their bows at the ready managed to get one off before Gortan and Korsand were able to engage them. The arrow struck Joshkar at the very center of his chest. He slumped down to one knee and then to the floor. Peter yelled and ran to him, oblivious to whatever danger remained.

"Joshkar!" He cradled him in his arms, blood seeping steadily from the wound and spreading quickly out onto the floor. "Joshkar! Oh dear God!" he cried, the sounds of fighting still echoing through the temple. "Don't you leave me," he blurted. It took all of Peter's strength to resist the urge to shake him, so angry was he that his friend had got himself shot. "I need you," he pleaded. *"Don't...."*

Joshkar struggled to form words, crimson liquid sopping through the gaps between his teeth. "The ring," he gasped, striving to lift his hand for Peter to see. "You promised."

Tears streamed down Peter's cheeks. He pressed Joshkar's arm back down. "Yes, yes. I haven't forgotten."

Ah well, he thought. *I shall die 'the lord arbiter imperial.'* That made him chuckle. *What would Aunt Generosa and Father have to say about that?!*

END BOOK I

Joshkar licked at the blood pooling behind his lips. "Biscuit king…" he whispered. Peter pressed his forehead to Joshkar's, sharing his last breath. His friend shuddered and was gone.

"Oh God!," he wailed. "Oh dear Lord!"

It took Peter some time to realize that the temple was silent once again. Still holding Joshkar in his arms, he looked up to see Lord Manthar, Princess Aixûs, Equerry Korsand and Master Guardsman Gortan standing over him. Except for the guardsman who nursed a nasty gash on one arm, the others appeared unscathed.

Lord Manthar placed a hand on Peter's shoulder. "There's nothing more you can do for him. We must go."

Anger swelled within him. He cared for nothing or no one. *Who are these people, and what do they matter to me?* he thought. He wanted nothing more than to be left alone.

"*Please,*" said Princess Aixûs, looking to him for hope.

It was enough to bring Peter back down. He wiped the tears from his face. Taking Joshkar's hand in his own, he pulled the empty band from the bowman's finger and then reached over to retrieve the moonstone from his pocket.

"All right." He stood up and went over to where Bonnie was tied.

"Whom do you wish to ride his horse?" asked Cestus Lord Manthar, cautiously.

Peter stared at him, unable at first to absorb the question. "You take it," he said at last. "He wasn't very fond of the animal."

Joshkar and Gortan had managed to scrounge gauntlets and oversized riding cloaks to disguise the Ulfair nobles. They put them on, burying their faces deep within the hoods, tying indigo scarves over their muzzles for added measure. Dressed like that, they reminded Peter more than a little of the strange but hospitable gatekeeper that had sheltered Bonifacia and himself their first night after coming through the portal.

Gortan re-donned his imperial livery at the insistence of Equerry Korsand. *Arrogant fools,* thought Peter. *We shall stand out like sore thumbs.*

He climbed into the saddle still reeling from the loss of his friend and more pessimistic than ever about his own chances of survival.

Ah well, he thought. *I shall die 'the lord arbiter imperial.'* That made him chuckle. *What would Aunt Generosa and Father have to say about that?!*

END BOOK I